TRAPPED
BY THE CANNIBAL MOUNTAIN MAN!

Narcissa White heard the front door rattle, and realized that someone was trying to force their way in.

A knife poked through the crack between the door and the frame, the blade hacking at the hinge, and Narcissa heard an animal-like moaning from the other side.

Sliding across the wall toward the rear of the house, she reached the kitchen as the knife snapped through one hinge and began to bite into another. She was trapped, and knew that in moments the cannibal would cut his way through and be upon her. She ran to the door and put all her weight and strength against it as the last hinge gave way.

Then the door pushed her back and a large hand reached inside. She pushed with all her might, and as the fingers withdrew she glimpsed the grotesque face, the snaggle-toothed mouth distorted in rage.

A burst of fearstricken strength from Narcissa pushed the door back, and for a moment all was quiet and still.

Suddenly, the door erupted against her shoulder, the impact stunning her. When the pressure eased again, she knew he was backing off for a final lunge.

With her heart beating wildly, Narcissa braced herself for the last time, knowing she had no strength left to hold him off again . . .

The
WOMEN WHO WON THE WEST
Series

TEMPEST OF TOMBSTONE
DODGE CITY DARLING
DUCHESS OF DENVER
LOST LADY OF LARAMIE
FLAME OF VIRGINIA CITY

Angel
of
Hangtown

Lee Davis Willoughby

‿e§

A DELL/JAMES A. BRYANS BOOK

Published by
Dell Publishing Co., Inc.
1 Dag Hammarskjold Plaza
New York, New York 10017

Dell ® TM 681510, Dell Publishing Co., Inc.

ISBN: 0-440-00117-X

Printed in the United States of America

First printing—July 1982

1

THE wind, a ferocious, unseen warrior, howled over the rim of the pass, its violence forbidding the trespassers to take one more step into its private domain. The gale warned, threatened, and promised. It was the last formidable foe, and the three feeble figures struggled wearily against its awesome might.

The wind was winning.

It swirled great bursts of snow in brief explosions or drove hard icy pellets against exposed flesh, pricking the skin like frozen darts.

Sky and earth muted the battleline to a featureless white. Directions were meaningless. The intruders were disoriented and terrified. They were abandoned with no choice but to lean into the main thrust of the storm and hope that the surrounding hills were funneling the wind through a natural sluice leading in from the west. If the gale crossed the mountains at the lowest possible elevation, then heading directly into the worst of the wind would guide the faltering invaders over the pass. The pass would take them from the Sierra-Nevadas into the promised Eden of California.

The weather appeared to be putting up an all out final

attack against its enemies. The force of the wind far out-matched its weak opponents. The blizzard was like an army throwing all its armor against children and a woman alone.

Narcissa White's one hundred and two pound stature was weighed down with deer skin boots and a buffalo cape cinched tight to her waist under a rawhide belt. She trudged ahead, each step a tiny victory. The hem of the cape flailed wildly, allowing frigid gusts to flatten the long wool skirt against her legs. Cold penetrated the coarse homespun fabric and the layers of undergarments, and her legs stung with fiery pain.

Her long dark hair was crushed beneath a calico bonnet, a ridiculous remnant of a more civilized world. The bonnet was topped with a foul smelling bear-skin cap that covered her ears. The crude coat and the cap were Indian made, bartered for bolts of expensive cloth by savages grown crafty in the white man's commerce.

A scarf, frosted with her breath, was wrapped around the fair skin of her lower face and nose so only her sky blue eyes were exposed to the brutal weather. The skin below her eyes was smudged with burnt pine pitch to fight snow blindness, but she could lift her eyelids for only a few seconds at a time before the blinding whiteness and the dry, cold air froze the coating of tears.

Her calloused, roughened hands were wrapped in strips of cloth cut from the last dress she had discarded.

Every breath stole warmth from her lungs. Her body would soon lose the capacity to recreate heat. Every cone of mist puffed through the cloth face cover represented a visual spark of life that was flickering out. She was like a fire being snuffed by pelting rain.

"Keep going," she prodded herself. "Don't quit."

Determination had carried her past the threshold of endurance. Her spirit could no longer sap any more strength from her body.

She was dying and she knew it.

"God, please," she prayed. "Not yet." Eighteen years was not enough.

Her body wanted to quit, to admit defeat. Her will-power could drive her only a quarter of an hour more, a half at the most, and there was no reason to think she could reach shelter in so short a time.

At best she was postponing the inevitable. The tenuous thread of hope hardly warranted the ordeal of another fifteen agonizing minutes.

She should quit. She knew she should.

Nothing in her short life had prepared her for this. She had been reared in a protective cocoon—taught to cook, to sew, to embroider. Taught to serve tea to the ladies, to take pride in fine-ground white cupcakes, to extend her hand in graceful greeting, to stand erect, to whisper in the midst of sorrow, and to flirt with eligible young men.

She knew how to be dependent, to leave the decisions to the men, to flatter their strength, and to obey.

There had always been men around. Her father, her brother. She was female, younger and the weakest.

Until now.

She should quit, give up. But that was a man's decision.

She didn't even know how to quit.

"Cissie, please, Cissie." The child's weak voice was scarcely audible above the belligerent wind. "Please, let's stop."

The voice was Adrian's. Her nephew, her brother's son, was eight years old.

Adrian had been a robust, rambunctious seven when the family's three-wagon caravan had set out from their state capital at Iowa City six months before. His cheeks had been as red as the spring roses blossoming at the parsonage where the family had lived.

He had sat on the back of the last wagon, waving exuberantly to his playmates. So filled was he with excitement of adventure that he never considered he might miss the company of those his own age.

They were going to California—the new frontier, wrested from Mexican rule less than four years before in a war that concluded with the 'manifest destiny'—extending the nation from the Atlantic to the Pacific.

California—where the dream of quick and easy riches was a giant whirlpool drawing men from around the world. Gold nuggets the size of a big man's fist scattered about, waiting to be picked up by the quick and the nimble. Gravel so rich in ore that a single handful could produce enough to support a family for a lifetime. So the stories went.

California—where men were snatching fortunes in gold from clear, fast-running streams. The new paradise on earth.

Narcissa White had heard it all, even in Iowa, itself the 'frontier' a few years before.

The prospect of gold was enough to tempt even the most successful of the homesteaders from the fields of Iowa, the latest state to join the union.

California would be next, everyone said. The land of golden sunshine and rich, yellow nuggets.

But today, crawling over the mountainous wall that separated California from the rest of the nation, there was no gold and no yellow sun. Just cold, bleak, featureless white.

In the blizzard Adrian was a different child. Gaunt and exhausted, the freckles across his nose were lost in the red blood drawn to the surface by the cold. His once lively eyes were closed, the lashes frozen to his cheeks by a layer of ice that his body could not melt. His red hair was covered by a hat and his mouth, once the source of boisterous boyish laughter, managed only feeble whimpers.

He had never begged before, nor had he ever defied the youthful aunt he adored. But now his small mittened hand tried to pull loose. He wanted to sink into the snow and give in to the relief of sleep.

He knew that it was a sleep from which there would be no waking, yet he pleaded.

"Please, Cissie, please."

"No," Narcissa insisted. "Keep going."

There was anger in her tone as if their predicament were the child's fault.

She resented the boy's father, her own foolish adventurism, fate, God, the devil, or whatever force or turn of events it was that had lured her from a woman's proper activities and dropped her into a role meant for a man.

"I can't, Cissie. I can't."

She dragged Adrian along. He tried to lift his feet, but with each step, he sank into drifts up to his knees. Narcissa was doing no better. Her trail was not a series of footprints. Rather it was a pair of parallel tracks showing where she had stumbled forward in a zigzag path, no longer able to lift her boots clear of the snow. And there were regular indentations where she had slipped and fallen.

Behind them, the wind was working to wipe away their marks entirely, smoothing the white surface like a tidy housewife cleaning up moments after unwanted guests had finally departed.

"Hush, Adrian, be a man," Narcissa chided the boy.

Immediately she regretted the unfairness of the chastisement. She was asking the impossible. Adrian could not be a man; no doubt he would never become one. She could almost guess the yards left before she collapsed, taking him with her. Her body agonized in spite of the sinewy muscles she had developed during the harrowing months on the trail.

Her stomach was knotted around an empy core. Her lungs protested every breath of the chilling air. Her toes, fingers, and ears ached as if caught in an icy vise. They felt brittle as if they would break like slender icicles dangling from the eaves. Her lips were cracked, her eyelids a strain to move.

She had given up hope long ago.

She wasn't certain why she continued struggling toward the unattainable goal. Was it stubborness? Anger? Fear?

It could have been the ingrained determination of her religious upbringing. Beneath the veneer of propriety she had been molded to tolerate rude and penurious parishioners, to stand by the infirm and the dying. Although her life had been easy, there was always her father's preaching. Every conquest of adversity was a coin stashed away for buying one's way into heaven, he told her. Helping another across a river of trial and difficulty paid even more.

But those had all been words. This was cruel reality.

She must have a more realistic motive for going on.

So maybe she wanted the children to die quickly when she finally allowed them to drop in place.

Sarah, the boy's younger sister by a year, was the weakest. Narcissa had to lift her after each step.

The girl was a flawed child. Tiny, blonde, and beautiful, she made people smile until they saw her walk. She dragged one crippled foot behind her—the ball and chain the warden of fate had given her at birth.

Narcissa recognized that people treated the child differently. They adored her at first, then shied away when they saw her walk. As yet, little Sarah didn't understand. People, religious people in particular, carried part of the guilt for her infirmity. It was their God's will that had crippled her at birth. If she let the child drop now, Sarah would never know why heads turned aside, Narcissa mused, looking for an excuse to quit.

"Momma," moaned the child lost in smelly buffalo skin. Only the pitiful cry proved she was still conscious. "Momma," she sobbed constantly and her clear little voice was audible only when the wind momentarily relented.

"We can't stop," Narcissa said, trying to convince herself. "We must go on."

"What about momma and papa?" Adrian managed to ask.

Narcissa White finally stopped. The question cut deeper than the wind. She had gone on because her brother John had told her to save the children from the anguish of watching their parents die.

Through an entire hour the children had been calling for their parents. It was as if they could not struggle onward without knowing.

Should she tell them? Stop their nagging questions? Or should she say something comforting—that they would be with their momma and papa soon? And they would be if she let them sleep.

"Your momma and papa are . . ."

The last word was snatched away in the wind.

It was not for her to tell the children. It was for Him to

explain. Him. The aberration that had led her brother on this odyssey of pain.

She raised her head and held her eyes open as long as she could. She spoke with what vehemence she could muster from her waning reserve of strength.

"Damn you, God. Damn you to your own fiery hell for leading us here."

"No, Aunt Cissie," little Sarah said before she slumped to her knees. Immediately, snow began to fill in around the child. In a few short minutes she would be buried alive, with not so much as a mound in the snow to mark her grave.

"Don't talk to God that way, Cissie." Adrian's voice was stronger than it had been for hours.

"He enticed us here," she shrilled. "He got us into this. Let Him get us out!"

The outburst against her God was a first. Never had she questioned the Almighty or any other authority. It would not have been tolerated in her home. God was perfect. Men were wise.

But it *was* His fault. God had tricked them into this hopeless trail. He had smitten her brother with a mission, then mocked him by making the road impossible. God's cruelty contradicted all she had been taught, just as lashing out at him was a desperate repudiation of all she had believed.

God was not good. Men were not wise.

She made one more effort to move forward, then surrendered. She wrapped the children in her arms to give them what comfort she could, and to take what courage she could from their little bodies. She too was a child.

"Momma, papa," Sarah whispered. She would not have the strength to say it again.

"They're dead," Narcissa shouted in her bitterness. But neither child appeared to hear over the roaring wind. It was just as well. There was no need for them to know that their parents, her brother and his pregnant wife, were back there somewhere in the snow, crumpled in the lee of a tree where she had left them—their frozen bodies locked in the embrace of death.

They were only part of the debris her zealous brother had left scattered along the meandering trail that had stretched across half a continent.

Now Narcissa and the children would be the last of the wreckage to mark the farthest limits John White's madness had reached. And it was madness, Narcissa realized now that it was too late. She had followed a fool, pulled along in another's obsession.

The entire trek had been madness.

With the enthusiasm that he brought to every aspect of his life, John Whitcomb White had followed his father into the ministry. Wild as a child, flamboyant as a youth, he had always considered moderation a weak man's alibi.

Once ordained, he espoused a passionate evangelical calling that far exceeded the Presbyterian teachings he had studied.

When the church assigned him as missionary to the Pawnees living in Nebraska, a vast, sparsely populated frontier that promised only boredom and introspection, he flamboyantly declared a predestination that overruled the elders.

"I am going farther west," he announced dramatically, "to the gold fields. To California. I have the call."

Narcissa looked up from the dinner table, as shocked as were her father and John's wife, Melissa.

"Gold!" her father exclaimed. "You have gold fever and you dare claim that it's God's will?" The older man's face reddened. "That's hypocrisy."

John laughed. His was a hearty, healthy laugh. He saw humor others missed. "Gold and greedy men," he said. "The fundamental ingredients of evil. The alchemy of the Devil. Where else could the word of God be more necessary? It is predestined! We shall go." He turned to his wife who had gathered their children on either side of her during John's pronouncement. "We will take three wagons. One we will fill with bibles. The other with all our earthly belongings."

"And join a wagon train with an experienced trail master," his wife said hopefully.

John brushed the implied dangers aside. "God will be our guide."

Never one to seek advice or be a follower, he knew best. God spoke to him and who could deny it. A big man, he frightened away opposition or reduced it to feeble pleas, despite the fact that he had not struck another with his powerful fists since he emerged from childhood. His strength was in his righteousness.

"There is no time to stay with a train of other wagons. The gold might run out and the men disperse before I can bring them the word.

"We'll miss being real forty-niners by more than six months as it is. I want to celebrate Thanksgiving with the miners. By Christmas we will have a proper church. Before the first half of the century has run out its remaining months, we'll have built a congregation and raised a golden cross to God." He lifted his arms above his head, then lowered them to shoulder height, making a crucifixion with his towering body.

Narcissa felt herself being swept up in the tornado force of his enthusiasm.

Iowa City bored her. She had been born and reared in the East and sent here with her family only two years before. In those two years she learned the names and the moods of every eligible male in the area. They were few, and none of them interesting. Most of the state was being opened by young men with young wives and young children. Few single men came here. Most of the girls her own age were married.

The state legislators who came to the capital were older family men, although they did not bring their families for the brief sessions.

And nothing happened.

Men farmed. Women kept house and reared children. No one had time or strength to do much else except to attend church on Sunday.

She was stifling in Iowa.

She dreamed constantly of escape.

And awake, at the mention of California, she saw bustling towns filled with adventuresome men growing rich.

And she saw opportunities for women to hold jobs that men would avoid in favor of their search for gold. She could just imagine the excitement of a strike.

She wanted to go to California too.

"Go by ship," her father suggested, "and get youself established. Then send for your wife and children. The boat trip from New Orleans and the land trip across the jungles of Panama are arduous enough under the best of circumstances. Even after you board another ship on the Pacific side, you still have a hardy sail north to San Francisco."

John brushed the suggestion aside. "That's a fool's route. The entire England whaling fleet is rushing men to Panama. When they reach the Pacific, there are not enough boats to take them north. Hundreds are dying of malaria, cholera, hunger. Besides, would Christ have gone by ship except to fish? Would He have cowered before adversity? We will have three good wagons and all the good oxen in town."

"All the oxen?" the older pastor exclaimed. "They belong to our church."

"They belong to God." John spoke as one who knew he would have his way. "We have what's left of spring and all summer to make the trip."

"That's not enough time, I hear," his mother said cautiously from the stove where she stood in the crude cabin that had served as home for three generations.

"God goes with me. He will hold back the winter."

Narcissa spoke up. She rarely did. In a household of strong males, the eldest daughter kept her thoughts to herself as a rule. "If Brigham Young can take thousands of Mormons to Utah, John can take three wagons to California."

"The Mormons are starving, I hear," her mother countered.

"They will prosper in the land nobody wanted," John argued. "As I will."

"But take one of the most traveled trails," Narcissa suggested, suddenly feeling part of the mission. "Through Oregon or up from the south."

"No time," he said, squelching her suggestion. "We'll

take the Oregon route across the Rockies as far as Fort
Hall, then cut south. There's a pass through the Sierra-
Nevada mountain range that comes down right in the
heart of the mother lode. The California trail, they call it
now. We'll save weeks."

"But snow can close it by the middle of October," his
father warned.

Nothing would stop John Whitcomb White. He was
filled to the bursting point with a desire to spread his
strength and his faith in the wildest frontier within his
reach. The stories of men lusting for gold as zealously as
he lusted for God's truth drove him to scratching an out-
line of California on the rough-hewn table top with his
knife.

"Here is where I am needed. Near Sutter's mill where
the rush began. I feel it. I know it."

No one tried to sway him again.

His wife packed as she was told. All they needed to
travel for five months or more had to be compressed into
three prairie schooners. Smaller than the Conestoga wagons that her family had used coming to Iowa, the schooners were no more than ten feet by three and a half feet
inside. They were covered with hemp, waterproofed with
paint and drawn over large hickory bows. Draw strings
front and back could be used to leave openings for fresh
air, or tugged tight to keep out foul weather.

They had giant wheels to travel across rough country
and were loaded with bedsteads, a chest of drawers, a
stove, a spinning wheel, kitchen utensils and clothes, rifles
and pistols, gunpowder and loading equipment.

As John said, "God never said a man couldn't hunt for
food or drive off a heathen Indian unless he comes in
peace." He had insisted before coming to Iowa that the
women practice with the guns until they were expert
shots.

There were provisions: flour and salt, a butter churn, a
coffee grinder, chairs, a table, and bibles. Practically one
entire wagon was full of the bibles John hoped to sell, and
hymn books for his church.

Six oxen were chosen to pull each wagon.

"They're cheaper," John had confided in Narcissa when he had made his choice of dreys. "Slower than mules, but they eat off the land, no need for special feeds. And the Indians don't steal them like they would horses."

Narcissa had joined them in a last moment burst of recklessness and resolve. Surprisingly, her request had not been denied. Her parents, she guessed, preferred the risks of the trail to having an old maid on their hands.

She did not share her brother's religious calling, but she lied, a rare deviation from the dutiful daughter she had always been.

"I too feel predestined," she claimed. "I too belong among the greedy and the godless."

John had raised his hand to squelch parental protest.

"If she says it, then it is true."

Narcissa cringed. It was not God she was going to serve. She was striving to escape boredom. God would know it was the congregation of married men and their families, the farm boys who teased or ignored her that she wanted to leave behind. It was the prospect of following in her mother's path to housework, polite teas and reverent handshakes that she could not bear.

There had to be more to life.

But what?

She didn't know. She just wanted to laugh, to become excited, to seek adventure like her brother. Home would have been even more dull and dreary without his booming voice and his relentless good nature.

A woman had a right to do something besides have babies, wash clothes, cook, sew, and have more babies. Men had all the excitement. She wanted something different. She didn't know exactly what she wanted to do, but she would never accomplish anything in Iowa City. If she stayed she would be strapped in the same harness with the other women—having babies, washing, cooking, sewing, having more babies.

So she had gone along. Off to California.

John's spirit and the oxen had pulled them across the prairies. It had been beautiful at first. When she ran ahead, she could look back and see the wagons and imagine they were ships sailing across a sea of grass. Warm nights under star-filled summer skies had salved the muscle aches of trudging beside the wagons through the heat of the days.

Her brother walked the entire way, to the left of the animals, goading them with shouts and large cracks of his fearsome eighteen foot whip above them.

Narcissa or Melissa usually took turns riding at the front while the others walked. Adrian ran alongside much of the time, but Sarah generally occupied the lazy seat, a board extending out one side from the bottom of the wagon between the wheels. However, even she helped push when a hill was steep or rain created rivers or mud.

The Rockies tried their stamina without breaking their determination. But all along the Oregon trail they could see troubles ahead. The trail was a long cemetery of dreams. The carcasses of dead mules, the ghosts of broken down wagons, and possessions discarded along the crude path became a constant grim reminder of the still long trip ahead.

Once Narcissa had come across human skeletons. After her first cry, she had controlled herself, told John to stop the wagons, and helped him bury them without telling the children.

But they knew, of that she was certain. They were beginning to sense death.

Still, Narcissa kept up her spirits. If men could cross this way, so could she. Although she wondered how many women had left the Oregon trail to take John's shortcut to California, she remained determined. She would be the first if need be.

The children cried when food ran short, but John could walk off the poorly marked trail at dawn and return before nightfall dragging a venison or slabs of meat cut from buffalo humps and tongues. In the cold of the higher altitudes they traded cloth with the Indians for hides they should have brought for themselves.

They left their first casualty while descending from the continental divide. The older oxen collapsed from the strain. One fell and the others followed. They died still in harness. The first rolled on it's side and the others gave up. The children cried as their father slaughtered and salted what he could of the leathery meat. A day was spent unloading the wagons, disputing what to discard in order to save the bibles, and reloading the two prairie schooners with what remained.

Short of water, they plunged across the desert.

"It will be cool in September," John reassured them. "It's fall back home already."

But the sun laid a skillet of hot earth for them to cross. Sand clogged the oxen's noses, mouths, and eyes. The women and children tried walking backwards against the abrasive winds. When the children faltered and had to ride, a few of the bibles were reverently buried beneath the sand.

Fine dresses, prized furniture, and family heirlooms were buried when more oxen faltered and another wagon broke down. It then had to be cannibalized for firewood as the nights perversely chilled the bodies that were baked by day. More oxen died or were left too weak to work.

"We'll be back for our things," John promised resolutely while he covered the children's dolls and toys beneath pyramids of rock and hid his wife's most cherished belongings behind brittle stands of chapparel.

There was doubt in the children's eyes and Melissa turned aside to cry. Everyone knew they would never return for their things.

They had passed the point of no return. California was closer now than Iowa. They would run out of strength and supplies before they could retreat to civilization. They had to go on.

When the last keg went dry, the surviving oxen were turned loose in hopes that they would smell water somewhere in the vast isolation.

Later they came upon the animals, covered with flies and ants feeding on their rotting meat.

"God will provide," John promised, and he made crude packs for each to carry.

When the women and children stood at the foothills of

the last mountain between them and their destination, they sagged with fatigue. They were certain they had finally met an obstacle that neither God nor John Whitcomb White could help them to surmount.

But John stood there, spreading his hands. They would discover the Lord's latest gift, he promised.

"Water. There will be plenty of water pouring down from the summits, cool streams and clear lakes filled with fish for the taking."

"Yes," Narcissa had agreed cynically. "Water like we've been drinking all along—filled with tadpoles or leeches and mud."

"No, never. Look there," he pointed to a low point between the towering peaks. "There is the pass. Follow me for God leads me on. Come."

Drawing on new strength, his small band marched upward into the Sierra Nevadas, confidence restored. He couldn't be misled. Not John. Although his once strong body had been reduced to sagging flesh where muscles once bulged, he was still a commanding figure as he found a stick and used it to lift himself higher and higher into the mountains.

"A little farther," he said repeatedly. "Just a little farther and it will all be down hill from there."

And when the temperature fell and the rain began, he dropped his stick and spread his hands, opening his mouth to drink in the thirst quenching water.

"Not much farther now," he promised. "Only a little rain makes its way across the peaks of the Sierras. We must be near the summit. We're near the top of the pass. Come on, children. Hurry. We have the Lord's work to do. You too, Melissa, hurry before the new child slows you down. And Narcissa, be my disciple. Tell everyone we meet how I found His way."

Every hundred yards he promised they would soon peer down into the Sacramento valley, down on the Mother Lode. But with every hundred yards, they discarded more from their packs until they carried only themselves and their clothing.

The rain turned to snow. Tiny flakes at first, then fluffy bits of cottony wetness, a thrill for the weary children.

Later the winds came and the snow no longer cast a beautiful white ornamentation to the trees. It weighted and broke their branches and hid the rocks. It began to bury the mountains for the winter.

It was mid-October. Somewhere, the world was still warm, but in the narrow circle their vision could pierce, they were battered by the storm, imprisoned in a frozen white nothingness. They walked through the night, afraid to stop. In the morning Melissa quit.

She begged the others to go on.

"Save the children," she pleaded. "John, just this once, do as I ask."

But he had lifted her in his arms.

"I know the way," he insisted. "It's predestined. Thanksgiving with the miners. Christmas in our church."

A half mile later he too slumped to the ground. With his last strength he pulled his wife into the lee of a tree. It was the only modicum of comfort he could give her.

"Go on, Narcissa," he said. "Take the children. As far as you can."

She was terrified. How could she continue without a man to follow? A woman alone? The idea went against all she had been taught, against all that was natural and right.

Yet he insisted, and there seemed no other choice.

She was confused and frightened, awash in a sea of fear and anger. Her brother was not a man after all.

"You fool," she told him, surprising even herself. "You egocentric, pious fool! What have you brought us to—a cold miserable death?"

He looked up at her, humble for the first time in his life.

"Please take the children. As far as you can."

"Why?" she quarreled above the wind. "What good will that . . ."

She stopped herself, knowing what he wanted—the children taken from their mother's sight. In the end, the only humanitarian gift he could give was sparing his wife the sight of their children's death.

Narcissa White had taken two small hands and drawn them away. She cried with the children as they wandered into the dimensionless world of snow.

And now she rose one more time. She lifted Adrian to his feet and picked up the sleeping girl child.

A black object fell from Sarah's coat, and Narcissa stooped to retrieve it, half expecting to find some bit of food her niece might have stashed away.

But the devil wind riffled the pages of paper between black covers.

A bible!

Through their horrors the child had saved a bible.

Her last shred of hope buffeted away like the flurries of snow that surrounded them. "You carried this?" she sobbed at the child. "When you had the strength to carry a half pound of food? How could you? You fool! You're as crazy as your father."

She lifted the book above her head in frustration as if to strike the child. But Sarah slumped into the snow, somewhere between sleep and unconsciousness.

Narcissa tossed the bible aside, a symbol of the foolishness that had brought her here to this freezing hell. Religion. It had killed her brother and Melissa, claimed a child that would never be born. Soon it would take her too. At eighteen, she was still a child herself. To never have known a man, to never have had a home of her own or children,—that's what the bible had done for her.

"No, Cissie, you can't do that." Adrian floundered away from her and retrieved the book. He clutched his arms across his chest to hold the book safe.

"As fanatical as your father?" Narcissa grabbed for him, her mind churning like the waters of a swollen stream. Eddies of thought, memories, dreams, and lost faith broke her final calm with mounting turbulence.

Why was she here, fingers and feet aching, her stomach gnawing on itself?

It was Adrian's fault. And Sarah's. And the bible's.

John's obsession. God's lure that had brought her to this painful end.

"Give me that," she shouted, grabbing at Adrian. She missed the boy and he backed away. She saw him drifting into the blur.

His cape was caked with snow showing the bible as the last blemish in the sea of white.

The boy retreated and fell.

"Cissie, don't. Cissie!"

She lunged once more, then stumbled face down in the cold, white powder.

The snow packed in her mouth and nostrils. She struggled to cough and spit, to breathe even though the air was painful, and as she caught her breath, reason returned.

"Oh, no," she cried. Why was she blaming the children? "Adrian, Sarah, I'm sorry."

She tried to reach out to him, but the boy was yards away.

He was screaming. At least, she thought she heard him screaming. It could have been the wind.

His back was turned to her and he stopped. He was staring upward.

It was then that she saw a giant bear of a man rising out of the snow.

2

She floated in a dream, awakening to find herself prone, yet moving forward as if drifting in a choppy sea. Darkness remained even when she opened her eyes.

"I'm blind," she cried.

It was not unexpected. Snow blindness was a hazard her brother had warned her about when he persisted in pushing forward into the higher altitudes. Frightened, she ripped away the cap that had been pulled down to the cloth covering her nose. Light poured in, brilliant and painful.

She was not blind, and her dilated eyes squinted against the fading daylight. Still, she saw his face.

A satanic gargoyle. Most of his face was concealed beneath a grayed, ice-caked beard that seemed as long and as shaggy as a horse's tail. His upper lip was also covered with hair, scraggly black hair that drooped down at the sides and lost itself in the beard. His cheeks were scaly from exposure to sun and rain and blizzard. Gray eyes squinted from slits under hooded lids. A squirrel-skin cap met bushy brows, the most arresting feature in the remarkable face. From the brows a fringe of tiny icicles hung like stalactites from a craggy outcropping.

Narcissa screamed.

The alien monster had her in its clutches.

Even when she realized it was a man who carried her, she writhed, her unexpected motion causing him to lose his grip. She fell into the snow, rolled, and tried to run. His big gloved hand reached for her wrist but she scrambled a step ahead of him.

"Let me go," she cried. "Who are you? Where am I?" John! She wanted to call out to her brother . . . but he was dead.

Tall as any bear she had ever read about and with a chest twice the width of most men's, the monster was swaddled in animal skins that held his arms away from his body when he let them hang limp at his side.

He was an ageless thing, ferocious and inhuman as the blizzard. Under scarred skin he could have been a young man or one in his sixties. His labored breathing sounded like the grunts of an animal.

He smelled of sweat and whiskey and poorly cured animal hides. Even the blowing snow couldn't carry away the stench.

He terrified her as he extended his hand again, a trap ready to snap closed on her wrist. The expression on the face was unreadable. It could have been cruel or kind, but its ugliness repelled her.

"Don't touch me." Narcissa stumbled backwards towards the trees. "Where are the children? Why don't you speak?"

That's what she wanted, the reassuring voice of a human, words to explain what happened, where he had come from since she last closed her eyes.

The man grunted and slogged after her.

What was he? Who was he? Nothing in all of her reading had described such a monster. He was not the devil as described by the bible. No horns, no tail as artists popularly portrayed Satan. Nor was he an Indian. Painted savages looked better than he. So did the beasts of the forest.

She fled, crying for strength from a body exhausted hours before.

She had no chance to outdistance him no matter how

desperately she tried. He wore snowshoes—heavy tree bark three feet long and twelve inches wide, lashed to the bottom of his crude boots by strips of hide. Crude as they were, the appliances kept his great bulk on the surface while she sank to her knees with every step.

When he overtook her, she shoved her hands behind her back, hoping to make it more difficult for him to hold her. Instead he caught her by the throat and lifted her until she reached around in a frantic effort to avoid choking.

Immediately he gripped her wrist.

"Stop it, tell me who are you?"

Weren't there any other men around to save her? There had always been men in her life when she needed them. But not now.

She beat at him with her fists, her futile blows as ineffective as if they were falling on the hard spine of an oxen.

When she stumbled and fell, he dragged her along behind him the way she had seen John drag the carcass of a deer toward the campfire.

A nightmare, she thought.

It had to be.

None of this was happening. She must be asleep in the snow, cuddling the children close to share what warmth she had left, and her mind was failing, creating this apparition from the hell fire within her own soul. When she stopped struggling, he paused to let her regain her feet. His awful face looked at her again, then pulled her along, down the slope.

She could not tell what direction he was taking her except that they were going down instead of up. The snow was not quite so deep here and the temperature was a bit more bearable, the wind less cruel. At times she could see a valley, glimpsed greenery, and she realized the bitter truth. John, by a short, cruel margin, had missed the pass that led to safety. A lower pass cut through the crossing where snow had not yet begun to fall.

The mistake had cost him his life, and Melissa's.

And his children's too?

Had God predestined all that suffering? Or had she caused it by her lack of faith?

"Please," she begged. "Not so tight." She used her free hand in a vain attempt to restore circulation to her entrapped wrist.

He seemed deaf. Or perhaps he didn't speak English. She tried a few words of Indian, but that was ridiculous. He was white. That was certain. And he had no intention of acceding to her wishes.

Finally she preserved her strength, deliberately falling and forcing him to lift her into his arms the way he had been carrying her when she first awoke. His breath was foul, but his hold more comfortable when she didn't resist.

"Just tell me where the children are," she said. "Are they dead?"

Perhaps it was best if they were.

Before, she would have sworn that she would welcome any human face, even an Indian's. Now she only hoped they had not fallen prey to this same hook nosed beast that carried her to his lair.

"God," she prayed. "What have I done to deserve this?"

Did He listen? Or care?

Had her blasphemy warranted this, a fate a thousand times more hideous than dreamy death in white blankets?

Suddenly the monster dropped her feet into the snow and pushed her forward. The shape of a cabin came into focus. It was the crudest shanty she had seen. Made of logs, it was without windows or any sign of ventilation. The logs that formed the roof were covered with dirt and pine needles, but the mud packed in the cracks along the side had fallen off in places, leaving big slits where the weather could penetrate. The door, hanging askew on rawhide hinges, was held shut by another short log wedged against it at an angle.

She shuddered. There would be no woman inside that isolated shelter.

A glance to the leeward side of the cabin erased any such concern. From the snow, fingers protruded like a tool left in an unattended garden.

"The children?" she cried.

He ignored her, knocked aside the log, opened the door and shoved her roughly inside.

Before her eyes could adjust to the dark interior, a weak voice called out to her.

"Cissie."

Praise God! It was Adrian!

She looked past a table made of a large sawed off tree trunk. The cabin had obviously been built around it. A single stubby log served as a chair.

The man lived alone.

The little red head rose from beneath a pile of animal hides, and she ran to the other side of the one-room cabin and dropped to her knees to embrace the boy.

Adrian whimpered, "Who is that man?"

She hugged him tighter. "Hush Adrian, he's just a man who saved us."

"He's so ugly," Sarah ventured cautiously.

"Shhh." The man was standing with his back to the door and she was afraid of offending him.

Ignoring them, the grizzled mountain man crossed to the large stone fireplace and took two pails from beside it. When he had gone out, Narcissa left the children and went to the entrance. She tried to swing it open, but it held tight. Their captor must have leaned the log against it.

She looked about, searching for an escape.

There was no other exit. The only openings in the walls were the cracks between the logs. Under them were tiny drifts of snow that sifted in with the wind. In the fireplace the flames leaped in a dance choreographed by the wind blowing across the chimney top and the free moving currents inside the cabin itself. Lit only by the darting flame, the room took on a crazed maniacal ferocity.

On the walls were several animal traps. They seemed to be large jaws ready to open and chomp down on her flesh with their giant shark's teeth.

She was a prisoner in a madhouse.

With the children.

And no man to help her.

The men in her life had always been strong of muscle

and quick with a gun. While hers had been a religious family, she had never doubted that her father or her brother would stand up against any danger, from man or beast. Now one was dead and the other half a year and a lifetime away.

There was a gun leaning against the stack of wood to the left of the fireplace and she went for it, confident until she hoisted the heavy flintlock to her shoulder. The weight pulled the barrel down, and it was pointing at the floor when the door opened again and the man came in with a pail of snow in each hand.

"Stay where you are," she ordered. "I'll kill you, so help me God, I'll kill you unless you tell us who you are!"

The man looked at the barrel, put down the pails, and pulled the door shut, latching it by tying a piece of hide around a peg pounded between logs in the wall.

Then he swung back his fur coat and put his hand on the handle of a knife. He drew it and held it wide to his right side. The bloody steel was threat enough. He had killed or carved something recently, possibly the body beside the house.

Narcissa pulled the trigger. The entire cabin exploded in an ear-deadening roar. Recoil slammed the rifle butt brutally against her shoulder and sent her staggering against the wood pile. The cone of black smoke that spit from the end of the barrel contaminated the entire cabin with its acrid stench. She coughed, but heard no sound. Her eyes smarted and glazed over with tears.

Adrian and Sarah crawled from the crude bed and wrapped their arms around her legs. They were screaming, but she couldn't hear them.

The giant stared at her with emotionless eyes. Then he picked up the pails of snow and crossed to the fireplace, balancing them on burning logs. He seemed unconcerned by her attempt to kill him, like an elephant attacked by an ant. But when she tried to run for the door, he grabbed her arm roughly and flung her onto the animal skin bed.

She gasped, for the first time realizing he was not intent on killing her. Instinctively she covered her womanly parts by pinning one arm across her breasts and her other hand over the place between her legs.

Rape.

She hardly knew what the word meant. She knew about babies, had assisted at their birth, but about men—men and women together—she knew little except that there was a woman's burden, the monthly curse, things men did and women endured, and rape.

She had heard the word, dreamed occasionally of monstrous men coming for her. In the dreams they never reached her. Even in her sleep she could not conceive of what they would do, those massive bodies and big powerful hands.

And . . . she didn't even know how to put it in words, those things boy children had between their legs that she didn't have.

"Watch the farm animals," a girl friend had told her once, but she stood staring into the fenced field of cows and a bull for hours and never learned a thing.

In her ignorance she could not even focus her fears except to conjure a vague image of a powerful man crushing her and forcing the breath from her lungs with his body. Rape must be like claustrophobia, she thought, like the time she had locked herself in the dark, spiderwebbed milk shed.

The children were beside her again, both of them crying.

The man hovered at the fireplace watching the pails as they turned red.

Determined to fight, she glanced about the cabin again, searching for another weapon, but there was nothing, not even a knife. A few animal traps hung from the ceiling along one wall, but she could not think how to use them except to swing them by their chains.

So the man was a trapper.

That explained his lonely existence, but it did not explain the body outside. The thing she had seen in the snow was a human hand.

But if the man were a trapper, if he lived alone for a normal reason, perhaps he would not harm her.

Hunger drove away the fear of rape as the snow in the pails boiled away and the smell of cooking meat began to overpower the other odors in the cabin.

Adrian and Sarah had dropped off into fitful sleep, but began to stir as the smell of food reached them.

"Would you feed the children?" she asked when Sarah and Adrian again awoke from their troubled napping and looked hopefully toward their captor.

The trapper, if that was what he was, finally took the two pails from the fire and placed them on the table. With a hand carved spoon, he scooped into the pail nearest him and slopped stew into his mouth. Bits of meat and watery gravy dribbled down his beard. He continued to eat until Adrian approached the table.

The trapper offered the spoon to him and the boy dipped into the pail.

Yanking her hand free from Narcissa, Sarah went over to join them. Narcissa waited while they ate and then she rose and approached the table.

"Eat, Cissie," Adrian said. He could assert himself now that he had regained a bit of strength. He was trying to be the man she had told him to be back on the trail.

He held out the spoon for her when he was finished. She stood looking down into the cooling stew while the children moved to the bed, drew the covers over themselves and went back to sleep.

"What is it?" she asked. "Venison?" The smell was unfamiliar. "Pork?" Yes she decided, from the color it must be pork. But when she took the first spoonful, she gagged, not so much from the unfamiliar taste, but from the reaction of her starved stomach. On the trail none of the three adults had eaten for days, saving what they had left for the children.

"Wild boar," she said. His silence made her desperate for the sound of a human voice.

Having given it a name she ate ravenously, still standing. He stood, still silent, watching her.

"My brother and his wife were behind us in the storm. Melissa couldn't go any farther," she said to the trapper.

"Is there any chance you could go back and search for them?"

The answer was more silence.

"No, I don't suppose you could. They're probably dead anyway. I should say a prayer for them."

She recalled the bible and found it lying near the children. Opening it at random, she read from Genesis.

"For dust thou art, and unto dust shalt thou return."

The appropriateness of the phrase intrigued her.

"Imagine, turning to that by chance," she said. When still there was no response from him, she pressed the question that was bothering her. "There's a body in the snow outside. Was that your wife? A friend? Couldn't you bury him . . . or her? No, I suppose not, with snow and the ground frozen. It will have to lie there until spring. How ghastly."

With the last spoonful gone, she gave in to a weariness worse than she had felt on the long march.

She stumbled toward the crude bed, pulled one hide away from the children, spread it on the floor, and slumped onto it. She curled herself into a tight ball and clutched the heavy robe to her, covering her face.

Sleep came instantly.

3

SHE figured it was the heat that woke her. More logs had been added to the fire and the cabin had become stifling hot. The flames were crackling and the burning wood was sputtering, cascading sparks popped out onto the dirt floor.

Her next sensation was the belt to her buffalo cape being loosened at her waist.

Her eyes flew open.

The trapper was kneeling beside her. His shape and size had changed, he was naked.

"No, don't!" she shrieked.

Her hands beat at his hairy chest. They were still covered with the rags she used as protection against the cold.

His body was a dirty gray. His stench was sickening. His hands were big and powerful and they spread the cape with ease.

"Stop it. Leave me alone. John! Father!" She called instinctively to those who had always protected her.

Her screams aroused the children and Adrian spoke sleepily from two feet away.

"What's wrong, Cissie?"

He slipped back into sleep at once. She squelched further screams. The children could not help. They must not see the horror that she sensed would come.

For one instant she stared into her attacker's eyes. There was a tenderness there that turned to rage when she resisted.

Then he was grunting and crushing one of her arms with his knees. She saw the seven-inch appendage between his legs and her terror mounted. Her free hand reached for his face. Her fingers crooked into claws and she raked down across his forehead, into one eye, and deeply into one cheek.

The deep gouge hurt him enough that he released his hold and she rolled from beneath him, running to the far side of the table made from the tree stump. Then he was on his feet, circling it, slowly at first then faster and faster. Taunting her. They were playing a grotesque game of tag and the monster was smiling, watching her lose strength.

She saw things around the cabin that she might use to hit him with—the traps, a pot, a gun—but everything heavy was far enough from the stump that he would grab her before she could snatch up anything useful to crown him with.

He extended his arms across the stump, laughing in a grunting sort of way. Then finally he lunged across the table. She wound her fingers together, making one fist with both hands. She raised them and used the force in her two arms to smash him in the neck. His face mashed onto the wooden surface, stunning him briefly.

"Leave me alone," she cried.

But he rose, face bloody and eyes fiery. He climbed onto the top of the crude table, ending the game. Before he could jump her, she ran for the door, unfastened the simple rope latch, and swung the heavy wood in time to hit him again.

Then she was outside, running in the snow. It was like running in quicksand, the wet snow sucking at her legs and holding her. A nightmare. Pursued. Feet weighted and body weakening rapidly.

"Help!" she called into the wilderness.

His hand tore the coat off her shoulders, nearly pulling

her off balance before she let it go and struggled on through the deep drifts. She was freezing, but he was naked and seemingly unconcerned with the cold. When she looked behind her, he was ploughing ahead with boundless energy, his hard manhood swinging between his legs.

He was leering.

Finally he caught her shoulder, slowed her, let her break loose once more, then spilled her into the snow.

He fell on her, pushing the back of her head into the drifts until snow fell on her face. She couldn't see, and her mouth and nose were being clogged. It was like being buried, she thought, the snow walling her in on all sides, his heavy body the slab that shut out the light, and the burrow made by her body was icy and damp like a grave.

She wanted to scream and gagged instead.

He emitted a garbled noise, blocked her free hand with his shoulder, and began working her dress upward. She writhed and twisted, her mind storming with frustration that momentarily erased her fear. She wanted to kill, to see him agonizing in his own blood, and for a time, she held her own in the silent primitive struggle.

Soon he had the dress above her waist and was pulling it over her face, adding darkness to her horror.

She could only feel her fist pounding at him, her knees pumping, trying to bruise him.

Her long legged undergarments were exposed. He was pulling them down, ripping them in the center. She could feel icy snow on her crotch.

"Please don't. Please!"

She was screaming again, but the dress muffled her cries. She was fighting for breath.

. . When she felt hard flesh against her opening, she gasped in surprise. His hard member was a cold bar trying to penetrate her.

The nightmare would not end.

It never got this far before, but it was like the dreams—the heavy weight crushing her body, the suffocating sensation, the helplessness.

Then pain, a hard rod being forced up inside her, stretching and tearing her flesh.

The pain shot far up into her body and it worsened as he withdrew and thrust, withdrew and thrust.

She prayed for unconsciousness, even death, but the nightmare went on. And on. Thrust and withdrawal. A hot poker being jabbed into her body again and again. And even when it stopped, he still lay on her, pinning her to the drift.

Eventually he stood up, looking at her, limp and cold in the snow. He took one wrist and drew her into the cabin. He would not even let her walk. He dragged her with no more regard than a hunter hauling a deer from the woods.

Inside he started on her again. She no longer possessed enough energy to fight.

All she could do was writhe and try to breathe. When he climaxed, he let his weight crush her until he drowsed.

When she managed to roll him aside, she only woke him again, and it started all over.

Three times, he tortured her, but at the last, just as he was about to withdraw, she felt a new, unwanted sensation rising in her body. It was *in* her but not *of* her, a thing that made her at once weak and strong, faint and agitated. Her body was not her own. Something was lifting her hips, driving her onto him. She was unable to control herself.

It was a mistake.

Her movements gave him new strength and he plunged into her again in a quick, brief frenzy before he rolled aside, letting her breathe normally for the first time in what had seemed an eternity.

She prayed—to God or the devil—she no longer cared which she would serve.

"Get me out of this," she vowed, "and I'll do anything. I'll do your bidding, I'll build your church . . . anything, I promise."

An unexpected calm soothed her.

She did not move.

The pain between her legs and in her lower abdomen was excruciating.

Then the trapper started to snore.

"Now," she said aloud. She had to escape now.

He lay on her right arm, stirring when she eased it free. She sat upright, studying her lower body. There was blood where he had forced himself into her.

She cried without knowing it and crawled to a little drift of snow that had come in through a crack between the logs. She washed away the blood and the thick moisture she found between her legs. The cold helped ease the pain a little, and she began to regain control of her mind.

She saw the gun and thought of beating the trapper's head until he was dead. But the first blows might do nothing more than wake him. She was too weak to strike a fatal blow. The religious implications of killing him never entered her thoughts. Escape was her only thought.

When she saw the traps again, her mind fixed on them. She took one from the wall. It had a chain on it long enough to wrap around a tree.

She knew immediately what she wanted to do.

But she wasn't strong enough to pull the powerful saw-tooth jaws more than two inches apart. She could wake the children to help her. But they might cry out and wake the monster who slept like a drunken cyclops against the wall.

Her confidence was returning. I can do it, she thought. There is a way. Somewhere in this cabin there is something that will work. So often she had had this feeling when coping. There would be a way out if you kept your wits, used your head.

With deliberate care she scanned first the ceiling, then the walls and finally the floor of the cabin. Her eyes fell on the gun. There. There it was. The answer.

She stumbled toward it, her torn underwear and clothes still twisted around her body.

She took the gun and inserted it between the jaws of the trap after she had pried them as far apart as she could with her hands. It took several attempts, using the gun as a crowbar, before the jaws jerked into the locked open position. The second trap opened much easier.

She took pride in her imagination as she looped the

chain around the stub of a log that the trapper used as a chair. She put the chained trap close to his feet, then she took the other around to his extended fingers. Setting the second trap open on the dirt floor, she gently lifted his big dirty hands.

He mumbled in his sleep and one eye came partially open just as she dropped his wrists onto the trigger device of the trap. The metal teeth made a loud click and the powerful jaws clamped across the backs of his hands.

A guttural, animal sound, a roar of surprised agony filled the tiny room and he flung his arms toward the roof. Blood rained in big drops.

Before he could react, she stepped over him, yanked his leg and forced his foot into the other pair of jaws. Again the primeval roar. His eyes widened and he tried to pounce upon her.

She evaded him, stepped to the crude bed and pulled the children to their feet.

"What's happening?" the boy cried.

"I'm sleepy," Sarah pouted, her eyes only partially open.

"Get out!" Narcissa ordered. Her tone brooked no argument. She pushed the two of them toward the door. "Go. Hurry."

The wounded trapper was trying to rise. He was between her and the children. She dodged and sidestepped as he regained his feet and lunged at her. He swung his locked hands down trying to catch her in the loop formed by his arms. Failing, he lashed at her with the chain.

The children were still inside, struggling with the door.

"Untie the cord," Narcissa called.

Adrian understood and freed the door.

They were outside. The first light of dawn, sick and pale, entered the shanty.

Narcissa looked past the trapper at the door, so near and yet so far. With the instinctive inhuman strength of an enraged bear, he moved toward her, dragging the heavy log chair with his chained foot. He was backing Narcissa into the fireplace.

Her skirt caught fire and she beat it out with her palms,

then snatched a small burning log and shoved it toward the trapper's groin, toward the thing that he had pounded into her body.

"Burn, damn you!" She yelled and darted past him.

She was at the door when he caught her buffalo skin cape. Spreading her arms, she let it peel away in his fingers. As she dashed through the door he lurched after and swung his trapped hands down in one final attempt to snare her.

With her back, she slammed the door shut.

"The log," she called to Adrian. "Give me the log."

The children scrambled to obey.

Behind her the door was slowly opening. She kept it partially closed by stiffening her body and straightening her knees until she had the log braced against it. She wedged it into position. With one end braced against the frozen earth and the other caught against a knot in one of the logs that formed the door, brute strength would not open it.

"Aunt Cissie, look!" Sarah said, pointing.

Narcissa turned.

Bloody hands protruded from under the door.

The trapper's hands.

She could see them wriggle, like the parts of a dismembered snake, trying first to retreat inside and failing that to push out. They were stuck.

"Good!" she said in a voice that sounded hoarse and unlike her own. "That's good."

The children gawked at her.

"Run," she commanded them. "Down the hill." The wind had died and no snow was falling. She pointed to the end of the snow line. That must be where the pass ran through the valley.

The children did not obey.

"What about mama and papa?" Sarah whined.

"They're down in the valley. Now go."

The children whirled, Adrian running full tilt. Sarah followed as quickly as she could, dragging her crippled foot behind her.

Narcissa hesitated.

Was there a trail below? Even if there were, did it lead to civilization? Could they make the distance?

Maybe, she thought. With the meal the monster had provided them, they might have the strength.

Then she remembered what she had seen when they first arrived—the hand in the snow beside the shack. The one she thought belonged to one of the children.

She went to the side of the cabin.

Snow had blown away from the top of the drift.

Her brother's frozen face stared upward, his brows whitened, his open eyes glazed with ice.

She sucked in her breath, surprised that no sound came out.

Throwing herself on top of the mound, she began scooping away the snow. Frenzied, ignoring the freezing cold and the sounds of the trapper trying to free himself from the door, she dug toward the bodies. There were two. She discovered that quickly when she uncovered Melissa's dress.

How had they come to be here?

The answer did not require much imagination. Obviously the trapper had found Melissa and John first. Whether they were dead or alive, he had brought them here before going back to discover Narcissa and the children.

The grunting and groaning from inside the cabin continued and it bothered her now. Could she leave a man trapped, his hands exposed to the cold? He would freeze if he couldn't free himself before the fire went out. But the humiliation and hatred were too much. She could not return to the door. He would free himself eventually. Perhaps too soon, before she and the children could escape.

Terrified he would come after her, with numb fingers she disinterred her brother's body from its shallow, white grave. When she could tear the cape off the corpse, she wrapped it around her own shoulders.

She had been reduced to that. Survival was more important than reverence for the dead.

She wanted the coat. That's why she dug into the snow. Was she any better than the trapper?

She turned to follow the children and then she stopped. Melissa lay in such a strange position. It seemed wrong. She fell to her knees, digging like a dog until she had exposed one frozen leg.

The flesh of the upper thigh had been hacked away with a knife.

And suddenly Narcissa White realized what she and the children had eaten. ᡓᢒ

4

At the lower altitude a soft, sad rain dropped into the limp grass and dead wild flowers. A stream ran down the middle of the pass, running west instead of east. It gave her hope. The trail must lead to California. There were hoof marks here and there. Horses had passed this way not too long ago, and there was a flat band of earth along one side of the stream wide enough for wagons to pass, although no marks remained.

Men had been there. Trees had been cut and dragged away.

It was definitely a wagon trail and in spite of the nausea in her stomach, Narcissa kept the children moving through most of the morning. By noon, they were soaked with the icy rain, they refused to go farther, and she was gathering branches to build a crude shelter when she heard a faint sound from the east.

"Haw, haw!"

An animal's cry?

No.

The children did not move.

"Stay here," she told them. She returned to the trail, cautiously retracing her steps.

Doubt assailed her.

Maybe it was the trapper. No, he wouldn't sound like that.

She heard the snorting of horses and the squeaking of wagon wheels. She ran another twenty yards and started waving her arms and shouting.

"Hello, hello, over here," she cried.

The first two teams of horses emerged from the veil of rain. Their nostrils flared and their muscles strained under a whip that cracked above them and drove them on.

Finally, she saw the hood of a covered wagon. It was a standard conestoga design, "a prairie camel" as some called it. Both ends were higher than the middle. The white roof was high and rounded, and the wheels were broad rimmed to prevent bogging down in the mud. A team of brawny horses pulled it forward. Barrels of water were strapped to the sides, as were rattling pots and pans and other gear. A man sat in the front seat.

Instinctively Narcissa drew inward at the sight of a man. She clutched her arms across her chest, frozen, unable to move closer.

The man was old and grizzled.

"Whoa," he called to the animals when he sighted Narcissa. "Whoa, you consarned, useless jackasses, whoa!"

The animals stopped, and the old man dropped the reins and drew a long barrel pistol from a saddle holster fixed to the side of the driver's seat. Narcissa took a tentative step forward.

"You whoa there too, lady, or I'll have to blow the nipples off your tits."

The language surprised her almost as much as the gun. "I'm lost," she cried.

"Yeah, and how many bushwhacking bloodsuckers you got behind you?"

"What's goin' on?" a voice asked from inside the wagon. Though it was coarse as gravel, it was definitely the voice of a woman. Narcissa burst into tears.

"Ma'am, oh thank God."

"Ma'am?" the old man laughed, lowering the fifteen inch barrel of the cavalry pistol. "We ain't got no ma'ams aboard this here wagon train, missy. A madam for sure, but no ma'ams."

Narcissa didn't hear.

She ran the rest of the way, reaching the front of the wagon. A fiery red head, yellowed in spots, poked from the opening in the tarp. The woman was in her fifties, or forties. Narcissa had learned early that the frontier, even Iowa, could age a woman before her time. But the hardness in this face was different from the look of farm women back home.

The redhead was wrapped in a beaver fur coat. Two gnarled and wart-covered hands held the coat to ward off the rain. There were splotches of red on the woman's puffy powder-pale cheeks. The color looked like rouge, but Narcissa dismissed the idea. She had never known any woman to use anything more than flour tinted with a drop of raspberry juice to enhance her complexion.

"Who the hell are you?" the woman asked. "In fact, what the hell are you?"

"Sounds like a girl," the driver said. "Looks more like the biggest, damned drowned rat I ever did see."

"My name's Narcissa White." In her relief, the words tumbled over themselves like water released from a dam. "I was coming west with my brother and his family and we got lost in the snow."

"Snow?" the driver looked up the mountain. From there it looked like a long way to the snow line. "What in Sam Hill you folks doin' up in the snow? Ain't no trail up there except for deer and bear."

"My brother wasn't much as wagon master," Narcissa tried to explain. "He was a minister."

"You betcha petticoats he was no wagon master. The high road don't lead nowhere 'cept to Trapper's, and nobody with half a squirrel's brain goes near that freak."

"Trapper? Is that what you call him?"

"He talks to squirrels," Old Gray said, "and the squirrels tell me he's crazy as a loon."

Narcissa tried to stop her voice from raising to a shriek. "He's a beast."

She couldn't say the rest.

The woman roared. "Then God led you up there, huh? You hear that, girls?" She drew her head back into the wagon. "Didn't I always tell you? Follow them preacher fellas and they'd lead you 'cross shit lake whether you can swim or not."

Another head looked around the end of the second wagon.

"What you got there, Old Gray?" a younger girl asked of the driver.

"Got some sheep, the good shepherd let run astray, I reckon." The man they called Old Gray leaned forward for a better look at Narcissa. "Shit, miss, you look worse than these whores after payday on an army post." He returned the pistol to its holster and Narcissa moved close to the wagon so he could see the fear in her eyes.

"Wh . . ." Narcissa couldn't finish the word.

"I'm Suzy Sunshine. Were there any other men in your train?" the girl on the wagon asked. Her hair was bright blonde and she ignored the rain that was turning it into snarls. "If'n we don't get us a better man than old Gray here soon, we're all liable to tighten up worse'n the hide of a drum."

Narcissa choked on her answer. "No, there were no other men. Just my brother and his family."

"Well, where's yer brother, honey? A preacher's better'n nothin'." Laughter pealed out from inside the wagon.

Narcissa hesitated. It took all the strength she could muster to say it aloud. "He's dead . . . so is his wife . . . Frozen to death." She said it carefully hoping the children were out of earshot.

"Did your brother die with a hard on, lady?" a voice giggled from inside the wagon. Another head drew her back inside and the older woman appeared.

"Well, better stand aside, girl. We gotta get to town before we all catch our death of cold."

"Missy, where's the rest of the family ya say yer with?" Old Gray spoke up again.

"John—my brother and his wife are—their bodies are beside Trapper's cabin." The words came hard for her. "They ought to be given a proper burial."

"What's left of 'em, ya mean."

He knew the trapper was a cannibal.

"You'll bury them then?"

"Not me, miss. I ain't crazy."

"But my brother was a minister. I can't. Have to look after his children. The trapper, he . . ." she stopped as she caught the old man's gaze. She wondered if he could guess what the trapper had done to her. Did it show on her face? She would kill herself if anyone guessed.

"Hey, Old Gray! We gotta get to town," a throaty young voice called out. "We're ruining our Sunday best sitting here." The wagon erupted into snorts and giggles.

"Town?" Narcissa's hopes began to rise. "Is that Sutter's Mill?"

Old Gray spat a wad of tobacco into the stream. "Sutter's Mill is a regular town now, Miss. They call it Sacramento. I reckon they'll be making it the capital when California becomes a state. So it's too good for these critters, missy. They're headed for Hangtown, all three wagons of 'em."

Hangtown. The name was foreboding. It would not be a place where God would have wanted her brother to start his church.

"What an awful name."

"Lotta places call themselves Hangtown. Helps scare off the riffraff. If the camp grows, they change the name to something fancy."

Narcissa stepped to the side so she could see around the first wagon. Two more prairie camels had drawn up behind the first as they talked. They were driven by women, dressed in men's trousers and shirts and with big wide-brimmed hats drooping over their eyes. The one in the second wagon had a pistol belt and holster strapped to her waist.

"That's Pistol Packin' Patricia," Old Gray said when he saw Narcissa's interest in the mannish girl. "Can shoot the eye out a needle at fifty yards and ride a man like he's a horse and she's carrying a message to President Taylor himself. So you don't tangle with ole Pat."

"Pistol Packing," Narcissa marveled at the name.

"Got us a Cotton tail, a Saddle Legs Sal, a Buxom Bertha, and plenty more includin' a Mary of Nazareth. She's the nigra that does the cookin' and cleanin'. Does a little humpin' too when business is good."

"Ah's a free niggah," a black face shouted from the last wagon. "An' don't you forget it, Old Gray."

"Free, hell. You charge as much as any these whores." Gray put his hand to the side of his mouth and whispered around it. "And she's better'n any of 'em in bed if you're askin' the only man who ever had a go at all of 'em."

Embarrassment was replacing some of Narcissa's agonizing memories.

The rain was letting up and more women were peering out from the front and the back of the wagons. Although all were young, there was a weathered look about them that had nothing to do with work in a field.

They were whores. She was not certain exactly what the word meant. They were women who spent time with men. She knew that much. But her mother and the other ladies of the church spent time with men too, and they were never called whores.

There weren't any whores in Iowa City that she knew of.

"I have two small children with me," Narcissa said. "They're hungry . . ." Her stomach turned at the thought of food.

"Feed 'em buffalo chips for all I care," the older woman said. "Just stand aside so you don't scare the horses. We gotta get to Hangtown 'fore another load a ladies gets there and has the men all dosed up."

Narcissa felt like flinging herself at the wagon and hanging on. She was ready to beg, argue, give anything to be taken along. She could not be left behind. The presence of a man, even an old man, gave her hope.

One old man? Why did she feel he could save her and the children when she could not save them herself? The question was a seed just beginning to germinate in her mind. But now she needed him, the children needed him. The other women could sound confident. They had their man.

"Ah, now Madam Lafayette, you ain't so hard-hearted you'd leave a mite of a girl and two younguns strung out on the trail," Old Gray interceded.

"Ain't the Madam's choice," a voice said from down the line. The girl driving the second wagon climbed from her seat and swaggered forward like a bow legged cowboy. "We got enough of us in these three wagons to keep a place bigger'n Hangtown hangin' limp twenty-four hours a day, seven days a week."

The girls began leaving the wagons, holding their skirts high and sloshing on the wet path to see the reason Old Gray had stopped. Along the trail, people were a curiosity; anyway, the least excuse for dismounting was welcome.

There were several dozen of them, she guessed. Few were really attractive. Most were pudgy or no longer fresh. One dark haired girl would have been among the most attractive except that her nose, cheeks, and forehead were tattooed with Indian curlicues and symbols.

"White Squaw," Old Gray called her.

Narcissa had heard stories of girls, some scarcely more than infants, taken by Indians and raised as concubines. Among the few who escaped or had been rescued, several had returned with tattoos over large parts of their bodies.

The berry-based dye permanently implanted on the girl's face bespoke nightmares worse than Narcissa had just survived.

Unlike the other women who chattered and even quarreled among themselves, White Squaw did not acknowledge Narcissa. The set to her mouth suggested that she spoke rarely, if ever.

God had treated White Squaw even worse than he had treated her, Narcissa thought bitterly.

"You're all women," Narcissa observed. "Except for him." She pointed at the driver of the first wagon. He had taken off his hat and was using a dirty rag to wipe rain from his forehead. His hair was the color of a dapple gray horse and there was a scar along the length of his forehead. She wondered if he had escaped scalping. "How did you survive the trail?"

Madam Lafayette answered for the group. "I've been running hog ranches outside army posts most of my life, girl. Trail ridin's a holiday by comparison, believe me."

Narcissa misunderstood. "Hog ranches? You're farmers."

Giggles rippled through the crowd slowly surrounding her.

"She's a whore madam," Old Gray said by way of explanation. "When she was younger, she could service a hundred men, two bulls, and an unbroken stallion in one day, and amuse herself with a tame rattlesnake before mornin'."

"Cissie," Adrian called from farther down the creek.

"Jesus Christ," the blonde haired girl said as the children came running toward them. "It's gonna take a while before he's ready to plunk down his gold dust for a screw."

The girl in man's clothing held a pinch of something dark to her nose and sniffed as she watched Sarah White hobble close to her aunt. "Gonna take the kid on for the dirty old men in Hangtown, Madam Lafayette?"

"Watch your tongue, bitch," the Madam chastized her. "We ain't takin' none of 'em with us."

"Gotta take 'em," Old Gray cocked his head. "It's a law of the trail."

"Fuck your law."

Narcissa winced at the word and drew the children to her side, trying to cover their ears with her hands and pressing them close to her hips. The fear must have shown on her face. She could not bear the thought of being abandoned again.

"Pay her no mind," Gray assured her. "She's so mean and in such an all fire hurry to get where the gold dust is blowin', she wouldn't take time to let the horses drink from a mirage."

Determined she would not be left behind, Narcissa reached up with both hands and withdrew the heavy pistol from the holster on the wagon seat. She put one hand on the round barrel and the other on the grips to aim the four-pound weapon.

Gray extended both palms as if to ward off a bullet.

"Oh, now lookee here, Miss. Don't go pointing that thing at me. That's Captain Sam Walker's presentation pistol you're pointing at me and I don't take kindly to that. I rode with the Texas Rangers at the battle of Salado in '42 and with Zack Taylor—President Zachary Taylor at Palo Alto in . . ."

"Don't try to talk me out of this," Narcissa cocked the gun. "I'm not being left behind."

". . . forty-six," the old man continued, "When twenty-three hundred of us beat off six thousand Mexicans, so I don't get scared too easy." He was extending his hand for the Colt.

"Reach another inch and I'll kill you," she said.

His hand withdrew. "Blasted if I don't think you would. Spunky for such a little thing, ain't you?"

"Spunky enough to get this far," she said. "I don't intend to let the children die this close to a town."

"All right," he said. "Climb aboard. Only give me the gun first."

She weighed her chances and decided to trust him.

He took the Colt from her, released the hammer carefully and replaced it in the holster.

"Drive on, damn you," Madam Lafayette ordered. "I'm payin' your wages."

"You got a heap a learnin' to do Madam. If'n we leave her and the little ones, the good Lord will strand us up crap creek, eyeball high in the muck."

"I say, leave her and take the kids," said the girl in man's clothing, the one called Pistol Packing Pat. She took a tough stance with her hand on the butt of a pistol that dangled by her hip. "They can do chores for their keep until they're growed."

"We take them all," a softer voice said from the last wagon.

The girl approaching was prettier than any of the rest. She wore a skirt of blue broadcloth, a velvet bodice and leggings of scarlet. She held the skirt high as she walked, avoiding the wet and revealing a shapely ankle. Her hair fell over her shoulders in two thick braids. A scarlet silk handkerchief was tied at her neck. She was eighteen, nineteen at the most, with bright green eyes and full lips. Her complexion was unblemished and she wore none of the makeup that covered the wear on the faces of the other girls.

"Annie!" Madam Lafayette shrieked. "What you doin' in them clothes? Who said you could go diggin' in the trunks? That stuff's for workin'.".

"Whip her," another girl shouted. "That Velvet Ass Annie gets away with everythin'."

The pretty girl ignored the comments and a path cleared through the group as she walked toward Narcissa.

"My name's Annie," she said in a cultured voice.

"Cut the sweet talk," the blonde inserted. "You're a lady of joy like the rest of us whores. What else can a single girl do except wash and fuck?"

"I'm Narcissa White." She pointed up the hill towards the trapper's cabin. "My brother . . . his family . . ." She was on the verge of tears. "We got lost and there was this man . . ."

"Trapper," Old Gray added. "Shoulda stayed a day's buggy ride away from his kind. Some say he's a survivor of the Donner party. If you know what I mean."

Thinking back to the only meal she had had in days, Narcissa knew only too well.

"We can't go on alone." Tears welled up in Narcissa's eyes. "The children can't walk any farther and I . . ."

"You don't have to," Annie said. "I'll take the children with me."

"And you can ride up here," Gray said. "Looks like the rain's through for today."

Madam Lafayette objected. "What makes you so high and mighty?" she demanded of Annie.

Annie made a motion with her head toward the other girls. "Who else you got to play 'virgin'?"

The blonde argued again. "We ain't worked in weeks and you want to take a gospel-spouting crew into town. Look at that book. If you could read, you'd see she was carryin' the holy book with her."

Defensively Narcissa covered the bible with her arms. "My brother was a minister."

"Makes no never mind. Ain't no room in the same town for rabble rousin' evangelists and the likes of us. I say they get left where they stand."

"If they stay, I stay," Annie said softly.

"Same goes for me and my wagons," Old Gray added.

That brought a rustle of protest, but Madam Lafayette had changed her mind. "You sluts, shut up," she ordered. "Two days after the men start work on your flabby carcasses, they'll be lookin' for veal rather than you old cows. We gotta give 'em some fresh meat like Annie once'n awhile to keep 'em comin' back, and she can't handle a whole camp. So maybe we can talk this little lady into joinin' us."

"Me?" Narcissa cried.

"Climb aboard 'fore she changes her rattle brain," Gray suggested.

Annie nodded. "Do as he says, honey."

"But, I could never become a . . . a . . ."

Annie had already taken the children's hands. They looked up at Narcissa with questioning eyes. She nodded and they went toward the last wagon, chatting with the beautiful young girl was if she were a new-found aunt.

"Get aboard, you whores and sit light on your butts the rest of the way," Madam Lafayette ordered. "I want you lookin' good. By Saturday you might be workin'."

Gray reached out and helped Narcissa to the seat beside him. He yelled at the horses and cracked the whip, and the small wagon train began to move again.

Narcissa held her arms across her chest for warmth, and spoke when Gray was free to listen. "Are they all prostitutes?" she asked.

Gray shrugged. "They're women and that's one thing Hangtown ain't got. It ain't exactly Boston society, you know."

"But what that woman said about me joining them . . ."

"Consider yourself flattered. Mattie Lafayette runs a good clean house. Pays her girls fair. Everybody gets their due includin' me. That's why I went out Dakota way when I learned Hangtown was missin' one of the most important institutions a place has gotta have, a pleasure palace."

"My brother was going to establish a church, bring the word of God to the miners."

"Mite early for that, miss. A new mining camp ain't no paradise right off. And in hell, it ain't the good folks who has the fun. It's the devil hisself that runs the church. So join him and sing, or fight him and burn, I always say."

"But I couldn't . . ."

Gray shrugged. "Hangtown's already got three Chinamen on suds row. Hangtown ain't no cheap place to live. No minin' camp is. Soon as these danged fool prospectors strike paydirt, along comes these other fellers that knows there's easier ways to get at that pretty yeller stuff than standin' in icy streams or breakin' your back with a shovel fifteen hours a day. These smart fellers take to sellin' booze fer two dollars a shot, a shovel for twenty, cackleberries for ten dollars a dozen, flour for its weight in dust, and dosed up women fer maybe five dollars every ten minutes. So you need money, young lady, a bottomless well full a money. And since the Chinaboys got a decent woman's rightful business sewed up tight, I don't know what you could do to feed yerself and the young'uns, except live with the first man that asks you, and that don't seem much different than what the ladies of the night is doing if'n it ain't a proper marriage with a preacher and all."

"We were going to Sutter's Mill," Narcissa said. "Surely that's more civilized."

"A mite, yep. Not far but do you got the price to buy a horse and buggie to make the trip? Things come high out here. Most men can't drag themselves away from the streams. In the beginnin' three miners took out seventeen thousand in gold in one week. Place got so crowded a dog didn't have room to bark. That glitter of gold blinds men faster than staring at the sun. But if you've got the money, I understand a chap name of Studebaker gonna set up shop buildin' wagons and carriages. A real craftsman, that Studebaker."

"I don't have any money. I left what little we had on my brother's body."

He looked across at her.

"And I wouldn't wash clothes or do anything else that you men consider too demeaning except for a woman," she added.

"Sounds to me like you're gonna spend your nights on your back, Missy. Just like the rest. Better get some rest if you can. A man who ain't had hisself a woman as long as these gold-fever bums can be kinda hard on a girl, mighty hard on a girl."

Narcissa shuddered, but said no more. She leaned back, resting her hips across the upright at the rear of the seat.

Her mind was filled with a jumble of images, a dozen men, all with the face of the trapper, pawing at her, thrusting their naked bodies at her. The pain inside returned, searing as it had when the trapper first violated her.

She wanted to leap from the wagon, to flee, to run until she dropped from exhaustion. She wanted to lie in the mud until life drained from her soul. Until oblivion released her from a life that had become a hell.

"Course you could always go back wherever you came from," Gray said.

Go back! Narcissa cringed. Go back! The last six months all over again. Could she do it even if she could find someone who could provide her with transportation?

There was no going back. It would be bad enough writing a letter, telling her parents and Melissa's what had happened on the trail.

"And what about them younguns?" Gray asked. "Minin' camp ain't too bad for the boy, but I don't know about the girl. You gonna support them too?"

The children.

They were stones weighing her down in a sea of adversity. They were the peak on the mountain of struggle she still had to climb.

"I could start a church," she said weakly.

Old Gray laughed. "No chance, girlie. The devil already staked out Hangtown for hisself." ໑ຣ

5

THE three wagons wound down from the mountains through stands of black oak, conifers, manzanita, holly, and evergreen toyon. In the foothills the stream took on more water and became an icy torrent flowing into the vast valley extending far to the south and to the west.

In the early morning of her fourth day with the whores, the wagon bounced and rattled onto a flat clearing beside a fork in the river. She saw the smoke of a campfire as heads poked from the front of the wagons. The girls fought with Mattie Lafayette for a look at the first sign of civilization they had glimpsed in weeks.

"Oh, glory be to God," Narcissa whispered.

She looked down at the children running alongside. They were going to be all right.

She had done it. She had brought them through to safety. No matter what lay ahead, that much had been accomplished. The children had been saved.

"What did you say?" Old Gray asked from the seat beside her.

She felt the need to express herself. "Who coverest thyself with light as with a garment? Who stretchest out the heavens like a curtain: Who layeth the beams of his chambers in the waters? Who maketh the clouds his chariot? Who walketh upon the wings of the wind: Who makes his angels spirits, his ministers a flaming fire?" She was letting the wagonmaster be God's ears.

"What's all that gibberish mean?" Gray asked with a scratch of his nails at the back of his head where his gray hair was the longest.

"I was just thanking God for getting the children and me this far."

"You love them kids, don't you?"

"Dearly. They're all I have and I'm all they've got. But on the trail when I thought we were going to die, I lashed out at them, blaming them and God. It was so unreasonable, I don't know that they'll ever forgive me."

"I don't know about God, but kids are forgivin' little rascals. So don't worry about them none." He raised slightly in his seat. "Look ahead," he said.

A man in a weathered hat, Levi dungarees, and heavy boots peered up from the fire after flipping a frying pan and turning over a single large flap jack. His whiskered countenance seemed hostile until he spotted Narcissa.

"Hey, Jake," he called as he lowered the frying pan onto the rocks surrounding the fire, "get your ass out here and see what's coming."

From a small tent near the fire a figure emerged in dirty body-length underwear.

"Jezus!" the second man exclaimed, his hand running down his front checking his buttons. "I'll be damned if that don't look like a woman." He grabbed a pair of trousers, and was pulling them on, while he hopped along behind his partner, who walked, then ran to the lead wagon.

Narcissa thrilled to a bit of sacriligious vanity. She had primped in Annie's mirror after breakfast. She knew she looked presentable to the men coming from the tents and huts. For weeks her only mirror had been the still water in a pool or a bucket.

"Howdy, ma'am, the name's Sawyer," the first man said. He walked alongside. "Placer Pan Sawyer they call me.

What you doin' with Old Gray? You married? Got your man aboard?"

Ignoring the man, Narcissa asked Gray, "Doesn't anyone go by his real name?"

The old man snorted. "A man likes to think he's startin' fresh as a new laid egg out here, and the whores are always afraid kin will hear what they're doin', so they change their names. Indians called me Gray Eagle when I was livin' with them once. When they started callin' me Bald Eagle, I figured I best be movin' on before they scalped me."

The young woman with the carrot colored hair, the one that went by the name Featherlegs Fanny, stuck her head from the covered part of the wagon. "Well, hello, boys. Got any nuggets for a girl with legs as pretty as gold dust?"

"Hot shit!" The man called Jake slapped his leg. "There's two of 'em."

"Three wagons full of 'em boys," Old Gray announced. "Don't ever go sayin' I done you no favors."

"Holy mackerel!" Jake slammed his right fist into the palm of his other hand. His excitement was boundless.

From the wagons, girls peered around the back or lifted the canvas sides to expose their faces and much of their bare decolletage.

Sawyer flung his hat at the ground and roared with approval while his partner dug in his pocket and held up a nugget of gold for Narcissa to see.

"Goddamn, if you ain't a sight for a horny fella's eyes. Jump down from there, young lady, and this here nugget's all yours."

Narcissa withdrew when he put up his hands to help her down, but her silent refusal did nothing to dampen his spirit. "You just jump down here and before you can say Jack Robinson a couple hundred times you'll have earned yourself breakfast and this here nugget."

"She ain't one of the whores," Old Gray said, "not yet anyway."

"Whatta you mean, she ain't a whore? That's what you went for wasn't it?"

"How 'bout me, miner?" Featherlegs Fanny called to him.

"Shit, why not?"

"No, you don't," Madam Lafayette commanded. "Nobody gets off the wagons."

"Why not?" the girls cried.

"Look ahead. Men enough for three hours work," Cottontail said laughing.

Narcissa, still recovering from the shock of being considered a prostitute, looked farther along the stream.

It was alive with men. Each man had staked his legally allotted claim and a few new claims were evident, marked by tools left behind while their claimant had gone into town to pay the filing fee.

Some men were still cooking their breakfasts, the smoke of their campfires rising like steam in the cold autumn air. Others were in the stream, working cracks in the bedrock, searching around boulders, roots, and fallen trees, anywhere that the water had slowed. Still others stood waist deep in pools surrounded by dark sand.

Some were shoveling gravel into fifteen-foot sluice boxes, the troughs built of coarse sawed lumber into which they poured water from buckets or diverted the stream itself. While water washed away the lighter soil, men bent over the sluice runs, looking for the heavier gold dust, flakes, grains, or nuggets that stayed on the bottom. More worked with pans, even frying pans, scooping up dirt and gravel from the stream and swishing it carefully in a circular motion until everything spilled over the side except the heavier metal.

Above the high water mark, two Indians were working a twelve foot pit rimmed by red dirt. Near them, three blacks, evidently slaves, dug while a white man watched them from a campfire.

This was hardly the gold studded paradise Narcissa had heard about. The men were not plucking giant nuggets from the surface. They were wading knee deep in the icy stream and wallowing in mud like pigs. They were hollow eyed and desperate looking, like men whose savings and hope were being washed away faster than the worthless sand and sludge.

"Color in the pan," a man called from farther down stream. He held up a nugget, then spotted the first two miners and the wagons filled with girls. "Women!" he shrieked, his hands flying up in the air like a sports spectator when his favorite team scores. The nugget sailed from his fingers and into the ferns and tall grasses. "Aw, shit!" he cursed. He plunged into the weeds, frantically seeking his bonanza while the rest of the miners dropped their tools and ran toward Old Gray's cargo.

The valley echoed with shouting and laughter. The men fell in beside the wagons, anxious to touch a feminine hand. The girls made vulgar jokes and promises that shocked Narcissa and made her worry about the children overhearing.

Sarah and Adrian were out of the wagons, running with the men who picked them up in their powerful hands and kissed them before passing them on to the next miner.

"Men miss the kids as much as they do the women," Gray told Narcissa. "Was in a camp awhile back when a tourin' band of players was puttin' on a show. Right in the best part the only decent woman in town brought in her newborn boy child. The little one lets out a yelp and the whole play stops. 'A hand for the baby,' a man calls out, and the others gave the kid a standin' ovation. More'n they gave the actors."

Gray snapped his whip over the head of a toothless miner reaching for for the skirts Narcissa had borrowed from Velvet Ass Annie.

Narcissa was awed by the excitement, terrified of the men, yet excited with the gaggle of white faces. She had seen only Indians during most of the trip across the prairies, desert, and mountains.

"Up there's the man for you," Old Gray said as he pointed above the miners.

Narcissa followed his whip arm toward a pit above the high water mark where the stream had run in ancient times. Red dirt rimmed the pit, and the diggers paused in their work but did not join their frolicking neighbors moving with the wagons. On the highest point of the rim stood a tall, rough-cut and taciturn man in his late twenties. He wore expensive boots and a suit jacket with vest and tie. His hat was neither soiled nor marked by rain.

"That there's George Hearst, smartest lad in these parts. Mark my words, if anybody makes a fortune out of this here earth, it'll be Hearst. Never stands still, wanders from camp to camp, stakin' claims, hiring other men to do his diggin' and prospectin'. And over there," Gray continued and pointed to another man who had not joined the clamor. He was wearing bits and pieces of an army officer's uniform. He was panning and did not stop. "First Lieutenant Ulysses Grant, hero of the Mexican war. Done ran straight up a street lined with snipers at Monterrey just to get a message through. But as a miner he's a failure. Ain't found nothin' 'cept a little dust and fool's gold."

"Fool's gold?"

"Pyrite, Missy. Useless Ulysses, the boys call him. Can't get it through his West Point head that pyrite floats, shatters, and don't shine in the shade. But then there's plenty soldier boys desertin'. Can't blame 'em. Six dollars a month for doin' their duty weighed against maybe seventy dollars a day diggin' in the gravel."

As Narcissa watched, Grant stopped and drew a bottle from his pocket. He took a drink and watched the wagons pass.

"Drinkin', that's what Lyss Grant does best. Be goin' back to his post soon's his leave's over, I reckon."

Narcissa found it hard to hear the wagon master over the boisterous voices of the men and the women they trailed.

She looked ahead and felt her hopes rise.

She was staring off into the valley of the Sacramento and American rivers. It was a sight her brother had mentioned often, luring his little caravan with promises of lush green fields and tall trees.

He had not lied. He just had not lived to see his vision turn to reality. Her heavy sadness was lifted by yet another sight—the semblance of a town.

It was crowded into a flat area where the stream had

made a wide sweeping curve. Two dozen or more cones of smoke were rising into the chill, spicy air.

"A city!" she cried. "A real city!"

Old Gray snorted. "That sure ain't no city, Miss. That there's Hangtown. Nothin' but a tavern in a tent when I left. And look at it now. Growed like a weed. And a weed she is, Missy. All these minin' camps. Nothin' but weeds, chokin' everythin' pretty, stranglin' everythin' except gold and greed. That's Hangtown, sure 'nough. That ain't no city."

Whatever it was, camp, town, or city, she was entering it alone. There would be no familiar face to greet her, no family to wrap her in a nest of love and caring.

Narcissa White was alone in a strange world. No, not alone—there were two children depending on her." ❧

6

"Women comin'," called a self-proclaimed crier as he ran into the town ahead of the wagons. "Women comin'. Must be a hundred of 'em."

On her seat at the front, Narcissa White was both surprised and depressed. It was like the circus parade she had heard about and never seen.

The covers on the wagons had been lowered and the whores were dressed in their finest. They wore gawdy colors, red, purple, green, and short skirts which many of them pulled higher to expose their black stockings. Narcissa was more sedately dressed with borrowed clothes. She wore a straight calico frock, plainly made without hoops, the bodice lined with canvas for extra strength and warmth. Her head was covered with a slat bonnet which was stiffened with removable wooden splints. A cloth cape decorated with sewn blue roses added a touch of bright color.

Dozens of the miners still accompanied the girls, exchanging catcalls with each other and occasionally grabbing a quick feel of a calf or a thigh.

"That'll cost you a dollar," Madam Lafayette demanded as she spotted one of the men sampling the merchandise.

The miner protested. "For a little feel? I ain't gonna pay it!"

"Then you're barred from my place," Mattie Lafayette decreed.

The offender conceded. "All right, all right, only it ain't fair."

His friends jeered and Old Gray began playing a harmonica, handing the reins to Narcissa to control the slow moving horses.

Although her clothes, a gift from Annie, were modest, each new man assumed she was with the other girls. She was mortified, her face red, her chin held high. Her throat choked when she attempted to rebuke the men's remarks. Each time Gray came to her rescue, and the men's faces darkened briefly with disappointment before they switched their attention to the others.

It was Annie they wanted most. She still had the innocent look of a virgin, and only her haughty attitude gave the other girls a chance.

"Bait," Gray said of the favored girl. "Guys will come to Mattie's place drooling in anticipation of gettin' Velvet Ass, excuse me, Miss, then they'll settle for whatever is available."

"It's awful," Narcissa remarked. "Vulgar and disgusting. I can't believe what I'm seeing and hearing. Those awful men. Those vile women."

Gray did not quite rebuke her. "It's God's way, Miss."

"God's way! How can you say such a thing?"

"I brung the girls, Missy, and I'm a God-fearin' man. Tain't natural for men to be alone."

"But these are prostitutes."

"Ain't seen many a you nice ladies rushing out here to marry the menfolk. Oh, you'll go to San Francisco, maybe Los Angeles, or Sutter's Mill, but you won't be stayin' in Hangtown overnight if'n you can avoid it."

"But God . . ."

"Didn't see nothin' of God here 'for I left, neither, Miss. Just men with gold fever, yellow fever, California mania, gold mania. Whatever you call it, they got it. I seen 'em walk here from Maine, and ride in carts with a mule and an ox trying to pull together. Another feller I met on the trail was pushing a wheelbarrow with his things in it."

Narcissa tested her own thoughts.

The women were sinners. The men too, for that matter. At home her father would have roundly condemned any behavior approaching what she was witnessing.

It was beyond anything she had been prepared to witness.

And yet . . .

They were people.

The long lonely trail ride had put a canted perspective on what she was seeing.

Her heart went out to the men, lusting for gold and the women. The women too, lusting after the appetites of the flesh.

But what were they in the eyes of God? He had let these people live while he had taken the lives of John and Melissa. That did not seem fair.

Or was there a message in the contrast of the dead preacher and the live whores?

Then she thought of the children. Was she supposed to bring them up in such an atmosphere? Such a town?

As quickly as she criticized the others, she denounced herself. She was being judgmental, thinking of herself as better than all the rest.

Was that what her father had taught?

She could not imagine what his reaction would have been upon entering such a scene. On the pulpit he preached a fiery hell and damnation type of sermon. But only from the pulpit.

"It's all crazy," Gray was saying.

"Plain hysteria," Narcissa observed.

"Yep, plain hysteria."

Narcissa straightened herself and watched Sarah and Adrian mingling with the miners. "Perhaps John was right in wanting to establish a church here. Certainly there is a need."

"Here?"

"Sutter's Mill," she admitted.

"Figures. Like I was sayin', God forgot these miners too, so don't be bad mouthin' the girls who come to do their part. Takes real stuffin' to come here in the middle of nowhere and make a life for themselves. Few years from now, most of them girls will be married proper and raisin' kids, foundin' a town."

"Married!" Narcissa dismissed the idea as outrageous.

Hangtown was an unplanned collection of tents, half built structures, stores and saloons with false fronts and broad sidewalks along mud roads. Most of the crude structures, often built at odd angles, were along one main but twisting street with a single sign on a post proclaiming it as *Broadway*.

The new Eldorado, the promised land—it did not look like much, except confetti and serpentine laying on a floor midway through a party.

Strangely enough, the first thing Narcissa saw was a printing press standing outdoors on a plank floor. A tarpaulin lay nearby to cover the paper, press and type in case of rain.

One of the two men working at the makeshift newspaper came running with pad and pencil. He shouted questions to Mattie Lafayette above the uproar.

"How many girls you got, Madam, and what are their names?"

"Got it all writ out," Mattie replied. She handed down a folded piece of paper. "Girl's names, ages . . ."

"All eighteen years old, I suppose," the reporter said cynically.

"Of course. Names, age, and descriptions. Save the boys time makin' their choice when they get to the parlour."

"This your lead girl?" he asked, nodding to Narcissa. His face was clean shaven, and he had a glint of lust in his eyes.

"Maybe," Mattie responded.

"No!" Narcissa said emphatically.

"What's your name, girlie?"

Gray came to her defense. "She ain't no girlie, and her name's none of your business. Why in hell do you want to put a story in the paper about this mess, anyway? Ain't no need. Everybody will know Mattie Lafayette is in town."

The reporter, jogging alongside replied, "Not the boys in the outlying stakes. Besides, those that know will want to read about the girls anyway. They'll pore over the paper until they get their money together. Never can print enough papers in a mining camp, you know that, Gray."

"Yep, and I'll bet there's a town promoter hiding in the woods somewhere paying you to print what a paradise Hangtown is so he can send word back east to the suckers."

"Every camp's got its promoter, Gray," the newspaper man said. "How else would we get all us fools here? You and me included." He switched his attention to Mattie. "These dance hall girls, too Madam?"

"Nope, they do all their dancin' in bed."

Embarrassed, Narcissa covered her ears and called the children to join her on the wagon, but they were caught up in the excitement. There was no getting them to mind.

From ahead came the sound of hammering and sawing. Some of the men continued at their jobs of building the town until their curiosity lured them to the crowd. It was a larger town than Narcissa expected. A man emerged from a tent with shaving cream on his face, and a barber's sheet hanging from his neck. A butcher appeared in his bloody apron, one hand holding a cleaver, the other clamped on the legs of a headless chicken that jerked in post-mordial spasms and showered blood onto its captor.

There were shacks sharing common walls and others set at odd angles to the street. Most of the commercial buildings, including stores, assay office, bank, and professional offices, were built narrow in front. They were compact in structure to save walking in mud and slush. Peaked roofs were hidden by square false fronts. Most had porches where a man could stomp off the dirt from his boots or take shelter against the weather.

There was a restaurant, a bakery, three laundries, a bootmaker and a tailor.

The main road was busy. Oxen dragged logs in from the forests. Construction men wielded hammers, picks, and shovels along the route. Mules plodded everywhere. Horses were scarcer. The town smelled of droppings.

The overall mood was stirring and bustling. Wheelbarrows rolled as hopeful profiteers put the town together with the same verve that others panned the icy waters of the streams or dug in the hard rock for their obsession.

When the wagons finally drew to a stop, it was outside one of the few two-story buildings, the Hang Dog Saloon. It was built with a permanence that exhibited more confidence than the other shacks.

Its porch was narrow, but the uprights that held the railed roof were lathed into attractive designs and angles. The windows were stained glass. Curtains veiled off the interior, although the swinging doors covered only the middle of the entrance. More males appeared, from inside. Some of them were mean looking, but less hardened and dirty than the miners.

The men were a cross-section of the world—whites, blacks, Indians, Chinese and men with foreign accents. Narcissa had expected that. Ships had been bringing adventurers to San Francisco for more than a year. Drawn by the lust for gold, the passengers and crews alike had left the ships rocking in the harbor and streamed inland to a hundred places like Hangtown. Ranches and orchards were deserted. Fruit rotted on the ground.

As they stopped, the girls were lifted from the wagons and escorted into the Hang Dog saloon. Before Narcissa could stop them, the children were heading inside.

"Sarah, Adrian! Don't you dare go in there!"

Narcissa fought against another fear. So many people, all strangers. She knew only those riding in the wagons and she had no one she could call a friend. The loneliness of the trail had been better than this.

Strong hands suddenly lifted Narcissa to the porch of the saloon.

Brown eyes twinkled down at her and the lips beneath his black mustache grinned. He was handsome and clean in a white shirt and black trousers. He wore a hat with the brim pinned up to the crown, revealing his thick black hair. He was in his thirties, she guessed, with strong fea-

tures. Something about his expression exuded enjoyment
of life. He was a man who would not take life too seriously.

Narcissa warmed to him instantly. He seemed to have
stepped from her dreams. A strong man with a bent for
fun.

She smiled for the first time in months. She wished she
had taken more care in the way she dressed and groomed
herself this morning, but she had not anticipated there
would be anyone like him in the camp. And she thought
she had been soured on men by the trapper. Instead she
enjoyed this man's touch.

"You one of the bloody tarts?" he asked in an accent
she mistook for British.

"What did you say?"

"Whores."

Narcissa exploded. "How dare you!"

She slapped at him and missed.

"No need to take offense," he said.

"We were going to set up a church," Narcissa said with
a haughty toss of her head.

He laughed. "That's a new name for it."

"She's serious," Old Gray said as he joined them on the
porch.

"You bloody well think God sent you, Miss? About all
you can do here is pray none of those bawds has crabs or
the clap. But pretending you're going to set up a temple
here in Sodom and Gomorrah, that's a giggle."

His power to offend her was greater than she would
have guessed possible. She had assumed he felt the same
about her as she did about about him—that there had
been a bond the moment they met.

He was not just another of the miners. She certainly
was not one of the whores.

Instead of friendship, animosity was building. She
would try to forgive him and restore the conversation to a
more agreeable tone.

"You're outback, way outback, Sheila."

"Outback?" She didn't understand. "Where's outback?"

"Out west, girl. Out in the never-never where the crows

fly backwards. West of sunset and farther than beyond, where men are men and women are as scarce and more in demand than your religion. Well, it's way out back. You can't miss it."

Narcissa looked to Old Gray. "Never give him a mind, Miss. He talks 'Strine. Orstralian, Miss. Don't listen to him. Them ducks will charm the skirts off a lady and not so much as leave her a tip."

"Call me Drover, Miss. Got other names but they're best forgotten. My mother says I was sired by a Koala Bear and nursed by Wallaby."

"You came from Australia to hunt gold?"

"Ah, six thousand of us came over. Those we left behind told us not to go. Had a poem for it. 'Then pause, ye heedless voyagers and shun the golden snare. Oh listen to the warning voice that cries, beware, beware.' "

"But you came anyway," she said.

He quoted another poem. " 'When you start for San Francisco, they treat you like a dog. The victuals that you're compelled to eat, ain't fit for a hog.' But I came anyway. Glad I did . . . now."

Narcissa felt a shiver. From the moment the wagon train had encountered the first miner, her hopes had plummeted like the sun at eventide. Her brother and sister-in-law gone, two children left, and the dreams of a young girl drying up and blowing farther away with each dirty face along the stream and in this purgatory called Hangtown.

Was this why she had risked her life to come West? For men like the miners and the townsmen who flocked to the whores like bees after a flower's nectar?

The Australian seemed different. He was tall, clean, and broad shouldered, with a devilish grin that suggested gold was not his god. There was a glint in his eye, a wry note in his speech, a sort of a wait-and-see attitude, as if he took nothing seriously. He stood with his thumbs in the tops of his trousers, a lean figure who would command respect even in Iowa City. But despite his pleasant demeanor, she sensed that wise men would avoid crossing him.

"Been livin' in Sydney town," he said, "where everything was coming up apples at first."

"That's in San Francisco," Gray explained.

"Had to leave when California became a state."

"California a state now!" Gray was surprised.

"More than a month now," Drover replied. "Thirty-first state in your union."

Narcissa did not understand. "But what does that have to do with you leaving San Francisco?"

"Law, Miss. Law and order. People get fussy about the law when they get more government hanging over them. Anyway, it seems my mates got to burning the bleeding town so they could loot and steal rather than work a mine or tend a bar. Five Strines were hopping like Roos from the end of a rope the night I left."

"How awful."

"It was right enough. Most of them deserved a bit of neck stretchin'."

"That's barbaric."

"It's a man's world, Miss . . . ah . . ."

"White. Narcissa White."

"Well, like I was saying. This is a man's world, like outback at home. I just hope you don't expect to bash me mates ears with religion, Miss White. You'll be bitterly disappointed."

"She's going on to Sutter's Mill," Gray said for her.

"Perhaps eventually." Her answer was unexpected, even to her. Suddenly she was not so anxious to escape the camp. "What did you do in Australia, Mr. Drover?"

"Just plain Drover. I was a ranger around Gundaroo, where folks toes turn up climbing gum trees for koala bears and honeycomb when things get hard."

"You were in law enforcement then?"

"Something like that."

A roar of laughter went up from the tavern, and Narcissa remembered the children.

"Mr. Gray, would you fetch the children, please? I daren't go in there."

"Might as well get used to the pub, Miss White," Dro-

ver told her. "It's Hangtown's social center and courthouse."

"But I couldn't go in there alone."

The big Australian took her arm and led her to the
door. Inside most of the girls were seated on top of the
long fancy bar. The children were among the men. Adrian
was awed by the nude painting above the mirrors and
Sarah stood on a roulette table while fatherly looking men
talked and joked with her.

A piano was playing, men were stomping their feet
while others danced. Miners who had not been quick
enough to get a girl grabbed another man and were dancing together.

Narcissa did not know whether to share the wild excitement or to be appalled.

"Any you ladies going to set up in suds row?" one of
the men asked from the crowd. "Damned Chinamen
charge half the price of a new shirt for a wash and press."

A friend tipped the man's hat down over his eyes.
"What do you need a clean shirt for, Sigle? What you figure on doin' tonight, you ain't gonna do half dressed."

"All you mud wallower's get to the Chinaman's before
sundown," Mattie Lafayette said from the end of the bar.
"My girls cater to a class clientele only."

"Whatcha chargin'?" a voice called.

"Five dollars gold for the regular. Ten for extras, and
twenty for the virgin here."

The attention switched to Velvet Ass Annie who sat at
the end of the bar, swinging her legs, her air of superiority
keeping the men at bay.

"What's your name?" Narcissa heard a young man
ask.

Annie looked at him and her haughty attitude changed.
She smiled. For a moment she was shy.

"Annie," she said.

"Velvet Ass Annie," the girl called Butterfly answered.
"She thinks she's better'n the rest of us. Thinks she's lined
with mink, she does."

"What's your name?" Annie asked back. "Samuel? I'll
bet it's from the Bible."

"David," he said as he rubbed his hands shyly on his trousers, drying the nervous sweat that dampened his palms and glistened on his forehead and upper lip. "Ain't seen nothin' like you since I left Missouri."

"You comin' to see me, David?" Annie asked.

The boy stared at the floor. "Ain't got twenty dollars. Don't never come up with anything except dust, and not much of that."

"You could come see me and talk," Annie said. "That's free."

"Like hell it is," Mattie Lafayette roared. "Ain't nothin' free at my place."

"Where's your place gonna be? In tents?" a miner asked as he wiped his hand back through his hair with anticipation.

"You'd like that because you can stand outside and listen for nothin'," a friend accused him.

"It'll be wherever Judge Russell says," Old Gray replied.

Immediately the room went silent and the men looked to the balcony that ran along the second story of the saloon. At the railing stood a man in his sixties. He was white haired, distinguished in a showy way, and wearing a dark suit and a shirt with studs with a narrow black bow tie. His most noteworthy item of apparel though, was a top hat. It was tall, black and completely out of place. While he stared down at the crowd, he pulled a cigar from his mouth.

"These are parlor ladies, Judge. They ain't no street walkin' strumpets."

"Can they stay, Judge?" a man asked.

"Can they?" The plea spread through the crowd.

"Come on, Judge. A minin' camp ain't a town unless it's got a whorehouse."

"Please." The word seemed as incongruous as the hat in these surroundings.

The Judge sought out Mattie Lafayette and the two negotiated with their eyes. He held the cigar in front of his trousers, bobbing it up and down, and Narcissa White felt herself blushing as an obscene thought entered her head.

After all the filth she had heard in the past few days, the thought should have meant nothing, but this dirty thought was hers alone.

"Forgive me, God," she said to herself.

"There's that big house, all fancied up, at the edge of the camp," Old Gray said. "I figured that's what it was for when I saw it goin' up 'fore I went to fetch the ladies."

"Can they, Judge?"

The man in black rolled the cigar around in his mouth. "For now," he said. Then he walked into one of the rooms that opened off of the balcony.

A roar of approval assaulted Narcissa's ears, and she remembered the gun going off in the trapper's cabin. The nightmare was still going on. She was in a madhouse where the arrival of prostitutes was cause for celebration.

"Then it's settled." Mattie announced. "You boys get yourselves cleaned up. And no standin' around outside moonin' 'fore sundown. My girls gotta fresh'n up."

The girls jumped down from the bar with help, flouncing their skirts as they were escorted to the door. None of them spoke until Annie came abreast of Narcissa.

"Coming?" she asked.

"I . . ." Narcissa glanced at Old Gray in panic. He only shrugged. "Is there a hotel in town?" she asked of Drover.

"Hotel, saloon. Same thing in Hangtown. There's plenty of rooms here, but they're no doubt rented out to miners who ain't yet lost their grubstakes." He wrinkled his brow in consternation and then grinned. "You could stay at my place, I suppose. You and the kids."

"I beg your pardon?" Narcissa was taken aback at the suggestion.

"Best I can offer. Nights get cold here for the little ones, you know."

"I'd rather freeze," she retorted. Taking the children by the hand she turned away.

"Don't get too high and mighty, Miss. Nobody figures you're the bloody queen just because you put on airs."

Again he had hurt Narcissa.

Annie took her arm. "You don't have any choice," she said. "You'd better stick with us for a night or two."

"But I couldn't! The children . . ."

"And you can't sleep in the open either. So come along."

"What'll people think?"

"People?" Annie laughed. "You'll be with Hangtown's high society 'til the good ladies and their gossip come into camp when the pickins are better and the life is easier. So come along. You and the kids have to stay somewhere."

"But will Mrs. Lafayette permit it?"

"She'll permit anything I want as long as she can sell my ass for a high enough price."

Narcissa caught Drover's eyes once more. "If you weren't one of them bloody tarts, Miss White, you'd accept my offer."

But Gray had her arm and was leading her to the wagons. Now every girl was carrying a bottle of liquor, each one open. Some drank as they climbed aboard.

At the lead wagon, Narcissa lifted Adrian into the rear, and took Sarah onto her lap. The child still clutched her bible. Her eyes were wide with excitement and in her hand she held a lollipop partially wrapped in paper. The candy was old and smudged with dirt, but the child's tongue licked at it with pleasure. "A man gave it to me," she said.

The wagons began to move when Narcissa noticed an arresting figure who would appear to be of a different class than the men around him. He sat on a stallion seventeen hands high, a glossy black animal that pranced nervously under the man's light hold on the reins.

The rider was tall and slender of build. He wore black engraved boots that had never stepped in mud. His clothes were eastern cut, a dark pinstriped suit with a vest to match over a fine linen shirt with diamond studs and a gold tipped string tie. He wore gold rings and a gold watch-chain. One thing was for certain. He was not afraid of being robbed. His hat was black and western, but the crown was low. The felt had never been soaked with rain or stained with bands of sweat. An intricate hand-crafted band of silver stretched around the edge of the brim.

The man himself was somber. His face narrow, his mouth a straight cut, his nose patrician, his eyes as deepset as if he were looking out on a crude corner of the world with quiet disdain. His irises were a cold steel blue.

He had an educated aura about him that Narcissa White supposed men of breeding carried with them like the robes of their matriculation.

She had seldom seen his kind, even in the east. The daughter of a minister had little opportunity to associate with such men. If she had seen few like him during her childhood, she had certainly never seen his type in Iowa. Iowa, where the state senators and legislators came to the still unfinished capitol building with its gold colored dome. Many tried to effect a similar air, but they were all older, and their ruddy cheeks and untanned foreheads marked them as men of the soil, even when they wore their 'go-to-meetin' clothes.

"Who's that?" she asked with guarded curiosity.

Gray knew who she meant.

"That's King. Walter King, only nobody don't call him anything except Mr. King, least wise nobody but Drover. That Aussie don't bow to nobody 'cept Queen Victoria, I guess."

"What's he do?"

"Drover?"

"No. Mr. King."

"Don't do nothin', far as I know. Just finances things."

"Things?"

"The Hang Dog Saloon. The judge owns it, but I heard King put up the money. Started in a tent and look at her now. King grubstaked twenty, thirty claims along the fork here and lord knows how much else. Story is he was a rich boy sent west because he got a girl . . . well you can't believe everything you hear. Anyway, he plays poker sometimes and goes to San Francisco when he gets bored." Gray considered his young traveler and extended the implications of her question to new dimensions. "The way I see it, a girl's safer with Mattie than she is with some dude like King."

"He looks like a gentleman."

"Maybe he is. Maybe he ain't. All I know is nobody fools around with King. Talks soft 'til he shoots the balls off a man who can't pay his gamblin' debt. Sorry, Missy. I still ain't used to a lady at my side."

King's left hand hung straight down and she noticed he had a way of folding his fingers into a fist and scrubbing his palm with the tips. It was a strange nervous habit for a man with his regal calm. His gaze turned to her. He was measuring her. In his eyes she saw . . . what? Respect? Interest? Or . . . desire?

Narcissa turned away, her face burning. She was at once flattered by his interest and angry with herself for her own weakness.

Gray snapped the reins and made a sharp clicking noise with his mouth. The horses started.

Narcissa looked up again at the man on the beautiful horse. Her hopes rose.

A gentleman.

There was one in Hangtown. One educated man amidst the rabble. Then she saw the belt across his waist. The gun on his right hip was hidden by his jacket, but the bulge showed it was not a little derringer.

Glancing up, she realized he was looking at her once more. All the other girls . . . prettier . . . more available at least, but he was studying her.

She lowered her gaze with embarrassment. Had he noticed her watching him, lost in the silly dreams of a young girl? The last one of the men she saw before the wagon jerked ahead was Drover frowning at her with disapproval.

Briefly she wondered why.

But Sarah and Adrian tugged at her and looked up at her with a pathetic confusion. The men had been nice to them.

She forced a smile. "It will be all right, children," she reassured them. "We'll be staying in a house tonight."

"A house?" Sarah was trying to remember back to the days when home was not a moving wagon.

A whorehouse, Narcissa thought. She was not offering the children much, but they would have to go along with the best she could do.

And somehow, God willing, she would be able to make a better home for them soon.

Maybe she would even make a better place out of Hangtown.

The enormity of that dream overwhelmed her, and briefly she put it out of her mind.

First, she had to get herself and the children through the night.　　　　　⌣§

7

THEY huddled in the attic of the newly built mansion. It still smelled of fresh-cut wood, and the furnishings in the first floor rooms were as elegant as anything Narcissa would have expected in San Francisco.

Here among the clapboard buildings, tents, and shanties of Hangtown, the "Parlor" as Mattie Lafayette dubbed her new castle, was a palace of baroque red wallpaper and plush overstuffed chairs and couches. It was dimly but richly lit by whale oil lamps with decorated shades. In the main sitting room, Mattie's girls arranged themselves in tableaux of seductive poses. Then the door was opened and the miners, freshly scrubbed and in clean shirts, crowded in.

Narcissa had sent the children to the attic immediately after the dinner she had helped prepare from food donated by the market.

They came in like gentlemen, speaking in soft voices, and holding their hats in their hands.

Briefly Narcissa thought she had misjudged them all.

It was almost like courting in any town, until the men allowed inside first had made the rounds of the parlor, sizing up the merchandise. Girls like Featherlegs, Cottontail,

81

and Annie attracted two or more men. They were polite to all of the callers, but eventually selected their first choice.

Then the mood changed. Cottontail stood and began pressing close to Placer Pan Sawyer, putting her arms around his shoulders and rubbing gently against him. Featherlegs drew her first choice to the couch beside her.

The girls ordered drinks and money began to exchange hands as the girls who had worn men's attire on the trail began producing bottles of champagne. Corks popped. Girls giggled. Men laughed. Hands began to probe the girl's intimate parts, and Narcissa stood at the top of the stairs, gawking.

"Oh no!" She shouted and captured the attention of the entire crowd. "Oh, no, this isn't right." Her innocence captivated the men. "You shouldn't be doing things like this. It's bad enough between husbands and wives." Her thoughts returned to the words of her father, and her upbringing within the sheltered walls of the parsonage. Her whole life had centered around the teachings of the church. What would they think now? She was sincere when she said, "You should all join me in a prayer for forgiveness."

Placer Pan's partner Jake howled like a coyote then said, "Preacher lady, you solve my problem and I'll join your church."

He began unbuttoning the front of his trousers.

"Cut it out Jake," Sawyer said as he shoved his friend to the floor.

"I'll take that deal," another man offered.

"Me too."

"You going down on your knees for me, preacher?"

"Marry me and I'll never enter another whorehouse in my life. I swear on a stack of bibles."

Then Madam Lafayette glowered from the base of the stairs. "Enough," she commanded. "Next man makes a remark, goes to the back of the line."

"Aw, Mattie, we was just funnin' her a little," Cottontail said.

"Fuck the fun. You're here to work. You, girl," the order was directed at Narcissa, "get up in the attic like I told you or you sleep in the cold. You're holding up business."

A stunned Narcissa White retreated.

It was not like her to push her religious convictions on anyone. The outburst had been completely atypical, but then she had never seen such goings on.

She cowered, her eyes closed, trying to recall an appropriate prayer.

She had gone to hell, that was it.

She was in the devil's power.

Should she fight? How could she? One girl against a town ruled by Satan himself.

In her turmoil, she glanced only briefly at Adrian and Sarah, assuming from their positions that they were asleep where she had left them.

But as the melodian began to play and the laughter grew raucous, the children sneaked down to the top of the first landing, where their aunt had earlier peeked at the party below. It wasn't until Sarah tittered uncontrollably that Narcissa discovered the pair and hustled them back to the attic.

"Why can't we watch, Cissie?" Sarah asked. "You let us watch grownup parties at home."

"This is different," Narcissa replied, still shocked by the men cupping the buttocks of the girls or burying their faces between the exposed mounds of the whores' bosoms.

"Why?" Adrian demanded. "Isn't it a party?"

"Not a christian party."

"Why?"

Narcissa flushed. She could not begin to explain to her two small charges what was under way in the room below them. "You two must go to sleep now. It's late. Under no circumstances are you to go down stairs." Her firm tone of voice discouraged any protests or further questions. She kissed them both and sent them back to their makeshift bed.

Natural curiosity tugged at her, but she had an innate prescience that the party would grow more bawdy, although she was still not sure what would happen next.

Perhaps it was like rape.

Maybe the men were going to rape the women like the trapper had forced himself on her. Yet the women were not crying for help or fighting to escape. It was as if they were looking forward to the act.

That was unthinkable, but she could imagine no other explanation. She remembered her own experience. With so many being raped at once, would the house be filled with screams and male grunting? Would the children hear? Would they visualize what was transpiring?

She went to join the children in the makeshift bed Mattie Lafayette had provided for the three of them. Both children were still awake, listening in the darkness to the party below. She sang a nursery rhyme, softly and soothing, but loud enough to cover some of the noise. Her efforts to distract the youngsters met with limited success. An hour passed before their weary eyes finally closed and she could pinch out the solitary candle that provided the room's dim illumination. Outside the dormer windows it was dark. There was no light in the street.

When she was sure the children were sleeping, she sneaked from the room. She crept down the attic stairs to the second floor. Along the corridors leading in three directions from the stairs, were doorways close together the way Narcissa imagined the hotels she had read about.

Ingenuous, she watched as pairs of males and females came up the stairs. Some went directly into the cubicle rooms. Others paused on the steps, kissing, fondling each other before they disappeared from view. Some stopped at the doors, the girls tantalizing their customers with brief delays, pretending they were innocents as the men thrust their groins at the still dressed ladies or ran their sand-paper rough hands with blackened broken nails down half exposed bosoms. In their haste the occupants of two rooms left the door ajar. Transfixed, Narcissa watched as men's bare rears pumped up and down, seemingly driven by the female legs wrapped around them. In one case the couple was half on the bed, the man standing, the girl's legs spread to greet him.

From another room a girl raced out, stark naked, her

customer whipping at her exposed buttocks with the end of his belt.

"Hey, Buck," a friend remonstrated. "What'd you wanta do that fer?"

The one called Buck, still in his underwear with his male appendage exposed, shouted his answers indignantly. "Damned bitch, so good with her hands, I didn't get my due."

Men, all smelling of whiskey, wrestled him to the floor, rendered him unconscious, and dragged him into the night.

Sin.

The word finally affixed itself to the din of music, laughter, shouting, grunting, and groans.

Sin.

This is what her father and brother had been preaching about. Men and women, doing such things to each other. Here was real hell.

Narcissa had never been truly religious. The bible had become nothing but meaningless stories read over and over. Prayers at meals. Prayers at night. Church on Sunday. Meetings and picnics on Saturday. Her menfolk standing at the pulpit raising their arms and calling God down upon the sinners that lurked somewhere in the town of Iowa City, the sinners that lurked everywhere. Sinners that the sheltered daughter of a minister began to doubt existed because she lived in a world where they did not.

Sin. She had never guessed it was like this.

It was all confused in her mind. What the others were doing was wrong, but why? They weren't lonely. They weren't miserable.

She was.

But what they were doing was wrong.

She had to discover why. She had to do something about it.

"May the strength of God pilot me," she found herself recalling from her repertoire. "The power of God preserve me today. May the wisdom of God instruct me, the eye of God watch over me."

"Narcissa," Velvet Ass Annie spoke to her from the second floor. "Did that boy show up?"

Narcissa blinked in surprise. Annie had just come from one of the rooms. She wore only her merry widow top and her underpants and hose. In her hand was a golden nugget and a miner in his forties was making his way to the first floor, buttoning his trousers. Another man, five years older, was being held at the foot of the stairs by Madam Lafayette.

"You ready, Annie?" Mattie asked. "Can't keep this mob waitin' down here. We want 'em pannin' for more gold in the mornin'."

"In a minute, Mattie." Annie came part way up the stairs. "You know, the one who called himself David."

Narcissa experienced cross-currents of emotions. She had seen, rather she had felt that same expression she saw now on Annie's face. When? She couldn't recall.

Yes, she remembered, in the makeshift schoolhouse her last year. There was a boy who stirred sensations inside her when she just glimpsed his face or passed close to him during recess. She had experienced it more recently too, but when? Annie had the same look.

But she was a whore. She couldn't have the same sensations as a decent girl, could she?

Another wave of feeling washed over the minister's daughter.

Was she decent anymore? Had the trapper soiled her in the eyes of God? She never remembered rape being discussed in church, leastwise whether the victim sinned as well as the man. And what if she had enjoyed it toward the end for a fleeting moment? Had she? Was she condemned to hell?

Maybe she was already there. Hangtown—the hell of the West.

Then another couple emerged from a room. Cottontail and a drunk. The man was arguing, holding up a brass medallion the size of a silver dollar. Words were stamped across the coin, but Narcissa couldn't begin to read them from such a distance.

"What'd you mean it ain't worth nothin'?" the man was

arguing. "I won it fair and square in a poker game. Says right here," his finger pointed to the lettering. "Good for one screw."

Cottontail finished the reading for him. " 'At Madam La Fifi's, San Francisco.' Get walking if you wanta use that thing, digger. We deal strictly in gold."

Another man came up to take a turn with Cottontail. He had left a small bag of gold dust with Mattie.

"Narcissa, did you see him?" Annie asked again.

"No, no I didn't."

"Damn," Annie sighed. "How come every time I see a boy I like, he can't come up with the money."

"You!" Madam Lafayette jabbed a finger at Narcissa. "Find yourself a room. I'm sending a man up."

"What?" Narcissa cried. "But I can't . . ."

"Can't hell. Any woman can lay on her back and spread her legs. There's more men down here than we can handle if the girls fuck all night. Be a riot if we don't get 'em all through."

"No." Mattie was disappearing into the living room. In minutes she would be back. In panic, Narcissa turned to the two girls on the floor below. "I can't," she cried. "I can't."

"Shoulda knowed," Cottontail said. "When Mattie took you and the kids in and fed you, I figured she'd have you on your back sooner or later, but not like this. A girl has to break in easy or it ain't no fun."

"Get the kids," Annie directed. "Hurry."

"But . . ."

"Hurry. Get the kids."

"What about my screw?" the man waiting asked Cottontail impatiently. "I paid with good dust for you."

"Well, tell the Madam I'm demanding double because you look big enough to tear a little girl like me apart."

"Me?" The man's face beamed with pride. "Aw, no. I ain't never done much comparin', but I ain't nothin' special."

"The hell you ain't," Cottontail said. "Double for a big man like you."

Narcissa ran upstairs and roused the children. Sarah's

eyes couldn't open and she had to be carried. Adrian, pulled by his aunt, staggered along down the stairs to the second floor, wiping the sleep from his eyes and trying to take in what was going on in the rooms around him.

From the far end of the hall, Annie signalled and held a door. It opened on stairs that led to the kitchen and out the back way.

"But where will I go?" Narcissa puzzled.

"Try the wagon parked at the south end of the town," Annie said. "I heard there was a couple of religious nuts down there. Judge told them to be out of town by morning."

"Why didn't you tell me that before?"

"Because . . . because, hell, who do I have left when you're gone? Not even David can buy his way in here. Go," Annie said, "and ride out of here in the morning before you're trapped like the rest of us."

Narcissa carried and led the children into the dark. Behind her she could hear a ruckus and the slap of a hand hitting a face. Madam Lafayette's voice was angry and high pitched. It was like a whip driving Narcissa away from the house. She wore no jacket and the night was cold. Her feet broke through a thin layer of ice to the mud below and she again felt the biting chill of the mountains.

A few men standing around the big house called to her and blocked her path. They were frightening the children, making crude remarks.

"Hey little girl, where you going?"

"Leavin' before we got our turn?"

"Send the kiddies away and let's go to it over at my tent."

They were on all sides of her, closing in. Shadows rather than recognizable men. She couldn't tell if they were serious or toying with her. She tried to run but a man pushed her to the center of the circle. The children were crying. She was demanding the drunkards leave her alone.

It was then that the Australian's voice overwhelmed the others.

"Leave her be, mates. The Sheila's mine. Bought and paid for."

"That's not true," she insisted.

But Drover pushed into the circle, shoving two men aside.

"Hey, we staked our claim on this one already," she heard one of the tormentors object.

"A claim is as strong as the man who files it," the Australian insisted.

A man swung and Drover plunged a fist into his belly.

The fight quickly engaged all the men, and Narcissa took the opportunity to run. She could tell the Australian was taking a beating, but not all the grunts and groans were his. He was taking a toll before the number of the opposition proved too much.

Another drunkard. She thought of Drover fighting over her as if she was a nugget found along a claim line. Or had he come to her rescue?

No, she convinced herself. Drover was no better than the rest.

She ran, stumbling once more and coming up caked with mud. She was crying.

The nightmare would not end.

The trapper chased her, so did Mattie Lafayette. Men with gold nuggets in their hands smirked at her and told her to spread her legs.

She remembered the pain and the other sensation too. One was as cruel as the other.

She didn't understand.

At the end of town she found a lone covered wagon sitting near a fire where only a few embers still glowed. She could barely see.

"Where are we, Cissie?" Adrian asked.

"I don't know," was the only answer she could give.

"Why can't I sleep?"

"Is this where mama and papa are?" Sarah asked. Then she cuddled down in her aunt's arms and drifted back to sleep.

Adrian sat where he was and leaned against the front wheel of the wagon. A horse tied near by whinnied nervously. The sounds from the whore house seemed far away.

"Hello," Narcissa said to the wagon. "Is there anyone here?"

There was a stirring inside, then a man's voice replying. "Who's there? That you, judge? I told you we were leaving in the morning."

Narcissa began to move away when a woman spoke from the wagon. "Heavens, it's a girl, and with children. Wait, child. Don't run."

The voice was gentle.

Within minutes, the man appeared wearing trousers over his nightshirt. The woman came out behind him with a blanket drawn around her. Neither was more than a silhouette framed by the dying embers of the fire.

"We're the Clappes," the man announced.

"Church folk?" Narcissa asked nervously.

His wife answered for them. "Yes, we've been spreading the gospel through these heathen lands. And you?"

"My father was a preacher. Presbyterian. My brother too. My brother was coming west to establish a church only they," Narcissa lowered her voice, "perished on the trail."

"What a horrible story. What did you say your name was?"

"Narcissa White. I rode into town this morning with the girls."

"The girls?"

Even in the darkness, Narcissa could tell Mrs. Clappe was looking toward the house.

"I'm not one of them."

"I should hope not."

"But they aren't all bad."

"Loose women like that? Even loose is too kind a word to describe them."

"They saved us. We'd have died, I think, if it hadn't been for them and Old Gray."

Mr. Clappe laughed. "That old reprobate. Goes to church once a year on Christmas, I hear. Puts a nickel in the collection plate and figures he's saved for another twelve months."

"If that bunch saved you, dear," his wife said, "it was only for one reason. But never mind, bring the children into the wagon."

They carried the boy and his sister inside. Then Clappe hoisted Narcissa in with his wife.

"I'll sleep out tonight," he said. "Keep an ear open in case any of that rabble comes looking for you. Can't be too careful with these types."

In the wagon, Mrs. Clappe made room for Narcissa to curl up and rest her head on a stack of bibles covered by a blanket.

"Better rest, dear. You'll need your strength. You'll be going back to San Francisco with Mr. Clappe and me in the morning. I'm afraid Hangtown is our one defeat."

"Oh?" Narcissa said through a yawn.

"We've traveled these trails for months, bringing the word of God to these poor men, isolated from everything good. And we've always been welcomed. Our services are crowded. The collection plate is filled with golden appreciation. Our bibles all sold before we were halfway through our trip. But not here. Not in this place where Satan rules with the strength of a hundred missionaries. We have to leave. We have no choice. No one comes to our services. No storekeeper will sell us so much as a pound of flour. We'll be living off the land before we reach San Francisco, but God will provide."

"Will he?" Narcissa asked, thinking of her brother and sister-in-law. Thinking of the children and the meal that had saved them.

"It's that man," Mrs. Clappe said. "The devil himself. That one who calls himself the judge."

Narcissa remembered the man in the top hat, standing on the balcony of the saloon.

"He rules like a king and nobody knows why."

Narcissa remembered. The men had turned to the judge. They asked if he would let the prostitutes stay. The decision was his. Obviously he ruled just as Mrs. Clappe claimed.

"Someday Mr. Clappe and I will return. God is not so easily defeated. We shall return, but in the morning, you'll have to go with us. You can't stay here. But let us pray before we sleep." The group knelt and Mrs. Clappe began to speak in a voice that seemed to reach straight to heaven. "Bless all who worship Thee, from the rising of the sun unto the going down of the same. Of Thy goodness, give us, with Thy love, inspire us . . ."

Narcissa's thoughts wandered back to the other phrase the woman had said. Can't stay here.

Can't stay here. The words echoed through her mind as Narcissa slipped into the first real rest she'd enjoyed in weeks.

And in her dreams she saw Hangtown.

Not all mud and cheap clapboard houses. Not drunken men and sinning tarts. She saw shops and women in fine dresses. Children at play. A school and a church.

The man called Drover and the one they called King.

She saw all that and more.

She saw the trapper's face and felt his weight crushing her, the thing tearing her body painfully, cruelly.

But there was more. A mixture of feelings. Hope. Determination. A need for revenge.

But revenge was sinful.

She remembered back to her childhood days when the family had lived in a small New Hampshire town. She had deliberately splashed mud on a boy who had pulled her braids.

She had been punished, forced to spend hours pretending to read the bible, and she had to apologize to the boy. Afterwards she had told him she had her fingers crossed when she asked his forgiveness.

But the thought of her days in New Hampshire were good memories. She remembered the tiny library. It seemed to have been filled with thousands of books. Reading as fast as she could, she could not get through them before the family moved on to another church and another town.

She wanted a library for Hangtown. How Adrian and Sarah would love that.

She wanted a park too, a square with a bandstand in the center. She bet there were more than enough men in the camp with talent to make up a complete band.

Socials too.

That was the best part of church. A naughty view of God's house, but true. In New Hampshire there had been lots of church socials. She and the other children could run through the adults talking and eating pies and drinking apple cider.

Those were happy times.

She could not go back. She would have to bring New Hampshire West. What a foolish, ambitious thought. Narcissa White could never accomplish so much.

But a church could. It transformed a town, her father often said.

If she could only get the men to set up a church.

Not these men.

Then who?

Herself?

She could not answer such a question, but she began to sense a premonition. Hangtown was going to have a church. She did not know why, but she felt this must be what God had pre-ordained for her. She must bring a church to Hangtown.

She sensed it with more assurance than she ever had for anything in her life.

Perhaps this was what her brother meant by a calling.

She would not be leaving in the morning.   ⊷ঌ

8

WITH their bellies full of breakfast cooked over the camp-fire, Adrian and Sarah became playful. They chased each other, the boy easily able to stay beyond the reach of his crippled sister in a game of tag. Narcissa waved at the Clappe's wagon as it rolled in a waddling motion along the rutted trail that led away from the stream in a south-westerly direction.

She had second thoughts. She should have gone with them. In San Francisco she could find work, find it easier and get a message of her plight to her family in Iowa.

She was not certain what or who had made her decide to stay in this den of sin. Did she think she could fight the entire camp, change it all by herself? The Clappes had tried and given up, and they were experienced evangelists!

They had offered to take her and the children with them, but they had not argued long, she thought. She had expected to be told a dozen reasons why she could not stay, but the couple had nodded and then loaded their wagon. It was still barely sunup when Narcissa strolled the street through the town. A haze hung in the valley, muting the best and the worst.

The whore house was quiet although a lone drunk slept on the porch. No hammers or saws stirred the silence. Smoke rose leisurely from a few chimneys.

Sunday, she thought.

Sunday had come to Hangtown. It meant nothing religious to anyone except herself.

The mud was frozen, making it easier to walk. Shortly after the sun had fully risen above the mountains to the east, the air would warm and the street would no longer crackle beneath her feet. It would turn to mud and drag her into its greasy mire. But for awhile the street was hers, and she walked it with a strange calm, the bible in her hand.

It was like Judgment Day, she thought. The Lord had come and gathered his flock. Everyone on earth had been taken to heaven and by oversight she and the children had been left behind.

She shivered, fought back the tears, and blurred the vision of loneliness.

At the first laundry, a tent with a sign above it, she saw a Chinaman coming out, carrying his load of wash from steaming tubs inside. He stood tossing his product over the ropes stretched between two trees, ignoring her approach.

"Do you speak English?" she asked.

He answered over his shoulder. "Washee-washee. No time talk."

She pretended not to hear his rudeness. "Do you know where the man they call Drover lives?"

She almost wondered why she asked. She had no idea what Drover could do for her. He infuriated her with his insolent assumptions, but at least he had not come to the whore house the night before. Almost every white man in town, except for King and Drover, had appeared sometime during the night. Nor had the boy David. She had forgotten the boy with the crush on Annie. He had not come.

The judge had been there. He spent longer with Annie than any other man, and Narcissa had noticed he was the only man who did not pay Mattie before going up the stairs with a girl.

"Washee-washee," the small yellow-skinned man replied. He wore tight dark clothes and a little hat on top of his head. His hair was tied in a long pigtail that hung down his back. There was intelligence and contempt in his slanted eyes.

"Drover," she repeated. "The direction to his house, please."

The Chinaman saw the children. He seemed to marvel at their presence, and his expression mellowed. "Children." He said the word strangely, mixing consonant sounds.

"Yes, I'm their aunt."

The yellow face frowned. "Children. Woman. Good woman bad for washee-washee man."

"Bad?"

"Come camp, marry, do washee-washee. No good China boy."

He busied himself at his work.

Narcissa straightened her back. She spoke more emphatically. "Mr. Drover's house, please."

He sighed and pointed to a clapboard house set off by itself in the shade of three towering oak trees. A horse was tied outside, but no smoke came from the chimney.

It was a slender, chastened girl-woman, not a zealous missionary, who uncertainly approached the house. What would she do if Drover turned her away? What did she expect of him and, equally important, what would he expect in return?

She should have gone with the Clappes, but that was of no consequence now. Drover was the only one left. Only he had offered shelter.

At what price, she could not guess.

With the little ones running free in the tall grass where the horse grazed, she climbed the rickety steps and knocked on the rough-hewn door. There was no sound from within. She knocked again.

She heard Drover grunting inside, then his footsteps thumping across the floor.

She retreated, stopping only when she heard the door open.

"Well, I'll be a bloody Abo," he said. His face bore bruises from the previous night's fight.

"You said . . ." she began.

"I know what I said, girl. Come on in before the dingos get you . . . wild dogs. Town's full of them, you know."

"Mr. Drover, I'd like to accept your hospitality, but that's quite impossible. I'm a decent woman . . ."

"Come on in," he said. "No such thing as a decent woman, man neither, for what that's worth."

"But . . ."

"Come on in, lass. Before I freeze my crackers and cheese."

"Your what?"

"Knees. Crackers and cheese. You Yanks don't do much for the Queen's English. Just use it like you copied it out of a book."

She entered cautiously, calling the children in with her, purposely using their presence to thwart any designs Drover might have on her.

The house was larger than she had expected. There were two bedrooms, one empty, one with a homemade bed, and a combination living room and kitchen. The windows were real glass. Among the furniture, sparse and all of it homemade, was a table covered with shell loading equipment. She had helped her father load shotgun shells, but this setup was for pistol ammunition.

In spite of his religious calling, her father had taught all of his children to be quick and accurate with shotguns, rifles and pistols. Indian attacks were rare but nevertheless an ever-present threat in Iowa, and her father had often said he could find no reference in the bible that condemned a man or a woman for self-defense against heathens.

It was really a surprisingly nice house for a single man, she noted. The floor was wood, instead of the dirt she had expected to see. The kitchen even had an indoor pump and there was an icebox too. With the mountains so close, ice to supply it with would not be hard to come by.

It was more than a miner's shanty. It was meant to be a home. Drover had been expecting a woman to share it with him, she guessed. Did he have someone in mind already? The question asked itself in her mind.

"She isn't coming," he said. He must have read her thoughts.

"Who?"

"My girl, a she lass as we say it, from Gundaroo. Patrick Dyce was her father, a good Scotsman with a thousand acres along the Yass river. Finest country as ever was seen, admirably watered, and fine, brick-red soil. Only he wouldn't let her join me after all, not a bushranger like me."

"A bushranger? Is that a lawman?"

"Wrong side of the legal coin of the realm, Miss. But I've been playing life straight and tidy hereabouts. Got a little stake down river that brings in more than enough." He shoved a hand in his pocket and sorted through a handful of small nuggets. When he found one the size he wanted, he handed it to Adrian. "Buy some lollies, nipper, for you and the jilleroo here, and find a dilly bag with tucker."

Narcissa sighed. "Drover, can't you speak plain English?"

"Speak it clearer than the Queen's tongue itself."

"I think he means we should go to the store and buy some sweets, Cissie," Adrian volunteered.

"I believe he does."

She was not selfish enough to refuse them. Although she knew it was not proper to be alone with this man, surely no one was looking, and in this town, not many would care anyway.

Adrian darted for the store, with Sarah behind him calling, "Wait, Adrian, wait for me."

Alone with the Australian, she felt pleasantly nervous. She had expected to cringe the first time she spoke to a man alone after the affair with the trapper, but Drover went to the fireplace to poke up the grayed embers and add small, quick burning tinder. Then he placed a coffee pot on the grate and turned to face her.

"Let's sit here at the table," he said. "I'll have a cup of brew for you shortly. Isn't exactly Billy Tea, but a Strine can't expect too much here in the bloody bush."

"I didn't come to stay," she said, but she sat down.

"Aye. I noticed you brought no swag."

"I had nothing to bring. But I thought . . ." She cleared her throat and then continued in a strong, clear voice. "You see, I know of no one else to turn to."

"How did you come by the nippers?"

"The children?"

"Yes."

"I told you. I was traveling west with them and their parents. My brother wanted to set up a church at Sutter's mill. But they died of exposure and we were taken in by a man who . . . He was . . . a . . ." She could not say the word.

"Cannibal?" he said for her. "That's the trapper, but I wouldn't say he was a cannibal. They eat their own kind. Trapper isn't one of us. A breed apart, he is."

"You mean he's not human?"

"There's a species lower than man."

"And higher. God is higher," she pointed out.

"I suppose. So like I was saying, there's a species lower than man and some higher. Then there's those that are just different."

"He grunted and made the most awful sounds."

"Trapper can't talk. Had his tongue cut out long ago."

"Oh, merciful God."

He misunderstood her exclamation for approval. "Wasn't God's work, Miss. The Indians did it. But I suppose you could say the Lord wasn't on the job that day."

"I want him brought in," she said. "Tried and convicted. That is another reason for staying in Hangtown."

" 'Vengeance is mine, sayeth the Lord,' " he quoted. He paused, but did not ask her the nature of her grievance against the trapper. "There is nothing I can do about the poor bloke. You'd have to see the judge about him."

"Then I will." She picked up her bible and stood. "Can you at least direct me to a place where a decent woman with children can stay?"

"No place in Hangtown that doesn't go with a man, Miss. Might as well stay here."

"But I can't stay with you."

He sighed. "Best I can offer."

She kept her tone carefully matter-of-fact. "Well, you see I don't know quite what to do. I don't even have any other clothing. Nor money for food." It sounded like begging, but more than anything else she was laying her troubles in the open for herself to see. The magnitude of them overwhelmed her.

He took a can of gold nuggets from a bench, picked up her hand, and poured them in. "Follow the nippers to the store, stock up on food for yourself and the little ones. Buy some clothes and ask the shopkeeper if he knows where you could stay, a place more proper than a foreigner's." The last was deliberately abrasive.

"I can't take money from you."

"Miss, around a mining camp, salt pork sells for two hundred dollars a barrel. Flour, two dollars a pound; potatoes, thirty a bushel. You don't have that kind of money. You only got one thing to sell, and I gather you prize that above the going price. As for borrowing without collateral, I wouldn't waste a leg searching for a loan. So take the charity from me and see the store clerk. If my luck runs true, you'll spend my swag and give yourself away free to some hairy miner who hasn't shaved in a month."

The insult infuriated her. "What kind of girl do you think I am?"

"A prettier one I never did see."

"And decent," she hissed at him, and her hand swept out, knocking the can of gold off the table. Little bright spots speckled the unswept floor.

Tears were stinging her eyelids, but she could not let him realize the power he had to hurt her.

"Miss, I'll show you a good time if you stay."

"I'm afraid I prefer gentlemen." She whirled and sailed out of the room, chin held high.

He stood at the door, calling after her. "All right, I'll throw in ten per cent of my diggings."

"I'll beg or borrow first," she retorted.

"Borrow and you'll have to put up the same thing as collateral." He strode alongside her.

She swung at him with the bible.

"You'll end up at Mattie's place, girl. So don't play that bible bashing role with me."

"I am not that kind of woman."

"Oh, come now, Narcissus, or whatever you call yourself. You spent last night some place."

She stopped, staring at him, appalled that anyone could think of her as loose.

He softened his approach. "I might not be much yet and I might talk a bit strange for your ears; but, believe me, there isn't anyone in camp that will treat you and the children better."

He touched her arm and she felt a strange tingling under his fingers, a feeling that surprised and confused her. She pulled free, as much in denial of her reaction as in rejection of him.

"I hate you," she stormed. "I hate you worst of all." She knew she sounded childish, ineffective, but for the moment reason was submerged in emotion.

"Me? Why?"

"You'd never understand."

She was walking away from him again, and he tried once more.

"Look, let's go back to my place and talk this over."

"No. Never!"

"Just for the day . . . by afternoon you can do as you please."

"And you'll pay me well?" she said sarcastically. "I get to sweep up the gold off the floor, I suppose?"

"That isn't what I meant. I'm just suggesting you stay off the streets today. The way I hear it, Madam Lafayette and her fairy belles got the boys stirred up so much last night they're gonna wake up with aching heads, fiercer than a constipated bear. And they got a bit of settling up to do for themselves."

"Settling up?"

"Neck stretching, Miss."

"Hanging? But who?"

"Who knows? One less miner won't be missed more than one less wallaby climbing in the rocks. Best stay inside some place."

"But not with you, bushranger."

"All right, Miss." He nodded, pulling the corners of his mouth down and tightening his jaw in a peculiar expression of assent. "Take your own trail through the bush. A Strine doesn't drag a bird to his nest against her will."

He touched her hand briefly and was gone, and she looked down at several pieces of gold lying in her palm. She was tempted to fling the hard pellets after him, but a quote from the bible inserted itself in her mind.

"A good man sheweth favour and lendeth." She was surprised that she remembered the psalm.

A good man? Drover?

Generous, yes. But why did he deliberately infuriate her so? How could he hurt her so easily? He meant nothing to her.

She hurried away from the house, following the children toward the store. The street was softening and she was glad to reach the boardwalk. Inside the store, she found a proprietor squinting at her with eyes that bespoke a massive headache. His mood was as foul as his breath, which reeked of last night's whiskey.

"I'd like to see your selection of women's clothing," she announced.

"You're wearing it, lady."

A glance around confirmed his answer. The store was stocked with men's working apparel, simple foodstuffs, a few household items, and mining paraphernalia. There was nothing for women or children.

"Tell me what you want. Bolts of cloth? I can have it here within a month."

"I can't very well wear the same dress for a month."

"See the judge," the proprietor said.

"And I need a place to stay."

"See the judge," he repeated. "If anything needs fixin', doin', or undoin' in Hangtown, you see the judge." He retreated behind his counter and began pulling a length of rope from a spool. Before she left, he was making a noose at the end.

She remembered what Drover had said about a hanging, and she backed away from the merchant and his rope, Adrian and Sarah at her side.

Outside, the center of town was springing to life. Hungover men were carrying boards and tools to the intersection of Hangtown's two main streets. More than twenty men were laboring to reassemble a gallows that had apparently been built previously.

"Come on, loves," she said, urging the children along. If she stayed, it would be impossible to buffer them for long from life and death as it was here on the frontier, but she was not ready to cope with that problem yet.

Maybe they were going to hang the trapper, she thought, and the pain and humiliation gushed up inside like a fountain. Although everything she had been taught denied her the right to seek vengeance, the trapper deserved punishment. It was only right.

In contrast to their conduct during the previous day's welcoming celebration for the prostitutes, the men ignored her presence today. Sexually satiated, at least temporarily, they were working off their hangovers on the gallows.

At the swinging doors of the saloon, she paused, gathering her courage to enter.

There was a bench near the door. She set Sarah on it and admonished, "Now, you stay there until I come out. I have to find us a place to stay."

"Don't worry, Cissie," Adrian said, enjoying his role as man of the family. "I'll watch her. These lollipops will last a long time. I got one for you."

She ruffled his hair affectionately and went inside. Nearly empty, the tavern was far less festive by daylight. The sawdust on the floor was fresh, but the air stank of stale beer. The nudes on the walls were less artistic now, as they stared down into brown-stained spittoons. Down at the end of the bar a teenage boy was polishing one of the receptacles, restoring it to mirror-bright lustre.

The roulette table was still, the ball lying in the double-ought groove. It was a night-time game that promised, without effort, the fortune miners sought by day in the cold and mud. At other tables cards were spread face up in neat fans on the flat surfaces, a reassurance of honesty. At the piano a man in a straw hat was practicing "Hangtown Girls"—the playing excellent, the instrument slightly out of tune.

Woodworkers had reached the pinnacle of their art in carving the tavern's fixtures. The bar was decorated with scrolls and sculptures of women cut into fine-grained wood and stained to a rich, dark color. The back bar, with its mirrors and shelves for bottles, was framed in wooden pillars, turned with precision. Red plush draperies closed off a small elevated stage, and fancy chandeliers hung from the ceiling.

"Beer a dollar a mug. Whiskey two dollars a shot," the one sign in the saloon proclaimed.

The place was a surprising bit of elegance in this remote mining camp. Its decor surpassed anything Narcissa had seen before.

She was about to speak to the bartender when the doors behind her opened and a little man skittered in. He seemed built close to the floor, his shoulders narrow as if he had been squeezed into a crevice where he could hide from a herd of pursuers. He wore a hat, but he took it off and held it by the brim at his chest, the way Narcissa had seen many men enter the parsonage or the church when they had not visited there often enough to satisfy their own consciences.

He scurried directly to the bar.

"How much whiskey can I get today with a pinch?" he asked and with shaking hands he fumbled at a tobacco pouch that probably held gold dust.

The big bartender shook his head. " 'Tain't for sale."

"What do you mean, not for sale?"

"Runnin' low. Can't be wastin' it until we get another load in. What with the shindig last night and the hangin' this morning, the town will be dry."

"For God's sake, Max," the man whined, "it's me they're talking about hanging."

"Ain't talk, Wee Willie. It's for sure. No use wastin' good whiskey on a dead man."

"Oh!" Narcissa whispered from her position by the door.

Wee Willie turned. He crouched a little lower. Sensing a sympathetic ear, he exploded with his woes. "They say I stole a man's money, his dust."

"You stole it, all right, Willie," the bartender confirmed. He finished drying glasses and began wiping the bar. "You spent it in here. Left the bag with me before you passed out. I knew it was the Irishman's dust soon as you put the bag on the counter and ordered your first drink."

"Then why didn't you stop him?" Narcissa asked.

The little man whirled hopefully. Perhaps she could bring Max around to his side.

"Not my place to play policeman."

"Then whose is it?"

Max shrugged. "Nobody's. Got no law, except Judge Russell. Be real law here soon enough. Best enjoy freedom while we can."

"Then I gotta see the judge," Willie cried. He had the eyes of a catfish but his loose-lipped, flaccid mouth dominated his face. His nose was shoved off to one side. "They're rebuilding the gallows."

"Judge won't see you," Max said, neither glad nor sorry.

"But he has to." Willie started for the stairs.

Max took a pistol from behind the bar and laid it on the counter with a loud, threatening sound. "Judge says shoot you if you so much as take a step up them stairs, Willie. He don't want to see you."

"But you can't hang a man for stealing!" Narcissa objected.

"It ain't me, Miss. It's the whole camp. Besides we ain't got no jail."

"I'll pay it back," Willie whimpered. "Convince the Irishman, Max. He's better off if he lets me live and pay back what he says I stole."

"You convince him. I know every fleck of gold you find will pass over my bar an hour after you dig it out of the pan. He knows you'd never pay him back if you was to live."

"Has there been a trial?" Narcissa asked.

"No sense having a trial. Wee Willie is guilty."

"Why don't you run, Mr. Willie?" she asked. "You'll get no justice here."

"Run where?" Willie slumped forward, his elbows on the bar. "Anybody sees me near a horse, they'll shoot me before I can get a foot in the stirrup. If I try to run, somebody will step in my path. I'd have been dead yesterday if'n it hadn't been for the girls. I thought the boys would forget it. But they're stirrin' themselves up for another run at the whorehouse by gettin' ready for a hanging. Mine. But any hanging would do."

"Aw, hell, Willie, it ain't that bad." Max relented and slid a bottle down the counter. "You ain't sober enough to know whether you're alive or dead most of the time anyway."

Willie uncapped the bottle and lifted it to his lips.

"Well, the judge will see me," Narcissa said. "This is outrageous."

"He'll see you, Miss. Pretty as you are. But I wouldn't get too wrathy with him. You're liable to find yourself sentenced to a couple of months service, cleaning his house so to speak." She was halfway up the stairs when he added, "Third door to the left. And go in smiling. The judge ain't the sweetest tempered man west of nowhere."

"There's a wild man loose in the mountains, a vicious beast," she said before she continued up the stairs, "and you men are going to hang a poor, helpless drunk."

She stopped at a half-opened door. A familiar voice came from inside.

It was David, the boy who had taken a fancy to Annie. He was inside the room pleading his own case.

"Please, Judge," the boy was saying. "Can't you understand? I love her."

"Saw her once and fell in love?" an older voice mocked.

"I'll work. I'll pan gold, do whatever you say to buy her from you."

"The girl is a Mother Lode working where she is, boy,"

the Judge said as Narcissa entered. When the old, immaculately dressed man saw her, his mockery turned to pity. "Besides, she doesn't work for me, boy. You can't think I condone such licentiousness. Good morning, Miss," he acknowledged Narcissa. "What can I do for you?"

David spoke before she could respond. "But it's your house." Then he turned to Narcissa. "Tell him. Annie and I love each other. You know Madam Lafayette. Tell him to make her set Annie free."

Narcissa said nothing, but the look she leveled at the judge was an accusation in itself.

The judge shrugged and stood. "All right, boy. I'll do what I can. Now leave me and this lovely thing alone before I change my mind."

"Oh, thank you, Judge, thank you." David backed from the big desk where the judge had been sitting. "You, too, Miss White. Thank you. I'll repay you both somehow."

Then he was gone and the judge was motioning toward one of the captain's chairs that faced his desk. His office was sparsely furnished, completely void of the law books she had expected to find.

"Well, what can I help you with, Miss White?" he asked politely. It was a condescending tone, although there was nothing in his manner that could be pinned down as compromising.

"You know me?" she asked.

He held his cigar in his lap, its position a deliberate sexual symbol.

"I know everybody in camp and all along the river. I know you left Mattie's place, spent the night with those fanatics I had to chase out of town, and I got word you're cozying up to the Australian. You thinking of setting up your own place?"

"My own place?"

"Your own whore house. You know what I mean."

"You are a crude, foul-mouthed . . ."

"Easy, Miss White. I'm the law in this town."

"Law. There's a frightened man downstairs and other men out in the street building a gallows to hang him. For stealing."

"So I hear."

"And you've refused to see him. To save him."

"That sounds right too."

"You can't hang a man for stealing."

"Oh, now, Miss White. Don't get yourself worked up for nothing. The law's got to hang a man in a camp every week or so if it intends to keep some semblance of order."

"You'd hang a man as an example?"

"You all fired up to save him?"

"Of course. I, my brother, was headed here to bring the word and the mercy of the Lord to the miners."

"And the Almighty let your brother die on the trail like a sparrow with a broken wing, I hear."

The girl's strength drained away. What he said was true. The Lord had let her brother die, had left her to be raped, had not even come forward to save the children from starving. A wagon train of whores had done more than God himself.

Or could God have sent the wagon train?

"If you're so set on saving this thief's life," the judge said, putting his feet up on the desk, "then why don't you repay what he owed?"

Her spirit wilted again.

"I . . ."

". . . don't have the money?" He smirked. "You could have earned that much in an hour working for Mattie Lafayette last night."

"I'm not that kind of woman."

"Too good to save a man's life?" he taunted.

His argument bothered her, like many of the religious debates she had heard at home in the parsonage, questions with no answers, one moral code weighed against the other.

"I don't . . . I don't know."

"Can't stand the thought of all those men lining up to have a go at you? A man's life isn't worth a little discomfort to you. Why should you expect me to risk my reputation for firmness to save a drunk?"

"But it's different."

"Is it? All right, I'll tell you what. You want me to save

Willie's life, and you don't cotton to a gang of men banging away at you. So how about raising the money the easy way? Just you and me. Here. Alone. Nobody will know the difference."

Her chin came up and she stared at him, stunned. Drover had been right in what he said this morning. The judge, however, was looking past her shoulder. He was no longer the confident old monarch demanding her body in exchange for a man's life. He was cowering.

"Miss White," a velvet voice said from behind her.

She turned quickly.

Walter King stood in the doorway. He wore the same pin-striped suit, a fresh shirt with ruby buttons, and an expensive cravat in place of his string tie.

"I think you'd better come down to my office, Miss White," he added.

Without waiting, he left the frame of the door and disappeared.

Narcissa rose, ready to follow.

But she had not forgotten the drunken Willie and the waiting gallows.

She spoke to the judge in a firm, determined voice. "If that poor man dies today," she threatened, "I'll build a church in his memory. I'll gather a congregation so large, so powerful, they'll carry you out of the town on a rail, tarred and feathered. Do you understand me?" She held up the bible. "I swear it on the holy bible. I'll finish what my brother set out to do. I'll bring God to your heathen wasteland."

The judge rose and nodded, his courtesy a denial of his recent offer. "Nice of you to visit me, Miss White. I will see what I can do to accede to your wishes."

"Do that," she said.

Then she was in the hall, her face hot with anger, her jaw tight with determination. She called to the little man slumped over the bar, his sobbing audible from her position on the balcony.

"You'll be all right, Wee Willie. They won't dare hang you now. The judge has promised to intercede for you."

The figure below did not move. The bartender took the

bottle from the man's hand and placed it with the others along the back bar.

With restored confidence Narcissa headed for Walter King's office. Her heart was pounding hard in her breast with the exultation of accomplishment and the expectation of seeing a man who was all she had expected, even in her dreams. ﻬ

9

HER concern must have been obvious to the handsome easterner who held the door for her as she stepped into his office.

"A problem, Miss White?" Walter King asked.

"You know my name?"

"You knew I would," he said. "Now what is the problem?"

"I came to see the judge because neither my niece and nephew nor I have a stitch of clothing except that on our backs. No money. No place to stay."

One corner of his mouth quirked up. "Madam Lafayette's wasn't quite appropriate, was it?"

"Hardly. We stayed with the Clappes."

He nodded knowingly. "I heard. I apologize for not having recognized your predicament sooner. I never believed you were one of the girls. The difference is obvious."

"Thank you!" That was more than the Australian had recognized. "If there is a married couple in town, or a church, I'm sure they can help us."

King shook his head. "Neither, I'm afraid."

"I went to the store and the man sent me to the judge, but in the turmoil about that poor man . . ."

"Perhaps I can help you," he interrupted. He rubbed his fingers against his palms as he stood in the office door and called to the bartender. "Max, select several dresses for Miss White. The most sedate you have. And bolts of cloth to make children's clothes." He closed the door. "There is an entire wardrobe backstage," he explained. "You will have to take off a few frills and add to the skirt hems, a handkerchief to the bodice perhaps, but I'm certain you will come up with something. And the Chinamen can sew clothes for the children."

"But I understood the saloon belongs to the judge," Narcissa said, confused.

King smiled. The tips of his fingers scrubbed at his palms. "It does. But he has no dancing girls and he owes me a favor."

"You realize I can't pay," she said, "Not yet."

"Consider it a loan.

He touched her arm, turning her toward his desk.

The office was that of a successful eastern banker. The floor was covered with a huge, rich Persian rug. The drapes at the two windows overlooking the camp's main street were made of velvet. On the walls were original oil paintings of New England coastal scenes and boats rocking at anchor.

The mahogany desk was large and the chair behind it was leather with a back tall enough to reach King's head when he sat. There was a leather couch, chairs for guests, and a safe that stood at three-quarters of Narcissa's height. The top of the desk held a ship's compass, a box of cigars, plus a bottle of ink and a quill pen.

Taking her elbow, he led her to the couch. Beside it was a table on which sat a model ship complete with riggings and sails.

When she sat down he asked, "Coffee?" He reached for a silver carafe beside the ship. A silver sugar bowl, creamer, spoons and several delicate china cups stood near the carafe.

"No, thank you." She knew her curiosity might seem presumptuous, so she phrased her question carefully. "I hope you will forgive my asking, Mr. King, but your office, it seems incongruous . . ." She was pleased that the word came to her. She had read it often but used it only in letters. ". . . out of place in Hangtown—so beautifully decorated, like the house where the girls are staying."

He nodded toward a side door. "My living quarters are through there. I had everything shipped to the Isthmus of Panama, carted across that narrow land bridge, and sent north to San Francisco on another ship, then across country to Hangtown when I first heard of the strike."

"But I thought the judge owned the saloon."

"I financed him."

"Is that what you do?" she asked.

"A financier? Yes, I guess you could call me that. Someday Hangtown will be a city. I'll own the choice property. I already own several of the placer mines and have grubstaked most of the more successful miners."

"But to live in a saloon?"

"This is more than a saloon. It's the best restaurant in camp, the hotel, town hall, courthouse, and the church for those who might want to pray for relief from a hangover come Sunday morning."

She studied him before she spoke. He was handsomer than she remembered him astride the powerful stallion when she first saw him the morning before. His eyes were impenetrable pools, his lips smiled with a mysterious tilt that suggested he was in no way revealing himself. Yet she was drawn to him. Of the men in town, including Drover, only he came close to appearing like the men she had known at home. He was more polished, of course, than the farmers. He was more like the Iowa City bankers and the new governor of the state. Except that King was young and appealing. He also seemed well educated, like her father and her brother, who had studied for the ministry.

"Are you here to stay?" he asked as he poured a cup of coffee and sipped it.

"My brother was a preacher. He intended to establish a church at Sutter's Mill. I suppose I will have to stay here, but I don't know what I would do. I could be a nurse. I helped tend the younger children in the family. But I would need things."

"Such as?"

She ticked off remedies from memory. "Salt for toothpaste. Gunpowder for warts. Turpentine for open cuts. Goose grease, skunk oil, and lard for liniment. And let's see, sunflower seeds, wild cherry bark, wahoo roots for tonics."

King raised his hand in restraint. "Whoa. My memory doesn't work that fast. See the storekeeper. Tell him I sent you. He can help you order some of those things."

"Or perhaps I could start a church. That is probably my only hope, with the Chinamen monopolizing the laundry and tailor business."

"Time enough for a church when the gold has run out and the men have turned to farming," he said. "Then we'll have women, churches, and schools."

"You have women now," she said. He looked blank until she continued, "Madam Lafayette's girls. They're women too."

"Hardly ladies," he said.

"You degrade them, sir." To her the whores were fallen angels, easily lifted into the realm of respectability, although she wondered if John or her father, or anyone in Iowa City for that matter, would make the same appraisal of the bawdy girls.

"They degrade themselves. In any case, my interests lie in getting the gold out of the ground and building a city. Drunken men and ladies of the night accomplish neither."

"But the saloon, the house too, you financed them, didn't you?"

"It's better I finance them than have the men brewing their own rotgut whiskey or the girls working from tents. I want Hangtown to prosper, not wallow in mud."

"Then you will need a church, decent women, and a school," she said. A dream was slowly emerging from her despair. Perhaps she could make a living here until, until what? Until she married?

He repeated his position. "In due time. All in due time."

"I shan't wait," she replied. The decision came as a revelation, an experience her brother would have seized upon with verve and vigor.

"To start your church?"

"Yes." She surprised herself. She hardly knew the bible. For years she had closed her ears to the preaching that stifled her home and her life. But she wanted to stay in Hangtown, and she had vowed to start a church. Now it seemed her only hope. If the men would come . . . "No one will stop me," she said defensively.

He smiled, without apparent condescension. "I certainly won't stand in your way. In fact, there is an empty house . . . four rooms, one large enough for a meeting hall. You can have that for your church and home. It sits just past the hardware store."

"I have no money for a house."

"I do."

"But I . . ."

"You have nowhere else to stay," he said. "Do you know anyone in Hangtown besides Mattie's people?"

"No," she admitted weakly. "I did meet an Australian."

"Hmm." His lack of enthusiasm was plain.

Narcissa found herself coming to Drover's defense. "He's quite a caustic man. He had something to do with the law in Australia. He might help."

King's expression was a mixture of cynicism and disapproval. "More likely a bushranger, that Drover. That's what they call highwaymen over there. Bushrangers."

"I can't believe that of him."

He shrugged. "In any case, the house and clothes are yours, and your credit is good at the store. Just mention my name." Before she could question his motives, he obliquely answered without prompting. "You don't know how marvelous it is to have one of my own ilk, and an attractive young woman at that, to converse with in this town."

She was flattered and a little embarrassed. Hoping she wouldn't blush like a child, she thanked him profusely and stood, afraid to extend her stay too long. The man was just taciturn enough to ensnare her.

"How can I repay you?"

She regretted the question at once. It sounded like an open invitation to trade her body—the only thing she had to sell, according to Drover.

"By having dinner with me this evening."

"In the house?"

Had the refined King no more respect for a decent woman than the Australian did?

"No," he said. "I did not mean to imply anything improper. I suggest we have dinner in my apartment. In spite of the seeming improprieties, it's the only decent place for a lady and a gentleman to dine. My Chinese cook will serve as chaperon. Shall we say eight?"

"Nine," she said. "I must get the children in bed first."

"Nine then." His hand touched hers and held it. Her heart dipped and thudded.

He led her to the door, and she decided to push her luck a bit farther. "There's a boy named David who's intrigued with a girl at the house. And a man they were talking about hanging. Could you influence the judge?"

"About the girl, perhaps. But I think it's too late for Wee Willie." He nodded at the front doors of the saloon. A mob of men were bursting in.

"Get the thievin' weasel," the one in front shouted.

"Please," Willie cried. "I'll pay it back. I'll pay it back!"

Seconds later the saloon was filled with men, many with faces still gray from the previous night's over-indulgence. All of them seemed to be in an ugly mood. Probably they had blown their savings on one wild night and were furious in the realization that they would have to return to the back breaking work on their claims, to start all over again.

To them, Willie was a symbol of frustration. They were like prizefighters—men who would work and train and win the fight for many rounds, only to be felled by a single unlucky blow. They came close but never won, and they had lost again last night.

The unlucky Willie was there now to absorb their fury. Even more of a loser than the others, he resisted little as they lifted him over their heads and passed him hand to hand to the doorway.

"Stop it," Narcissa called out. "Leave him alone!"

The response was laughter. "Soon enough, Miss. We'll leave him alone at the end of a rope."

She appealed to King, and he stepped forward, but his voice was lost in the vengeful chorus. Drawn by the uproar, the judge emerged from his office and stood at the balcony's railing a short distance from her.

She ran to him and grasped his arm. She felt the same panic for Wee Willie that had engulfed her when the rapist trapper had suffocated her with his weight.

"Stop them," she pleaded of the judge. "You promised."

He quirked an eyebrow and spoke to a group immediately below him. "Any you boys think Wee Willie might be innocent?"

A few laughed. The others ignored the quiet question.

"Louder," she insisted. "They didn't hear you."

He lifted his voice an octave. "Anybody have evidence to give on Willie's behalf?"

He turned to her with a smile that was half smirk, half grimace. He had done what he could, it said. Holding his cigar over the railing, he flicked it with his thumb and let the ash flutter over the emptying barroom's floor. The victim had been carried from the building.

"Do something. Stop them!" Narcissa appealed again to Walter King.

"I'll get my gun," he said.

She ran down the stairs and into the street, where the scene and the mood had changed from that of early morning. Now the sun was bright and harsh, the shrouding haze dispelled. The rutted street was slippery and treacherous under the ugly, self-righteous mob that hustled Wee Willie toward the still-unfinished scaffold in front of the store.

Four men stood at the top of the gallows, waiting for the sacrifice to be delivered. The rope hung limp, tracing and then retracing a slow, narrow path in the lazy breeze.

Adrian and Sarah appeared at Narcissa's side, their eyes wide with excitement.

"They're going to hang a man, Cissie!" Adrian cried. "They really are."

Sarah understood less. "What's hanging?"

"Get away from here," their aunt ordered. "Go in the saloon. I don't want you to see this."

Adrian was adamant. "No. I want to see."

"Don't you sass me!" She narrowed her eyes and spoke each word separately.

"Aw, hell, we want to see."

"And don't you ever let me hear you swear again." She slapped his face resoundingly. He took his sister's hand and trudged reluctantly toward the barroom doors. His stay there would be temporary, she knew, but she could not wait to enforce her edict. Although Willie was still some distance from the gallows, his time was running out.

"Stop this," she urged, clutching the nearest man's arm. "The man had no trial."

"Who are you, my little beauty?" the big miner smiled. "Didn't see you last night."

He stuck an exploring finger into her behind, and she leaped ahead. "You pig!" she stormed.

Another man explained. "She's the high-toned missionary who wouldn't fuck with anybody last night."

"Too good for us, eh?" the first man said. "If you weren't so high and mighty, a man might be more likely to listen to you, little girl."

She pushed away from him, her eyes sweeping beyond the camp to the mountains. Blue October sky, white-capped peaks, evergreen forested slopes, and the reds and golds of autumn along the creeks below. The only ugliness was the foreground, the product of mankind, the unpainted buildings, the muddy, gouged earth and most of all the crudely-built contraption of death in the center of the town.

Down the street Old Gray was leaning against a

hitching post, biting off a chew of tobacco and watching the show with mild interest. She hurried to him.

"Mr. Gray, you're not like the others," she said. "Can't you do something?"

He snorted. "Like what? Take Willie's place? Once the boys get riled enough to rebuild the gallows, they're gonna use it on somebody. Best you go hide and pray for his immortal soul, Miss White. That's all Willie's going to have left quicker'n a mosquito can bite."

Again she pushed on. Farther down the street she found the girls from the whore house, their faces weary and poorly made up in the harsh sun. They sat on the wagons that had brought them to town. There were no horses in sight, so apparently the men had pushed the wagons into position as a sort of grandstand.

"Madam Lafayette." Narcissa elbowed herself close so that she could be heard over the noise. "You could stop this. Tell them you'll ban the entire town for a week if they kill that poor man."

"Lose a whole week's business?" Mattie Lafayette scoffed with a laugh. "For what?"

"But Willie could be a customer." It was a weak argument and she knew it. The girls who heard laughed.

"Willie? His kind uses their own hands and saves their money for booze. Besides, after this is over, the men's blood will be running so hot we'll collect any dust left over from last night. 'Nother thing: you're the one run off last night when I could've used you. Now you're back whining for favors."

"Annie!" Narcissa found the younger girl standing behind the last wagon, locked in David's ardent embrace. "Annie. You've got influence. Help me."

The lead girl from the whorehouse pushed her beau aside. "Oh, hello, Narcissa. Did you hear? David talked to the judge and . . ."

"Annie save poor Willie. Please."

David answered for her. "Go against the judge right now? We dassn't." Then he wrapped an arm around Annie and pulled her away.

"Dear God, is there no one here who will help that poor man?" the newcomer asked silently. "Are they all uncaring about a human life?"

Up ahead there were cheers, and twisting about, she could see Willie being handed up to the men on the platform. He was fighting and squirming too wildly to be maneuvered up the stairs. They pinned him quickly to the wood planking and roped his ankles and arms.

But they did nothing to mute his screams.

"Miss White?" It was Drover making his way to her side.

"Got to thinking you'd be messing in this," he said. "Got a half mile out on the way to my claim when I decided I'd better come back."

"They're going to hang him." She pointed to the trussed-up figure now being placed on his feet atop the gallows. "Stop them. You're a Christian man."

"Don't be too sure about that, Miss."

"But you could try."

"Nothing to be done."

"Then I'll climb up there myself." She whirled away and was almost to the stairs when Drover clamped his big hand tight on her arm.

"You aren't doing Willie any good, bird. You go up there fighting and all you'll do is prolong his suffering."

"But Mr. King was going to help. He'll be here. He went to get his guns . . ."

"Fast as an emu can fly. Anyway, nobody can help once a mob gets its head. Best you can do is say a prayer for Wee Willie, for whatever that's worth to him."

She sagged. The Australian was right. She could not fight the crowd. They were dropping the noose around Willie's neck.

"Then let me do that," she pleaded. "Get me up there so I can pray for him."

"I'll try," Drover responded. His deep voice boomed. "Stand down, you bloody blokes. Would you hang a mate without giving him a chance to make his peace?"

The men on the scaffolding stopped their labors. The noose was in place and drawn tight.

A hush settled over the mob.

A big man with a gun strapped to his leg looked down at Drover and laughed. "You going to read from the good book for him, Strine?"

Two hangmen on the gallows wore guns. They were not dressed like miners. Their shirts were embroidered and their boots were muddy less than an inch up from the soles. They looked more like killers than gold diggers.

"No. The little lady's going to say the words," Drover replied. "Unless you want to mix it up with me afterwards, MacIntosh."

"Ain't seemly for a woman to come up on a gallows," the man standing next to MacIntosh said.

"Ah!" Drover smiled. "The two 'Macs' on a gallows together. MacDermitt and MacIntosh. Never knew two lads more deserving of a place on a scaffold. Be more than glad to say a few words over you two anytime."

"If you want words said over Willie, get your ass up here, Strine," the one called MacDermitt said.

"He don't need no praying," said MacIntosh.

Drover had Narcissa part way up the stairs when Old Gray spoke to the two hangmen. "I figure you two were the ones in town most like to approve bible shoutin' for a condemned man. You know, sure as beans make a man fart, that you'll both be danglin' from a rope sooner or later."

"But after you," MacDermitt shot back.

"Let her speak," Walter King said from the far edge of the crowd. He stood with his hand on his pistol, but the weapon was still in its holster. It was just as well. Narcissa realized now that no one man, not even five or ten, could change the mob's mind and live. Praying was the best that could be done for the sobbing unfortunate standing on the trap door to death.

MacDermitt motioned one of the assistants to step back and make room for Narcissa at the top of the stairway. Drover pushed her forward.

Slowly, on unsteady legs, she began the ascent. Eyes misted with tears, she was as fearful as the condemned man. She had never stood before such a crowd, never spoken in a church meeting. She even hated reciting at the tiny school she had attended. All she wanted now was to disappear, to melt away, to be ignored.

Looking up, she saw that Willie had stopped his sobbing and turned his eyes to her. Whether it was courage or resignation, something had given him the inner peace to cease his fruitless begging for life.

When she drew closer to him, he said quietly, "You ain't no minister or priest."

"True," she admitted. "Are you Catholic?"

"Damned if I know. Can't remember ever goin' to a church. Never knew my folks. Can't remember back more'n a coupla years. Drinkin' dulled my wits, I expect. Let's just get it over now. All right?"

"If you don't want me to pray over you . . ."

"Hell, yes, I want you to pray. You're all I got left, lady, and that ain't much. But say something. Tell me that there's something waiting for me at the end of this drop. Please. Tell me there's a God."

Narcissa felt her body bathed in her own perspiration, then chilled by a wind that seemed to sweep down from the pass through the mountains, down from the snow and the cabin where the trapper had used her.

Her mind groped backward in time.

What had been the words her father and brother said over the coffins of the dead, the comforting words that gave the family of the deceased the courage to continue?

They would not come. She must never have really listened.

When she finally spoke, the words were her own. "Oh, Lord, hear this poor man's prayer. Accept him into your care. Blessed are the dead which die for the Lord. Yea, saith the Spirit, that they may rest from their labors, and their works do follow them. And I looked, and behold a white cloud, and upon the cloud one sat like unto the son of man, having on his head a golden crown."

"That's enough," MacIntosh said. "Don't want him dyin' of old age."

He pushed her toward the steps. From behind her she heard Wee Willie say his last words. "Thank you, Miss."

Then there was a click, a thump, a cracking sound, a choking cry, and a cheer from the crowd.

Narcissa White did not look back.   ᴇᴈ

10

"A collection for the little lady," she heard Drover announcing. "Come on, mates. God's putting the bite on you. Boots and all there, boys. In the hat for the lady."

There was grumbling at first, but the mood improved as the hat passed. Drover was giving them absolution for what they had done.

Gathering up the children, who of course had missed nothing, she led them to the house that Walter King had offered her. Sarah was crying. Adrian kept looking back over his shoulder, dry-eyed in childish disbelief.

"Cissie! He keeps twisting, around and around, at the end of the rope."

"I told you not to watch."

"Does that mean he's still alive?"

She yanked his arm impatiently and forced him into the house ahead of her.

Sarah entered too, her tiny face wrinkled with bewilderment.

Narcissa leaned her back against the door. She put her hands across her eyes to blot out the picture of Wee Willie with the noose around his neck, waiting out his last seconds while she delivered her muddled prayer.

She had failed.

When she had spoken with the judge, she had been certain she had saved the condemned man's life.

"Cissie, does it hurt to hang?" Adrian asked.

"Yes, horribly," she replied.

"Then why did they do it?"

She found answering difficult. "For stealing. But it's not right to hang a man for stealing."

"It's a sin," the boy said emphatically.

"Yes."

"Then why didn't you stop him?"

"Because . . ."

The reason was more complex than she could ever explain. Obviously stopping cruelty in a mining camp was going to take more than a few words. She would have to change the men's entire way of thinking.

And she would, she vowed. She would change the whole town if necessary. But for now she had to think of herself, the children, and the house Walter King had loaned her.

As King had promised, the four-room structure was well built and adequately furnished. She wondered whom the house had been built for originally. For King himself? And a wife?

Had he built in expectation of someone joining him in Hangtown? A gift-wrapped package gathering dust on a counter and the unfinished interior told the story. Whoever it was he had expected had changed her mind.

She felt sorry for King. Such a noble man to be treated so cruelly.

On the other hand, Judge Russell had built a mansion in expectation of the whores' arrival and he was not disappointed. That fact said much about Hangtown.

The largest room was without furnishings. It was suitable for a small church, as Walter had suggested. In her imagination she could see pews, a pulpit, and perhaps even an organ. She could hear a choir and imagine her brother John preaching.

But it would not be John. It would be she in the pulpit, or no one.

"You preached at a hanging," she told herself aloud. "You sent a man to his Maker. Surely you can face a simple sermon, a wedding, a baptism. You can do that, Narcissa White. You can."

Feeling better with her determination spoken aloud, she examined the two bedrooms. Both had imported bedsteads. One was suitable for a man and wife, the other for a child.

Walter King had been planning far ahead.

Pleased with all she had seen, she entered the kitchen. There was a cast iron stove with wood and kindling stacked beside it. A butter churn, a fluting iron for the ruffles in her dresses, a coffee grinder in which she could add "stretchers" like rye and barley when the price of coffee was high. There were even some groceries in the cupboard, enough to get her and the children through a few days at least.

"Can we eat now, Aunt Cissie?" Sarah lisped, her memory of the hanging already tucked away for another day or some feverish night when the demons were about.

Before she could answer, Adrian was stepping aside to let Drover in the front door. He carried his hat in his hands. It was heaped with gold and coins. He held it out to her.

"This ought to give you a burl at staying in Hangtown."

His smile disappeared when Narcissa swung her hand at the hat, knocking it out of his hands and sowing the money across the raw board floor.

"Blood money," she snapped. "I don't want any part of it."

What was there about him that agitated her so?

Adrian and Sarah dropped to their knees and began to collect the scattered offering. It was a game for them.

Drover scowled. "I thought you were going to be a preacher lady."

"I never said that," she snapped. Had she? She no longer knew what she wanted. She looked down at the bible in her hands and placed it on the kitchen table. Then she sat down, folded her arms on the book, put her head down, and began to cry.

Despite her tears Drover was smiling again. "The money's yours," he said. "You earned it like any preacher."

His tone made her prayers for the condemned man sound like a sack of flour sold at the store.

"They hanged him anyway," she sniffed.

"Hanging Wee Willie was fair dinkum. Number eight of the ten commandments."

"Where does Moses say you can hang a man?" she said, reaching for the bible. "Tell me."

"The Miner's Ten Commandments," he said. "We had to write our own laws, and number eight of the commandments says, 'Thou shalt not steal a pick, a shovel, or a pan from thy fellow miners, nor borrow a claim, nor pan gold from another's riffle box. They will hang thee or brand thee like a horse thief with the letter R under thy cheekbone.' And surely the drongo Willie did more than steal a pick or shovel."

"It's still not right."

"Then teach them different. You probably got the only bible in town."

"I'm not a minister."

"And I'm no miner, but that's what there is to do here, and that's what I'm doing." Suddenly his chin went up and he looked around him. "What the bloody hell you doing in this house, anyway?"

"Mr. King is letting me stay here," she said. "He's sending around some clothes and cloth. I have credit at the store. I *am* going to set up a church. Here." She said it with more conviction than she really felt.

"It figures he would be the first cab off the rack with a new woman in town."

"What?"

"He's the first one to stake a claim on you."

Again she was angry, inordinately so. "Nobody is staking a claim on me. Mr. King is a fine man."

"Yeah, a fine bloke. Bought a rich claim from a stupid kid for a bottle of booze and a blind horse once. Got Mexicans doing his digging for beans and a couple of dollars a day."

"That's good business," she pointed out stubbornly. Her tone of voice surprised her. Certainly she owed King some loyalty, but why the vehemence? It was something about Drover—his size, his dominating presence, a magnetism that at once attracted her and made her fearful he would sense that attraction.

"He's the son of a wealthy family, the kin of eastern silvertails that kicked him outback because he was such a stirrer. Always in trouble, they say."

"And you were a highwayman in Australia," she countered.

"That's a bloody lie. Never bailed up a stagecoach in my life. King's the biggest bull artist this side of Black Stump, beyond the last billabong."

"He's a wonderful man. He intends to make Hangtown into a real city with churches and schools and . . ."

"And he's abso-bloody-lutely the worst big note man in the district! He's . . ."

The door opening from outside interrupted him midsentence.

Old Gray came in, holding his hat in his hand. He looked around as if he were afraid.

"This going to be the church?" he asked.

"Yes!" Narcissa answered.

"Oh, then you won't be needin' me," Gray said. "I was just headed for San Francisco and figured you'd want to escape this devil's roost."

"She's not going. She belongs to King," Drover said flatly.

"Don't be spreading that rumor," she fumed. "Mr. King will stand up for my honor."

"Imagine he will, what with him setting you and the kids up with a place temporarily," Old Gray said.

"He did not set me up—not in the context you're suggesting. And if that's the way people are thinking, I won't stay here."

"Sure," Drover said. That cynical brow was quirked again. "You'll make more wandering about California with your Matilda filled with bibles and you planting crosses wherever you stop." He stopped her retort by raising his voice and continuing before she could speak. "Anyway, you couldn't plan to stay long here. When King's fiancée finally comes West, he'll kick you up the street to Mattie's parlor."

"He has a fiancée?" Her confidence deflated like a sail with the wind spilling out.

"Drover don't know that," Gray said. "King don't tell nobody nothin'."

Narcissa believed the old man. Walter King was not a man to share his confidences with those he considered beneath him socially.

She reined herself in. She was being snobbish, and that was not a fit attribute for a minister, even a self-ordained one.

Gray advanced to the table, where the children were stacking the money, and added his own donation to the pile.

"Well, which is it, Miss? Are you goin' or stayin'?" Gray asked.

"I'm staying."

"Well, then I'll be moseyin'. But you be careful. A man like King, all the folks out here, they ain't no better nor worse than they is back in civilization, only here they unbutton their fine clothes. Then the fur of the real animal starts to show through."

"You're leaving Hangtown?" Narcissa folded her fingernails into her palms. If she could, she would have to clung to the gentle old man. She had nothing, no one else in California, except the children, and they were clinging to her.

She stiffened her shoulders the way she recalled seeing her brother do when he was about to make a pronouncement that no one would dare refute. She would not plead for help again.

"I understand there's a couple dozen more women in San Francisco waiting for a wagonmaster to take them where there's men," Gray said.

"More like Mattie's girls?" she asked.

"Not as I hear it. These is decent women looking for husbands. Gonna take them to Sacramento."

Gray's announcement brought a surge of hope Narcissa would not have believed possible minutes earlier. "Bring them here," she said. "There are plenty of single men."

Gray shook his head. "Couldn't be doing that, Miss. Mr. Sutter's footing the bill, and he's outside waiting now. Came into camp this morning."

"Let me talk to him." She hurried outside and found a well-dressed man sitting on a carriage in front of Gray's three wagons. Beyond, she could see that the hangman's rope was at last empty. Willie's body had been taken to a grave, and she wondered if she were obliged to say the final prayer at his burial site.

However, Sutter was her immediate concern. A small man, he had a forehead that was heightened by baldness, but there was plenty of hair elsewhere. Sideburns stretched down around his ears and merged with a mustache and goatee. His clothing was immaculate, with crisp white collar seeming to bite into his neck above a shiny black velvet tie.

Narcissa knew the man by reputation. Although it was a sawmill employee, James Marshall, who had discovered the first flakes of gold that flooded the Argonauts to California, Sutter was the man behind the events that were tilting the population of a continent.

Now in his late forties, he had come from Switzerland. He had headed to the American West to escape debtor's prison, and once here, he had announced his intention to establish a great colony at the point where the American River joined the Sacramento. He cleared land and pushed aside the wilderness when California was still a remote outpost of Mexico. He had called his empire New Helvetia after the ancient name for his native Switzerland.

Although he again sank hopelessly into debt, he attained a title as a great land baron. He had nearly lost everything for the third or fourth time when he rose once more on the flecks of gold found at his mill. At that moment, there were stories that he was fighting an influx of miners who were staking claims on his land, most of them refusing to pay the fees he was demanding. Still he was temporarily rich, selling his land in Sacramento, the new city that he and his son were founding.

The women Old Gray was being hired to transport were probably part of his plan to establish his city. They would give the men an opportunity to start their families.

"Mr. Sutter," Narcissa said as she walked to the side of his carriage, "do you own land in Hangtown?"

"And who might you be, young lady?" His accent and his manner fitted that of a man known as an outstanding host to immigrants and visiting dignitaries alike.

"Narcissa White. I'm going to start a church here."

"In Hangtown?" Sutter asked sounding surprised.

"And I'll bet you own land here, too," she said.

"Two years ago I ruled forty-nine thousand acres—Spanish land grants, a quiet, fertile paradise."

"Then you found gold too. What a piece of luck!"

"It was a curse. That damned Sam Brannan, you don't know him, but he brought a plague to my haven. He went around San Francisco screaming that there were fortunes lying on the ground just for the taking. Within days fleets of boats were bringing hundreds, thousands of men up the Sacramento River to *his* store. He became rich selling tools and supplies."

Narcissa could tell Gray had heard Sutter's harangue before.

"San Francisco was deserted. No mayor, no sheriff, no government. And the miners—they trampled my fields, butchered my cattle, and squatted on my land. Grain went unharvested. Fruit rotted on the ground. And that was only the beginning of the madness. They're still pouring into the area from all over the world, contaminating everything they touch."

"Most of your land, Mr. Sutter, is it more suitable for homes than mining?"

"Yes, farms and orchards. The land is fertile as a child's mind. However, I don't grasp your interest."

"It involves the women, the decent women, Mr. Gray is picking up for you in San Francisco. Let him bring them here, Mr. Sutter."

"To Hangtown? After what you've seen?"

"Women will change that, Mr. Sutter. Men won't plow or plant unless they expect to marry and settle down. They'll go on mining until they have a family."

"I don't see where Hangtown comes in."

"Don't listen to the bird, Mr. Sutter," Drover interjected. "She's daft. Thinks she's a man planning and thinking."

Narcissa scowled at the Australian. He was like the boys in Iowa. They did not want a woman to be independent, to think for herself.

"The men are here. Bring the women and I'll see that they meet. Most will buy your farm land, but others will make Hangtown into a regular city. A center where people can sell produce and buy agricultural supplies, and things women need. It will expand your business interests beyond Sacramento."

"It could," Sutter agreed thoughtfully. "Hangtown is already in the center of the mining district. It's on the mail route. There's lumber nearby for the mill. And men growing sick of breaking their backs for dust."

"The price for everything is outrageous," Narcissa said, deliberately sweetening the idea. "The men will expect to pay top price for your land when they want to settle."

Sutter grew pensive. "Got nearly enough women in Sacramento right now. But the boys here aren't doing me any good. They set up tents and squat on my land. They would pay for clear titles if they went to the trouble to build homes or plant orchards. A woman won't stay long in a tent."

"Right, Mr. Sutter."

Drover and Gray still stood beside her. Sutter ignored them while he made up his mind. Then he spoke to the wagonmaster. "All right, Gray, bring the women that agree to Hangtown. And you'll see that they get settled, Miss White. Married fast. A woman alone changes her mind mighty quick."

"They won't change their minds, Mr. Sutter. They'll change Hangtown."

"We shall see, Miss White. We shall see." He snapped

the reins and rode off down the street that led south of town.

When he was gone, Narcissa confronted Gray and Drover, her eyes flashing with excitement.

"Women!" she exulted. "Did you hear that? You'll be bringing women to Hangtown, Mr. Gray." Neither man expressed enthusiasm. "Don't you understand the importance of what you're about to do? Women will change this from a camp to a town, a decent town."

"There's them that won't be too happy about that, Miss White," Gray mused.

"Like who?"

"Mattie Lafayette for one. She was expecting a couple of years good run before the mines petered out and the boys took to farming."

Narcissa dismissed the argument with a wave of her hand.

"The judge and your Mr. King too," Drover added. "They'll be trying to make you pull your head in when they hear what you've done. They like things the way they are."

"Well, certainly not Walter King. He gave me this house in which to start a church."

"Church is one thing. Decent women is another," Gray mumbled. "But Sutter's payin' the bill, so I'll do like he says. Bring any woman who wants to come to this muddy mess. Only if I were you, I wouldn't be announcing anything until I get back. Getting rid of the ladies once they're here will be harder than turnin' me north while we're still on the trail." He climbed into the front seat. "The judge and Mr. King are going to hang out my carcass to dry for this," he said as he snapped the whip and the front horses began to move.

Two tired ex-miners sat on the driver's seats of the other wagons. They had the look of defeat about them. They were ready to work for wages, and they whipped the other animals into motion.

Narcissa waved to the departing Gray and then turned to Drover. "Why is everybody against Mr. King? I'll tell him myself that there are women coming. He'll be happy."

"You think you can change the way of the world, little girl?" Drover asked. "You think you're some kind of god?"

"No, of course not."

"You think it's as simple as the abos—that's the aborigines back in Australia. According to them, during the dreamtime, before creation, all was darkness and the earth was flat. No hills, no valleys, no trees, no birds, nothing until an old blind woman named Mudungkala rose out of the ground, carrying in her arms three babes. Crawling on her hands and knees, she traveled in a circle. Water bubbled up in her tracks and the bare land was clothed with vegetation and inhabited with creatures so that her children and the generations to come would have food and shelter. You think that's what you can do to this station of dirt pushers."

"Maybe I can't rise from the ground," Narcissa said, "but I can read from the bible and I can help good women come into town and I can . . ."

In her enthusiasm she was not prepared for the strong hands that suddenly grasped her arms and pulled her against Drover's broad chest.

"What makes a little twist of a girl like you think she can change the world?" he growled at her. "What you need is a man, not cracked ideas of grandeur."

He tilted her chin and kissed her. His kiss was as firm and determined as he was.

Her first reaction was shock, then pleasure, then embarrassment when she realized there were men walking along the street, enjoying the scene.

She jerked back and he released her at once. Part of her wished he had not relinquished his hold so quickly. Another part flashed back to the cabin in the mountains and the trapper's foul-smelling breath and heavy body suffocating her.

She pulled back her hand to slap the Australian, but his quick grin disarmed her.

"You'll never do that again," she said firmly. "I'm not

some hussy from Mattie Lafayette's pleasure parlor, you know."

"And I'm not one of her clientele," he remarked. "But if you're saving it for Walter King, so be it."

"I'm not saving it for him or you or . . ."

She was still sputtering when Drover went back into the house.

"Aw, bloody well forget her, Drover," he muttered to himself. "If it was raining gravy, you'd be the only one with a fork."

When she reached the door, he was coming out with his hat. Passing her, he leaned down and kissed her again, then jumped from the steps to the ground. He strode purposefully toward his own place, stopping only when she called to him.

"Drover," she whispered. She knew she was being silly, but she could still feel the touch of his lips on hers, and she wanted an excuse to keep him with her—without his knowing it, of course. "What's going on?" she asked, pointing down the main street. There a man in his fifties with a hard, stoic face, hair combed straight back, was walking down the street swinging his cane. A dozen or more men followed him like ducklings following their mother to a pond. "Who's he?"

"James Marshall," Drover said. "He must have come into camp with Sutter."

"But those men . . ."

"You never see Marshall without miners dogging his footsteps."

"He found the first gold, didn't he?"

"Yep. Tried to hold onto the land where he made his find. Only the boys run him off. So he claimed he had supernatural powers to find gold. Now the losers hereabouts threaten to lynch him if he doesn't lead them to a stake soon. Maybe he'll be your next customer."

"Don't say that. There'll be no more hanging here. There will be law and order, you'll see."

Drover shrugged. "I hope you're right, but I wouldn't sit up a gum tree waiting for the day." He tipped his hat and winked. "Soon as you see through that bastard King, with all his tickets on himself, let me know. That conceited finagler isn't good enough for the likes of Mattie Lafayette, let alone a lady like you."

From the doorway she watched him go. She wanted to call him back, but she knew from his determined stride that he would not come. Why was he that way, she wondered in frustration. Why couldn't he be more like Mr. King? Then she squared her shoulders and righted her thinking.

"You're on your own, girl," she reminded herself. "You don't need a man. They need you."

The scaffolding still stood down the street and slogging past it were men carrying shovels and pans of greed. Those who passed Narcissa avoided her eyes. They were embarrassed in the presence of this preacher lady.

What strange design had brought her here? She had never meant to be a minister. Women weren't even allowed ordination in the Presbyterian Church as far as she knew. Could she fulfill her vow to set up a church here? Even more basic, why try in a place where the seedbed was so poisoned with greed and sin that the sowing of truth might never bear fruit?

Still, there was something about Hangtown that was holding her, almost against her will. It was as if she had been predestined to bring civilization to this scar in God's valley. Others would beautify the paintless structures and level the deep-bitten gouges in the street. She would smooth the way for men's souls.

Be honest, though, Narcissa, she said to herself. There's something else keeping you here, someone else. You're just too confused yet to know who—Drover, the carefree Australian, or Walter King, as fine a gentleman as she had ever seen?

She smiled into the warm autumn sun. Despite all the uncertainties, all the problems ahead, it was an exciting time and place to be a woman.

11

THAT night, alone in bed, Narcissa was less woman than child, a lonely child staring into shadows that threatened and seemed to move. Silent tears slid down her cheeks and into her hair. Little Sarah already had awakened once, shaken by a nightmare. She had seen her mother and father hanging from a gallows and woke up screaming.

Narcissa was exhausted by the time her niece quieted and slept again. Adrian was tossing restlessly too. He pulled the covers from his sister in the bed they shared. Perhaps his dreams brought the same torture.

The hanged man.

Even Narcissa could not exorcise Wee Willie from her mind. She had put the children to bed shortly after dark, a dark that came early this time of year. Then she had set an oil lamp on the table and taken out the writing paper she had found in a drawer when she searched the borrowed house for kitchenware. Sometimes, in the past, writing had helped when she was troubled. Often the soothing words came in poetry, but tonight she would write a letter, one that had to be written sooner or later. And it might help to put the day in perspective.

"Dear Momma and Papa," she started. "I fear my first letter to you from California must be the harbinger of bad news. While the children and I have arrived . . ."

She was about to write the word "safely" but the quilled pen stopped in her fingers. Safely? No! Wounded . . . damaged forever. She would never be able to tell anyone of the rape or of anything that happened at the cabin, and the hanging would scar the children for life. They had no money except that which Drover had collected as compensation for her prayers and they had no home except for the house Walter King had seen fit to lend them.

No, they had not arrived safely. They did not have a true friend within two thousand miles. God seemed to have saved them only to let them flounder like fish thrown up on a shore.

Yet she could not write the truth on paper. She could never tell her parents what hell her brother's blind faith had brought down upon his family and herself. Even if she did, her letter would take months reaching Iowa, as would their response once they had heard from her.

It might be a year before she heard. Would her parents still be alive? Her younger brothers and sister, neighbors, friends?

The fire was low, the room cold by the time she replaced the pen in its holder. Leaning over the lamp, she cupped her hand, ready to blow out the flame when she thought better of it. If Sarah woke up again, the light would quiet her. She rolled herself in the feather comforter on the bed. Not a sound broke the ringing stillness. She had never felt so alone, so bereft of love, so abandoned.

It was then that the tears began to flow, escaping from a dam that walled off the panic somewhere at the back of her mind. Still, she did not allow herself to lose control. If she let it, the panic would inundate her and diminish her into a helpless thing, an insect that rolled itself into a ball of self-protection. Only the children in the next room could succumb to helplessness. They had someone—weak as that someone was—to lean on. Still, there was therapy in tears, and so Narcissa gave in and let them dissolve the tension that stiffened her limbs and body.

She might have dozed off when she heard the front door rattle. Someone was trying to enter.

"Yes," she called, rolling from the bed. "Who is it?"

A fist was pounding on the door, and she picked up the whale oil lamp from the kitchen table. It cast long, moving shadows as she crossed the unfurnished living room. At the door she pressed her ear against the paneling.

From the other side came the sound of heavy breathing.

"Mr. King? Walter, is that you?"

There was an answering mumble, and she knew who it was—the trapper!

The tone and timbre of the grunting was not cruel. It was soft. Shaped into words it might be pleading, even repentant. If it came from anyone other than the trapper, it would be reassuring. In daylight she might have opened the door to a man who spoke so gently.

But it *was* the trapper.

With the memory of his face came primitive fear.

"Go away," she said.

The door rattled lightly. He was trying to coax her into admitting him.

He's sorry. He wants to repent. That's what her father would say of the man. Every man had the right to cleanse himself in the eyes of God, father said.

But there was no forgiveness in her heart, no charity. Only fear.

The door rattled harder, impatiently.

The heavy breathing and moaning thickened into animal-like grunts. A knife poked between the door and the frame, the blade hacking at the hide hinges.

"No! No! No! Help! Someone help me!"

She slid along the wall toward the rear of the house, reaching the kitchen as the knife snapped through one hinge and bit into another. Her heart was hammering against her ribs. Her breath came in gasps—the way it had during the rape!

"Adrian! Sarah! Get up! Now!" She had to get them out. But how? There was only one door.

Through the windows.

She snatched up a knife and hurried to a window, the lamp still in hand. "Children. Please! I need you!" There was no response.

Frantically she moved the lamp up and down and across in the window, hoping to attract help. The flame wavered and dipped and threatened to go out. She peered out into the blackness through the wood-framed panes, panes so small and wood so strong that not even Sarah could escape. And the window had not been built to open.

She was trapped, and the knife was sawing through the last hinge in the other room. In moments the cannibal would be on her again.

She looked down at the knife. Could she kill with it? How did it feel to sink a knife into a human body? Like cutting cabbage? No, a cabbage would not feel like flesh. A tomato then. Did the red gore gush onto your fingers and stain your clothes?

The door was creaking. She ran to it and leaned into it with all of her strength just as the last hinge gave way.

The door pushed her back and a large hand reached inside. It was the trapper's hand, scabbed and sore where the animal trap had bitten into it.

The feeling of that hand on her body would never leave her.

"Help!" She heard the word, felt it come from her throat, but the sound was not human. It was the primal cry of a terrorized animal.

There was no response. She could hear the piano from the saloon, even catch the distant laughter of men strolling to or from Madam Lafayette's pleasure parlor. But no one heard her. No one would come to her aid. There was only herself.

With the knife she tipped off the glass globe that protected the lamp's flame and heard it crash to the floor. Next she moved far enough to the right to hold the unshielded lamp to the groping, swollen fingers.

There was a gutteral sound. The fingers withdrew and she glimpsed the grotesque face, the haggle-toothed mouth distorted in shock and rage.

A moment of respite. Then the door erupted against her shoulder. The impact stunned her. When the pressure eased again, she knew he was backing off for another lunge.

She could not hold him off again.

Before the impact came, she stepped back, letting the door fall flat against the floor.

The invader was already into his run, his shoulder forward to strike the barrier. He could not stop himself when Narcissa thrust the whale oil lamp at him.

He got his hands up in time, but the lamp broke against his knuckles and the burning fluid poured down his full length coat. He roared like a monster in a nightmare.

Narcissa backed off. The burning figure took two more steps toward her.

She could hear men shouting and running outside. The beacon of flame had brought help. Whether from pain or fear, the trapper staggered in a confused circle and then plunged through the entrance into the night, shedding the burning coat as he hobbled along. Even then he continued to burn, the flames lighting his way to the icy streams below. The merciful waters extinguished the human torch.

In the street there were loud, close male voices and pistol shots. The sounds hardly registered on the ears of the girl who was methodically stepping on flecks of flame glowing on the future chapel's floor. They were like gold nuggets come alive, she thought inanely.

Then Walter King was there, holding her in his arms, shaking her, urging her back to her senses.

"Who was it?" He shook her again. "Narcissa, who was it?"

"The trapper," she gasped. "It was the trapper," and she leaned against him him on legs unwilling to stand.

"Go after him," King ordered the men gathering at the door.

But no one moved.

"Ain't enough of us to go after that maniac in the dark, Mr. King," one said for the rest.

"You'll go if I tell you to," King snapped. In his voice was a new harshness.

Narcissa saw the gun in his hand. "Please. Don't force them," she said. "There's no catching him now."

She felt King relax. "Probably true. Never known him to come down out of the hills at night before." He surveyed the damaged door, then located another lamp and checked the cut hinges. The crowd outside had drawn closer and was staring in. "You'd better come over and spend the night at the saloon . . . you and the children," he added loud enough for the others to hear.

"I . . . ," she demurred.

"You're in no shape to be alone," he said firmly, grasping her arms in his firm grip. "You're still shaking."

But she looked past him.

Drover was pushing his way through the crowd.

"Narcissa," he called. "Are you . . ." There was real concern in his tone until he was close enough to see King holding her. "Yeah, you're all right. Should've known," he mumbled.

"Drover."

"Enjoy yourself, *Miss* White." He put a cutting edge on the "Miss." He dipped his head in an ironic little bow. "You too, Mr. King."

"Drover, wait." She wanted to run after the Australian, to explain that nothing had happened between her and Walter King, but the Easterner held her tighter, and the urge to redeem any misconceptions slipped away.

"Cissie!" Adrian said, coming from the bedroom. Sarah was behind him, wiping sleep from her eyes. "What happened to the door?" . .

"We'll talk about it in the morning, dear ones," she reassured them. "Now go back to bed."

"Why is everybody standing outside?" Sarah asked. "Is there another hanging?"

"No, darling. You go to bed and if you can't sleep I'll come in and lie down with you."

While she settled the children, King spoke to several of

the men, arranging for replacement of the rawhide straps on the door. "And fix a board lock on the inside so that maniac can't break in again."

These instructions were accepted agreeably, and while the men fixed the door, King followed Narcissa into the kitchen. He reloaded his gun and laid it on the table.

"If you insist on staying here, I'm leaving this," he said, "although the town will be more alert if you should call for help again. You could use a gun if you had to, couldn't you?"

She avoided the question. The thought of killing anyone, even the man who had attacked her, should have been abhorrent, but she could not deny she might take satisfaction in destroying him.

"If you're hesitant, I'll stay the night, outside of course." The last came as an afterthought.

"Thank you. But I'll be all right," she said and sat down and picked up the gun, cocking the trigger with her thumb. "I'll be all right," she said again.

"Yes," he said. "I believe you will."

The men were finishing with the door. "We're through here, Mr. King," the hangman called MacIntosh reported. "It'd take a dozen men to break in again."

Now that he was not standing on the gallows, MacIntosh did not seem so evil. In fact, he lost the veneer of menacing toughness here at ground level, even though he wore a gun. Few of the miners went around armed. If they did, they carried rifles for killing game. They did not swagger about with a pistol on their hip. It must be the pistol that gave MacIntosh the bravado he displayed on the gallows. Obviously his strength came from someone else. The judge, perhaps? There was a relationship between the two men Narcissa did not understand. So far, it appeared that MacIntosh and his more manly alter ego, MacDermitt, lived without working.

"All right, gentlemen. Thank you," King said.

"Yes, thank you all very much. Won't you let me fix you some coffee before you leave?" Narcissa offered.

MacIntosh seemed amenable to accepting, but King answered for him. "It's rather late for the men, Miss White.

They want to be up at dawn what with the days getting shorter, don't you, boys?"

They closed the door, and King covered Narcissa's hand with his own. She withdrew from his touch.

She bowed her head, trying to remember a prayer. "Grant us grace to rest from all sinful deed, O Lord," she said, and she put her head on the table and cried.

King was bewildered.

"What in hell are you asking forgiveness for?" he asked.

"For burning that man."

"Trapper?"

"Yes."

"He's an animal."

"He's a human being. A soul. I nearly killed him." She took a deep, shuddering breath, and looked up at King, who stood blurred beyond her wet eyes. "Oh, I'm so confused. One minute I think I'd feel good about killing him, and the next I'm filled with remorse. What's the matter with me!"

"You have to be ready to kill out here, Narcissa," he said.

"But I don't think I could. I'd fear for my immortal soul, that I'd burn in hell for an eternity. There is no excuse for killing."

"If it were to save the children?" he asked.

It was a question with convoluted answers. To kill to save another, the ultimate sin, the ultimate sacrifice. To give up one's soul to save another.

"I don't know," she said sadly.

He put his hand over hers again. The touch reminded her of the trapper, she told herself. She did not want a man to touch her so soon after the mountain beast's appearance. Again she pulled her hand away.

King pretended not to notice the rebuff. He understood, she thought.

"Good thing I was on my way over," he said matter-of-factly.

"On your way here?"

"We had a dinner engagement," he said with a smile. "Did you forget?"

"Oh, dear. I am sorry. So much happened today. The hanging . . ."

"Care to join me now? We could send someone over to mind the children."

"Not tonight, please." He recognized the polite dismissal.

"Another time then."

"Yes, another time."

She went with him to the door, and he showed her how to remove and replace the new barricade device. Then he turned and gazed down at her with a confident look. Was he going to kiss her?

"Thank you, Walter," she said. "I don't know what I'd do without you."

"It's nothing," he said and patted her hand. Outside, he hesitated, and to fill the awkward moment she asked a question.

"Walter?" It was the first time she had used his first name. Did he notice?

"Yes." He sounded hopeful. Perhaps he thought she might invite him back inside now that the street had cleared.

"Who was this house built for?"

There was silence. She could not read his expression. He stood beyond the glow of the lamp. He did not answer until he was ready.

"For you perhaps."

He knew that was not a reasonable answer, and she waited for a better one.

"I knew someone like you would come along eventually. There were miners down on their luck who needed work, and I could get lumber. So I had it built . . . in hopes."

"Walter, don't rush me. Please."

She wondered why she said that. A smarter woman would jump at the chance to catch the only Walter King in town. Why did she put him off, even if they had just met? This was not Iowa City, where people thought it was necessary to play proper social roles.

"Is there someone else?" he asked.

"No." She answered so quickly that it sounded as if she had anticipated the question. She hadn't. "It's just that I want to find myself."

"Find yourself?" She knew he was laughing at her. "Is that modern woman talk?"

"I don't know what you mean."

"The farther west you go, the more independent the women become. They say they want roles other than being wives and teachers. There's even a lady bullwacker driving eight yoke of oxen just like a man—filling their ears with curses and cracks of the whip. Talk of women getting the vote is rampant here too, but then there's only one woman for every hundred men in all of California." He smiled. "Couldn't hurt to let them vote, I suppose."

"Yes, I guess that's part of what I mean."

"Fine," he said. "I have no objection to your being more than a housewife. As long as you remain a woman."

"I will."

"Good night," he said. Then he was gone.

With the door locked, she poked up the fire and pushed the coffeepot onto the grate. When it was hot, she poured a mug of the steaming, strong brew and sat for a long time at the table. The gun lay beside the mug.

I should be shaking, she thought. But it was not the trapper who filled her mind and kept fatigue at bay.

It was Drover. She wished the Australian had not seen her with King.

12

WALTER King stood beside Narcissa watching the first posters come off the press. They had been ordered the day before.

The afternoon was clear, the bright yellow sun warming all that it touched. Yet in the shade, the air was still chilly.

California—a cold climate with a hot sun. That's what people said. It was particularly true in the foothills of the Sierra-Nevadas.

Alternate warmth and chill—that summed up her feeling for Walter King too, Narcissa thought. He had been so helpful and she had been drawn to him these past few days, but when he touched her, she still felt that instinctive withdrawal.

Give it time, she decided. Because she was young and unsure did not mean there was something wrong with Walter. After all, they had only just met.

She took the first card and held it up to the light, reading aloud.

"Hangtown Church. Services Sunday, 11 a.m. Bible study, Sunday 7 p.m. Prayer services daily 7 p.m. Narcissa White, preacher."

She frowned. "Preacher. That word bothers me. I shouldn't be claiming to be a minister. I'm not."

King put a reassuring arm around her waist. "You didn't say you were a minister. You said you'd preach. Anybody can do that. Besides, you're the closest thing we have to a minister in Hangtown, so you'll have to do." He picked up a stack of the posters and handed them to the printer. "Tack them up around the claims. We want all the men to know there's a church in town."

"What about here? Should we tack them up in town too?" the printer asked.

King said, "Yes. I want to be sure everybody in Hangtown knows. But the outlying miners are the hardest to reach."

"And who's paying, sir?"

"You shouldn't, Mr. King," Narcissa said as he led her from the clapboard shack that had been built around the printing press in preparation for the winter cold. "You've given me so much and so far I haven't had a single parishioner show up at my place, your house."

"Your church," he corrected her.

He walked with her through the main part of town, a possessive hand on her elbow.

It was Friday, a work day. The miners were working at their claims or at pits owned by men who employed them, yet the town maintained a bustling air.

Hammers pounded, saws rasped, axes chopped. With each day the town took on a new permanence not unlike that of many other towns that had prospered only to fade when the gold ran out.

She hoped Hangtown never became a ghost town. She was developing a perverse attachment for the place. Much of it was unsightly, muddy, and unplanned. Streets were determined by the mule trails of men going and coming from their claims. Yet the smell of newly sawed wood was invigorating, and a wagon load of paint had been brought in. The saloon and the pleasure parlor were being painted a bright, cheerful white. Other buildings had to settle for a cheaper metallic gray.

Narcissa might have deplored the whore house being painted first, but she didn't.

Narcissa found it hard to condemn anyone after the lonely horrors of the trail west. The tarts and their patrons were people. Madam Mattie's place was a sort of umbilical cord to the future. At least it was populated by women who in their own way were pioneers.

And the town was still an embryo not wholly formed.

It would be ready to start a proper life soon though, she thought, just as her new life would begin before long.

"The posters will bring the men in," Walter was assuring her. "Few miners work on Sunday. You'll see, day after tomorrow."

At the sight of her church, she came to an abrupt stop.

A cross rose from the peak of the steeply sloped roof. It hadn't been there an hour before.

"A cross! Who could have . . ." She turned to Walter in her excitement and planted a delighted kiss on his cheek. "You did it!" she exclaimed. "You do all the nice things."

He took her hand and contemplated the cross with her.

"Really looks like a church now, doesn't it?"

"How did you get it up there without my knowing?"

"Well, actually I didn't build it myself," he admitted.

"I wouldn't expect you to."

"I had several of my men build it and then put it in place while you and I were busy at the printer's."

His referral to "his" men interested her but she said nothing. Somehow she had not thought of him in terms of being an employer. He seemed to do nothing, yet money was plentiful. He had given her so much, everything she needed. It was a loan, of course, or a contribution to the church.

When he led her by the hand into the church, she felt obligated to follow him.

"The children home?" he asked, closing the door behind them.

"Why no. I should be tutoring them, but they have that pan you gave them and they're always at the river looking for gold. They find a few dollars worth every once in a

while. With winter coming on, they'll have to quit though.
I promised myself they wouldn't grow up without knowing how to read and write."

He took her other hand and held her with only a few
inches between them.

He was going to kiss her, and she was not averse to the
idea. It wasn't proper, though. They were alone in the
house. The children might not come back for an hour, and
Walter was handsome and clean.

Clean. Strange how important that had become. In a
town where men made their living by digging in the mud
or standing in the icy waters of a stream, the clean smell
of soap set a man like King apart. Not that alone, of
course. He was a schooled man, and as he held her fingers, he quoted Shakespeare.

"'Of nature's gifts thou may'st with lilies boast, and
with the half-blown rose.'"

"Thank you," she said with a small curtsy. "Quite flat-
tering from a man who is 'honorable, and doubling that,
most holy.'"

"If I'm holy, then I'm your first convert," he said. He
bent to kiss her lightly on the forehead.

She was disappointed. A kiss on the forehead was no
kiss at all. But she said, "I'm sure someone or other saw us
come in. It's most unseemly for us to be alone in the
house."

He brushed aside her observation. "In church. Your
church."

"Our church."

"Our church then. Who can say we are alone here?
Maybe there are other worshippers. And who can say we
would do anything wrong?"

Now he kissed her properly, and she rose on tiptoe to
meet his lips. For an instant the moment glowed. Then it
darkened, and something made her pull back.

"Something wrong?" he asked.

"No," she said, her eyes downcast.

"It's the trapper, isn't it? You're thinking of him."

What did he know about that? She had told no one. It
was not something you would put into words, even if you

could. But Walter was perceptive enough to guess a woman's secrets, and apparently she was not soiled in his eyes. She was grateful for that, and it eased her guilt. There was no reason to blame herself for what had occurred in the mountains, no reason to be ashamed, even for the involuntary moment of pleasure at the end. But old ideas died hard.

In Iowa City she could not have brought herself to speak to a woman who had been raped. She would not have known what to say.

"I'll have my men bring him in. They will take him to San Francisco and have him put away. Incarcerated."

Again Walter had shown his sensitivity. He wasn't suggesting the trapper be hung, only jailed to protect others.

"Forget him," he was saying. "The trapper isn't a man."

"Not like you," she said.

It was all the encouragement he needed. Now his arms were more eager, and his lips were warm against her neck. Foolishly, she expected the kiss to tickle. She was afraid she might giggle. Instead a shiver ran down through her body, culminating in an indescribable sensation. Pleasurable, but not like the taste of good food. Tantalizing, like a prettily wrapped gift, promising special delights. Frightening, like a child's venture into some forbidden woods.

"Please don't," she murmured breathlessly. The request was a sincere plea. To feel like this had to be sinful.

A sin of the flesh.

He kissed her lips. She closed her eyes as if she could shut out her responsibility by closing out the late afternoon sun coming through the windows. "God can't see in the dark." That was a joke her father used in his sermons.

Walter's hands ran down the length of her spine. The same feeling she had experienced briefly with the trapper, the pleasure in the midst of the agony, surged back in waves, far stronger than before.

She tried to hold King away, not because there was terror in his touch, but because she could not stop that gentle warmth spreading through her body. For the first time since she had left home, she was safe. Walter was

strong and righteous like her father. He could ward off
the devil, wrap her in safety and contentment with a
sweep of his arms. He took command as her brother had,
but Walter was not a dreamer, defying natural laws. He
was smart and pragmatic. He could protect her.

Then his hand was on her breast, and she felt her
nipples tingle and swell.

It was a sensation she had known before when she lay
awake at night, her two sisters already asleep in the bed
with her. When she stared into the darkness of the tiny
bedroom, she had sometimes touched herself, pretending
the hands were not hers, that they were those of a man.

She knew she was doing wrong. Her father sometimes
alluded to such behavior in his prayers, but he was a loving man, and he saved his righteous anger for more important sins. And she knew from what she could hear
through the walls that her father and mother did such
things in the sanctity of their bedroom.

Now Walter was doing it, and when her hand folded
over his with the intent of pushing him away, she found
herself pressing his fingers harder instead.

"I'll buy you a hundred Beecher Bibles," she heard him
saying as if from a distance.

Was he buying her? The lovely feeling vanished. Anger
rushed in to fill the void. She pulled loose, and he sensed
what she was thinking.

"I should pay God for bringing you into my life."

Pay God? It was she who should pay God. It was she
who should ask King's forgiveness for her thoughts about
him.

"I'm sorry," she whispered, and stepped back into his
arms.

Now his hands slipped to the twin swells of her bottom.
His eyes were open, looking into hers, and instead of re-
moving his hands from her body, she reached up and
closed his eyelids with her fingertips. At the same time she
closed her own eyes. The world was devoid of sight and
sound, except for the growing quickness of their breathing. There was his clean, masculine smell. There was the

swelling pressure inside her that yearned for him to press forward until their bodies met at the groin.

It was a shock at first, a repellent one, when his tongue parted her lips. Surely no had ever done that. Still it was pleasant, and she tried it with her own tongue, liking the feeling as it slid across his teeth.

Wrong! Sinful! For married couples only. But she was with Walter King, the man who financed the church. Could that be wrong?

"Walter," she gasped, "we can't do this. We're acting like a married couple."

"Well, aren't we close enough to being married?"

Was that a proposal? She took it as one. Her body wanted it to be, wanted an excuse.

His hands caressed her hair, then lifted her and kissed her in the cleft between her breasts. Next they were touching along the length of their bodies, one of his arms lifting her, and the other urging her into a slow, circular motion.

Did she float or did he carry her into the bedroom? Suddenly he was about to put her on the bed, and she squirmed free. He made no effort to hold her except for a light grip on the very tip of her fingers. She went back to him, and he kissed her again until she forgot it was a bedroom. All the sensations were new. She closed her eyes, making every movement part of the beautiful dream.

What they were doing was no longer sinful.

It was a dream.

And when he lay her on the bed, he did nothing wrong, only sat beside her stroking her hair away from her face, kissing her mouth, her cheeks, her neck, her breasts.

She felt his hand on her leg, not sure whether it was under her skirt or not.

Only when he slid her underclothing down did she panic again.

"This is wrong," she said aloud. "We shouldn't be doing this. It's a sin."

"It's love," he said. "The Adamic surprise, although I

don't know why we men assume that Eve didn't experience the same startling thrill."

The biblical reference to Adam and Eve eased her
doubts. They had sinned by eating an apple, or was this
the sin that had condemned the world?

No, Walter had said it right.

This was love.

"You and I," he said. "Building a temple."

Then the last of her underthings had been removed,
and she did not resist when he pushed the ruffled petti-
coat to her waist. How could she offend the only person
within thousands of miles who cared about her?

She wasn't exposed, she thought in her mellow dream.
Her skirt covered her, and when she felt his hand
touching her, she pretended it was her own. She was
home, in bed with her sisters, touching herself gently and
dreaming of nothing in particular, sure that the future
would be good.

The memory of the trapper came rushing back when he
tried to enter her. She cried out and rolled away.

But this was Walter King. Kind. Gentle. Patient.

He waited for her. She must not allow her thoughts to
confuse him with the beast.

She apologized and rolled back to him, eager to have
him touch her again. Then he was inside her and the pain
was over so quickly. She was rising and falling with him,
afraid he would leave her before she fulfilled the powerful
need that begged satisfaction.

"Oh, you're wonderful, Drover . . ."

She knew King heard her mistake, but he continued his
plunging and withdrawing, impatient to satisfy himself.

He left too soon. That aftermath of soft, glowing contentment—he should have stayed with her through that.

He left before she could say, "Walter, we can't ever do
that again, not ever. It's sinful."

She would have to bring up the subject the next time
they met. Indirectly, of course, subtly. Never quite refer-
ring to it as sex.

He would understand.

He would say, "Of course."

And he would apologize, hint at marriage.

Then the children came running into the house and directly to the bedroom.

"Cissie, look! Cissie, I found a big one," Adrian bragged. He held out a golden nugget larger than anything they had found before.

"It's worth a thousand dollars," Sarah announced, wide-eyed with joy. "We could buy dolls."

Narcissa hoped their enthusiasm blinded them to the embarrassment that flamed in her cheeks. "A thousand dollars? Who told you that?"

"Adrian. He's a real miner now."

"Yes," the boy agreed, "I'm going to stake a claim and go to work to support you and Sarah."

"You're going to school, that's what you're going to do," Narcissa scolded.

"There ain't no school here."

"There isn't any school here. And besides, there is. Starting Monday morning, you and Sarah are going to begin learning how to read."

Adrian was baffled. "Why? I can make my mark. That's all you have to do to file a claim."

"Because you're not going to be a miner."

"Yes, I am."

"Not always."

"What else is there to do in Hangtown?"

Narcissa stood before the mirror on the wall and tugged at her hair with her comb. "You could be a school teacher."

"That's women's work."

"There's no women's work or men's work."

"Yes, there is," Adrian disagreed violently. "And preaching ain't no woman's work."

"Who told you that?" Narcissa demanded.

"The men. All the men. They say you should be working for Mattie Lafayette. That's where you belong."

She slapped him and he swatted back at her, hitting her arm repeatedly while he cried angry, manly tears. "Ain't nobody coming to your silly church."

She did not fend off his blows.

"Yes, they will," she said quietly, "and the town is going to change. There won't be any more hangings. Men will stop digging in the mud and start farming. Mattie's girls will marry or go to decent work. People will help each other, and the men won't get drunk every Saturday night. They won't gamble away every cent they've earned."

"Who says?" Adrian challenged.

"God says so."

Why had that answer popped into her head?

She did not hear the boy's reaction to her proclamation. She was too enthralled with her own words.

God says so.

Had he spoken to her, a sinner like the rest?   ❧

13

ELEVEN o'clock came and Narcissa stood behind the newly built pulpit, waiting. Her fingers folded around the leading edge holding on, seeking strength from the firm, smooth wood.

The new pews were almost empty. Walter had them built, and she had so wanted to please him by having them full that she had wandered through the town and even out among the mining claims, inviting the men to church. They had all promised to be there except Madam Mattie, who had been adamant, even rude. She had laughed and slammed the door.

About the only person she had not reminded personally was Drover.

Sarah and Adrian squirmed in the front row. Behind them were MacDermitt and MacIntosh, the two men who had stood at the top of the gallows when the town hanged Wee Willie. When she asked them to take their gunbelts off and hang them at the back of the church, they had acquiesced without argument.

Their presence irritated her at first. She thought they sullied her church. Then Christian charity persevered, and she accepted that they, of all people in town, needed to be present. A few feet away from them was Judge Russell, wearing the smug, expectant expression of one who waits for what he is sure will happen.

Walter, of course, was sitting with her at the front, facing the others. An "assistant preacher" he had playfully labeled himself.

She had expected more, many more, people. The miners and the storekeepers, the girls from the parlor, they should have come. In Iowa almost everybody attended church.

"The best people are here," King assured her. "Once the men see who has come, they'll begin too. You'll see. Go ahead. Start the service."

Then the door opened and White Squaw, her tattooed face barely inside the door, peered cautiously in.

"Come in. Do come in," Narcissa said with as ingratiating a tone as she could manage.

The former Indian captive had taken no more than two steps inside before Featherlegs Fanny came in after her. The young preacher's hopes rose. Most of all she wanted the girls from the parlor to attend. They needed her more than did the men. But Featherlegs was reining in White Squaw, not joining her.

"Come on, you fool," she hissed. "Mattie saw you come in here. You're gonna get your ass whipped as it is."

"Let her stay," Narcissa said.

"Why?" Fanny asked. "What business has a whore got in a church?"

"We're all God's children. Besides she won't be a prostitute forever."

Fanny was skeptical. "So what's she gonna become? You know any man who's going to marry a tattooed lady?"

"She could become a teacher and give lectures on what Indians are really like."

"At ladies clubs?" the judge scoffed.

"Yes. Or she could become a missionary to the redskins. Let her stay."

Fanny shook her head. "Like I said, she'll get a beating just for coming down here."

"Speak to Madam Lafayette for her, will you, Walter?"

King considered the request before he denied it. "Mattie would just agree, then take her revenge out on White Squaw later. Don't press the issue quite yet."

Narcissa capitulated, saddened by White Squaw's fearful, chastened countenance as she was led from the church.

"Let's start the service," the judge said. "Nobody else is crazy enough to waste a good Sunday in here."

Narcissa fumbled with the notes for her sermon, still reluctant to begin.

The door opened once more and Drover appeared. At the sight of him, a hot flush of shame and embarrassment erupted inside her, oozing from every pore. Could he tell what had transpired between her and Walter? She did not want him to know.

Why was that so important? He did not matter to her. Not now.

"Take off your hat, Aussie," King called from the front of the small chapel. "You're in a temple of God. Or don't they have churches in that penal colony you come from?"

Narcissa cringed. "Walter, please," she said just above a whisper. She did not want a fight between the two men.

Drover surprised her. He removed his hat and said nothing. She could feel Walter gloating. Why had Drover taken the rebuke so meekly?

"Preach, dear girl," Walter said again.

There was no excuse for waiting any longer.

For days she had been planning the service, trying to recall the format she had sat through in her father's church for as long as she could remember. She was chagrined to realize she had never really listened. She had dreamed through every service she had ever attended.

Now what little she could piece together was scribbled on a piece of paper on top of the pulpit, but she could not concentrate. Her mind kept wandering to the end of the hall where the tall man stood against the wall.

Afraid she would stammer, she lowered her head and started with the one prayer she thought she knew.

"Join me in the Lord's Prayer," she said, "as we inaugurate this, God's latest temple, humble, but built with love. 'Our father which art in heaven, hallowed be thy name. Thy kingdom come, thy will be done in earth as it is in heaven.'" She paused. Only Drover and King were praying with her. The other three men were silent, and the children were making movements with their lips, just as she had done short years earlier. She continued slowly, "Give us this day our daily bread. And forgive us our debts as we forgive our debtors. And lead us not into temptation, but deliver us from evil; For thine is the kingdom and the power, and the glory for ever. Amen.'"

"Amen," the two men echoed.

Her voice cracked when she went on. "As we gather here today, so few of us, I make no pretense of being an ordained minister. I . . ."

The door to the outside opened and she saw only two silhouettes backlighted by the noonday sun.

"Miss White, Reverend White," a young man's voice said while the two figures started down the aisle. "We don't mean to interrupt or nothing, but . . ."

She recognized them. It was Velvet Ass Annie from the pleasure parlor and the boy Narcissa knew only as David. They were walking hand in hand toward the makeshift altar.

The judge was the first to speak, his tone flat and cutting. "What are you doing here, whore? This is a house of God, not tarts."

"You watch what you're sayin' to my fiancée, Judge," the boy warned.

"Fiancée?" The judge laughed. The two hangmen joined him. Walter King so far had not moved.

"We want you to marry us, Miss . . . Reverent White," Annie said. "This boy doesn't have all his marbles. Says he doesn't give a squat about what I've been."

"I . . ." Narcissa's knees were quavering.

She had been yanked from the fairy tale of her dreams into harsh reality.

"She can't marry you," the judge pronounced. "She's no proper minister."

"And who made you a judge?" the boy challenged.

"I did," the judge responded. "I'm the law here."

"David, Annie," Narcissa said. "I don't think you know what you're doing."

"We know," David assured her. "We've been seeing each other ever since she came to town."

"And no, I ain't been charging him," Annie said defensively.

"You belong to Mattie Lafayette," the judge interrupted. "Better get back there, girl, before she whips the hide off you."

"She ain't never whippin' Annie again," David declared.

The judge addressed the two Macs. "Take her back," he ordered.

Narcissa was surprised when the two hangmen left their pews and started down the aisle toward Annie. I should have known they worked for the judge, the young clergywoman thought.

"I wouldn't be touching that lass, mates," Drover advised politely.

"This has got nothing to do with you, Aussie," MacIntosh said, his tone an ominous warning.

Drover shrugged. "Just didn't want to see two nice blokes get their bloody heads blown off and mess up the new church, that's all, stickybeaks."

"Who you threatening? You ain't even toting," MacDermitt said as his hand went to his waist, where his gun belt usually hung. His face whitened.

"I am now," Drover said. He had sidled to the coat pegs on the wall and extracted both of the men's guns. "Now you boys just get down on your knees and pray while Miss White gets these two young ones married."

"You can't . . ."

Drover took aim.

The hangmen looked quickly at Walter King. It was as if they were waiting for instructions from him. His lips did not move but his eyes narrowed.

Narcissa said, "Drover, I can't marry them. I'm not a preacher."

"You are if you say you are. Self-ordained, they call it. Same thing happens outback in Australia. Just say some words over them. The courts will make it legal when they get around to this part of the country."

"Please," said Annie. "You're our only hope. Mattie will never let me go otherwise."

"Marry 'em, Cissie," Adrian said.

Sarah agreed. "Yes, Aunt Cissie. I've never been to a wedding before."

"You do and you'll be coated with tar and run out of town naked," the judge warned.

"Judge!" It was all that Walter King said. It seemed to be enough.

The two gunmen moved to take their seats.

"In the aisle and on your knees," Drover reminded them.

"Is that necessary?" Narcissa asked. "As long as they don't interfere?"

"Yes, Miss," the Australian said. "If I got to shoot them, I don't want to put any holes in your nice new pews. Now go ahead. These lads are volunteering as witnesses, aren't you, mates? I said, aren't you, boys?"

"Yes."

"All right, Annie and David," Narcissa said nervously. "I don't know how legal this is, but I'm sure in the eyes of the Lord what you are about to do is binding. And I don't know the words so we will have to make it short. Do you, Annie . . . Annie . . ."

"Driggs. Annie Marie Driggs."

"Driggs?" David laughed. "That's a funny name."

"What's yours?" Annie challenged.

"Ledbetter. David Ledbetter."

"Well, you better have led in your pencil," Annie joked, "or this ceremony ain't worth a thing."

"Annie, please," Narcissa scolded. "This is a church."

"Yes, ma'am. Go right ahead."

"Do you, Annie Marie Driggs, take this man, David Ledbetter, as your lawfully wedded husband, to love, honor and obey, until death do you part?"

"Long as he ain't any meaner than that bitch Mattie Lafayette."

"Annie!"

"Yes, I take him . . . long as he's kicking . . . and got all his other vital parts working."

"And you, David Ledbetter, do you take Annie Marie Driggs as your lawfully wedded wife to keep in sickness and in health for better or for worse?"

"I sure do, ma'am. I sure do."

"Do you have a ring?"

David blinked. "Been meanin' to make one. But I been spending my time sneaking down by the river with Annie when I should have been panning for gold."

"Well, we'll dispense with the ring. With whatever power is invested in me I pronounce you man and wife."

"Yahoo!" David yelled. He pulled Annie into his arms and planted a triumphant kiss on her mouth.

"Ain't legal," the judge mumbled.

"Can we get up?" one of the men on the floor asked.

Drover said, "Yes, and you can walk right past me, through the door, with your hands on your heads. If you keep them there and don't wait around outside, you might live to get married yourself someday."

"What about our guns?"

"Consider them a wedding present. One for the groom and one for me."

Of the two who had hung Wee Willie, MacIntosh was by far the more despicable. He was a coward with a mean streak, hiding behind a weapon. MacDermitt did his job with a tinge of regret. He had probably failed as a miner and now worked in law enforcement, albeit without enthusiasm.

"I'll see you in hell for this," MacIntosh threatened.

Drover smiled, but the pleasantry did not extend to his eyes. "One more remark and you'll be there waiting long before I arrive. Now move!"

The two men walked up the aisle with the judge following close behind. They paused outside the church until Drover stepped to the open door, aimed at their feet, and fired twice. Dirt splashed up on their clean boots. Defiantly slow, the three men walked toward the saloon.

"You, love birds," Drover called to the newlyweds. "Hide at my place until dark. Then get the hell out of town. Take my horse."

"But I can't pay for it," David said.

"I could," Annie offered with a grin.

"Another wedding present," he said as he tossed one gun to David and slipped the other into the holster on the wall. Then he removed the gunbelt and strapped it to his waist.

The lovers passed in front of him, and he came down the aisle where King now stood by the pulpit.

"That was none too smart, bushranger," the smartly groomed King said. "You may have just signed the death warrants for those two young people."

"You going to have them shot?"

"Hardly. But MacIntosh and MacDermitt . . ."

". . . won't do anything unless you tell them to," Drover finished for him. "They work for you."

"Like hell they do."

"Drover," Narcissa interjected, "why are you accusing Mr. King? Without him there'd be no church."

"Without him there'd be no whorehouse, no saloon with crooked dealers, and rotgut whiskey at two dollars a shot. Without him a man would have something left over after panning in icy water all week."

"And precisely what does that mean?"

"That he owns the store, the printing press, the barber shop, everything except the laundries. The Chinamen are the only ones jake enough to stare down this snake."

"That's ridiculous," Narcissa said. "He owns none of those places. He's not responsible for the high prices."

"And he owns you, you and your church. Only you're too dumb to know it."

"How dare you!"

"Narcissa, pay no attention to him," King said softly. "Now, if you don't mind, Drover, I think this is not the place for us to settle our differences. This is a church, after all."

Drover looked around him.

"Maybe it is. Maybe blood money can build a temple, I don't know."

"Drover, you apologize," Narcissa demanded.

He raised his head and looked at the ceiling. "Forgive me, Milapukala, if I offend thee."

"Mila . . . what?"

"An aborigine goddess. The cockatoo woman. Finally transformed herself into a cleft rock on the shores of Milapuru lagoon. You going to do that, Miss White? Transform yourself into a rock after King here has used you like he uses everybody in Hangtown country? Might as well because this bull artist will turn you hard as rock if you stay with him."

"Get out," she said indignantly. "Get out!"

He nodded and swung through the door, his hatless head clearing the upper frame by only a narrow margin even though he ducked.

Tears of hurt and anger stung her eyes. Turning to King for comfort, she found him dour and unpleasant. "You shouldn't have done that," he said coldly.

"What?"

"Married that whore. She belongs to Mattie."

"Annie's not a slave."

"Mattie took her in when the girl wanted to escape a brutal father. She fed her, gave her a home, brought her west. Now Annie owes her."

"You mean Annie's indentured? Is that what you're trying to say?"

"A case of simple economics. Mattie hasn't made her stake back yet." He started down the aisle. "No different than a miner taking a grubstake and then disappearing into the hills without trying to find gold."

"It's not the same," Narcissa argued stubbornly. "She's . . ."

"It's the same."

"Then I don't care."

"You made an enemy, Narcissa," he said, "and women like Mattie Lafayette don't like being cheated."

"I still don't care." She knew she sounded childish, but she didn't care about that either.

"You will. Sooner or later."

He stalked out and Narcissa was alone. Even Adrian and Sarah had taken the first opportunity to escape. Had she now turned even Walter against her? She had alienated Drover, angered the judge and the two gunmen, and now Mattie Lafayette. And by dark Annie would be gone, with her new husband.

"Just you and I, God," she said somewhat hopelessly, her eyes lifted to the ceiling.

But isolated as she felt, she was not alone. Men had gathered outside, attracted by the sound of gunshots. They had watched curiously as Drover and the newly-weds walked away in one direction; King and the others headed for the saloon.

Narcissa walked to the door thinking perhaps she could muster a congregation from the assemblage.

"Gentlemen, won't you join me in church? We can plan Thanksgiving dinner. Thursday's the day, you know."

The men, somewhat cowed and a little uncomfortable in her presence, pretended to be receptive.

"Like to, Pastor," one said, "but I got beans cooking."

"Later," another said.

"Thursday's a workday for me, ma'am."

"Next Sunday."

"But what was the shooting about?"

Narcissa lifted her chin. "I'll explain that in church."

No one, however, was that curious. And Walter had not looked back.   ❧

14

THE frantic beating on the door was enough to wake even the children, who seemed to sleep through almost any disturbance. Narcissa considered carrying the gun Walter had left after the trapper's appearance, but to do so seemed over-dramatic at least until she went to the door. Lighting a lamp, she went through the chapel and called to whoever stood on the other side of the bolted panel.

"It's David." The boy's voice was sick with pain. "David Ledbetter. They're beating Annie. Beating her to death, I think."

Narcissa opened the door, and he staggered into the light. His face was a black and blue mask. One arm, obviously broken, hung limp from his shoulder. He favored an injured leg and was doubled over from blows to his abdomen.

"David! Come in. Let me help you." Narcissa stepped aside.

"No time. They're beating Annie to death, I tell you."

"Where?"

"At the pleasure parlor."

"But you were at Drover's house."

"They caught us when we tried to ride out of town.

Beat me, beat Drover unconscious when he came to help and dragged Annie to Mattie's place. They're killing her. You can hear her screaming from here."

Narcissa stepped into the night. She could hear, or imagine she could hear, the cries of the new bride from the big house at the end of the street.

"You'll have to save her," David cried. "I can't." He held up the hand at the end of his good arm. "I can't," he sobbed.

His fingers were grotesquely broken.

"I'll try," she said as she started on the run to the whorehouse.

"What's wrong, Cissie?" Adrian called from behind her.

"Nothing. Go back to bed."

But she heard the children padding along behind her and knew they would not obey. Curiosity and fear and the bright face of danger—strange bedfellows that they were—kept them close to her.

The rest of the town was waking too.

Lamps blossomed in shack windows and through the canvas tents. A few men were stepping into the open wearing only their long underwear. Narcissa was not dressed in much more. She wore a nightgown, which covered her adequately, but flattened against her body in the stiff, cold wind. She carried the lamp as far in front of her as possible.

"What's up, lady?" the town barber called from his shop. Like most of the merchants, the back of his business served as his home.

A weary miner poked his head from a tent. "You one of Mattie's girls?"

"No," another voice said. "It's that uppity bible belter."

"Shut up. Leave her alone," David yelled. He could not keep up on his injured leg.

By the time they reached Drover's home, a small parade of curious townsmen followed her.

She found Drover regaining consciousness, painfully trying to sit up. She stooped to help him.

"Drover, are you all right?"

"Gone a million, I am. Some bloke got a king hit on me when I wasn't looking."

He tried to regain his feet and fell back.

Holding the lamp over him, she saw the lump on his forehead and the revolver lying in the dirt.

"Never mind him," David pleaded. "He'll be all right. It's Annie we got to save."

Drover rose. "I'll give her a go, boy, but I don't know . . ." He staggered and slumped down again.

"The gun. Pick up the gun," David shouted at Narcissa. "You'll need it."

"No!" She was no match for Hangtown with a gun. Besides, she was not sure she'd be able to shoot, even if the need arose.

"Go on," Drover muttered. "I'll be right behind you." When she hurried on toward the whore house, he was leaning against a tree, still half-unconscious.

The men from the camp were following, their number growing with each shack or tent they passed. Whether they knew what was happening or not she did not know, but they assumed a party mood.

By the time they reached the house, the front door was open and the prostitutes were running out. They wore little except the robes which they let hang open enough to show their legs. Men helped out with lamps and torches, and the laughter almost drowned the sounds of the girl screaming from the third floor attic.

"That's Annie!" David pointed toward the agonized sounds.

He followed Narcissa to the door. It was bolted from the inside.

"You in there," Narcissa shouted. "Leave the girl alone. Let her out!"

There was derisive male laughter from inside, and she pounded on the door with her free hand. When there was no response and the screaming continued, she circled to the rear and tried the exit there. It too was locked.

The screaming intensified, and Narcissa appealed to the men for help.

"Somebody's got to help," the man she knew only as Jake said. "Come on. Placer, let's give Annie a hand."

His partner hesitated. "Go up against Mattie? You crazy? We'd be banned from the parlor."

Jake succumbed to second thoughts. "You gonna service me and my partner if we help?" he taunted Narcissa.

"Hey," another chimed in, "can I get a piece of that deal?"

"Shut up, you lice," David bellowed. "You're talking to a preacher!"

"Seems like she's tryin' to wear bloomers on a job the Almighty most likely meant for a man," Jake responded.

"A real man wouldn't stand by while a woman gets beaten." Narcissa flung the gauntlet of challenge at him but he did not pick it up.

Several others might have helped. It was the girls, however, that discouraged them.

"Annie's only getting what she's got coming," Cottontail said. ". . . trying to run off and leave the rest of us with no virgin."

"But you have to help!"

The girls laughed at her; the men avoided her like a guilty conscience.

In desperation Narcissa ran to the porch and the closest window. "Kick out the glass," she said to David.

Awkwardly, he teetered on one foot and kicked. The pane shattered and the shards flew inside. They climbed through carefully, the lamp in her hands illuminating the room.

Rushing toward the steps, they found their way blocked by MacDermitt. Where did MacDermitt and his partner fit in the town hierarchy, Narcissa wondered. Hangmen, gunmen, bouncers at the whorehouse. She had asked, but no one except Drover would guess, and she could not believe him.

"Where you think you're going?" he spat at Narcissa. "And you . . ." He looked at David and pushed the battered boy back toward the door. "Ain't you had enough for one night?" He drove his fist hard into the boy's stomach. David doubled over in agony, unable to defend himself.

Threatening to use the same tactic that had saved her from the trapper, Narcissa raised the oil lamp above her head. "Hit him again and I'll smash you with this. You'll burn in the fires of hell where you belong."

The gunman scoffed and took the lamp from her. He knew she could not carry out her threat. Then the toughness in his mood seemed to soften.

"Look, Miss White," he said, "don't get involved. It's like this with whores, you know what I mean?"

"She's God's child too."

"Well, God didn't stake no claim on Hangtown. Wish he had, but this is Satan's country. Nobody's changing that."

"I am," Narcissa said. "Help me."

"Wish I could." He sounded sincere until Madam Lafayette called from the top of the stairs.

"Who's down there?"

"That hellfire and damnation bitch," the man replied. "She broke in."

The screaming stopped, but not the crying.

Mattie came part way down the stairs, where MacIntosh, the second gunman, joined her a moment later. She carried a lamp waist high. It cast upward shadows that turned the madam into a classic drama mask.

"Well, little miss virgin, the lady preacher. Who'd a thought you'd come running back here?"

"You were beating Annie and . . ."

"Beating Annie?" Mattie feigned incredulity. "Us?"

"I could hear her screaming halfway across town."

"You're dreaming, child."

"The hell she is," David said. "You were beating her like those bastards beat me."

"You hurt this boy?" she asked MacIntosh.

"Me, ma'am? It was me and my partner who saved this twerp from being killed. The little tyke was being run over by a colony of piss ants. The Australian fella too. Had to save the both of them, didn't we?"

"Yep," his partner said.

The black girl, the one who said her name was Mary of Nazareth, emerged from the attic.

"They got the girl. Beat her bad, they did."

"Mary!" Mattie snapped, "you want some of the same?"

"Don't much care," the black replied. "Just sick to death the way you treats us all, bitch lady." The Negro prostitute walked past and into the night. "Ain't comin' back, neither. Rather starve."

Narcissa feared for her. A glance between the madam and her two toughs boded trouble for the black rebel, but the girl in the attic was in more immediate peril.

"I want Annie," Narcissa said emphatically.

"We don't have any Annie living here that I know about."

"I want my wife," David demanded.

Mattie tossed back her broad head and laughed. "Wife? Well, that's one thing we sure as hell haven't got in this here house. But what about you, Miss Pure Ass White, you ready to join us? The devil pays more than your phony God. I'm sure you figured that for yourself by now. You can spend the rest of your life selling your gospel and not make as much as you can by selling ass here for a month. Now what do you say? Ready to be reasonable?"

"Let me see Annie," Narcissa repeated. She rushed for the stairs, but Mattie put a hand between her breasts and pushed. "Get them out of here," she shouted at MacDermitt.

The men took Narcissa and David by the arms and hustled them away. When they had been forced into the street, Mattie strode out onto the porch, fists on her hips, and shouted to her girls.

"You simpletons, get back in here! You're giving away free feels. Always wanting to give it away, you fools!"

"Just having a little fun," Cottontail replied. A miner pressed close to her, his arm draped around her neck, hand cupped over her breast.

"Fun, shit. You don't fuck for fun. That's business. Now get the hell in here."

"My God! Look!" a girl cried.

"Fire!"

Narcissa's eyes swept the house, seeing nothing at first, not until she looked to the second floor windows that fronted on the street. The light there was not the steady glow of a lamp but the flickering and prancing of flames running up the curtains.

For a moment the awful magnet of flame hypnotized the crowd. As men, women, and children had done for eons, the onlookers quieted and stared into the leaping fire. They were transfixed, carried beyond their mundane thoughts, their minds edging close to some eternal wisdom, some insight into the unknown. Narcissa had seen fire do that to people; even her otherwise effervescent brother became quiet and pensive at a campfire.

Those townspeople still arriving on the scene came at a run, then stopped, fascinated with the aura of fire.

The first to break the spell was Madam Lafayette, who did it with a burst of profanity. "The fucking bastard whore has done it! She's burning my place down!" She rushed for the front door. "Cottontail, you and some of the men surround the house. Don't let that Velvet Ass bitch escape!"

Mattie dashed inside.

David Ledbetter erupted with anguish. "Annie's in there!" Dragging his battered body, he tailed the madam through the door.

Narcissa ran in with them. So did MacDermitt.

"Bucket brigade!" The cry was echoed down the cold, dark street.

Narcissa was at the door when she felt a small hand tugging her night dress. The frightened Sarah was clinging to her. Picking the child up by the armpits, she passed her off to a whore. "Take her and keep Adrian away too."

Then Drover was there holding Narcissa back.

"No need you risking your life," he said.

He squeezed in ahead of her, but she charged through the parlor with more speed than his beaten body could muster. They all seemed to reach the foot of the stairs at the same moment. They met the same wall of fire. Glass at their feet told the story. An oil lamp had been flung from the upper landing, breaking midway down and splashing flammable fluid in a wide circle. The crazed Annie was breaking other lamps on the second floor. It was one of these that caused the flames the crowd saw first.

David was undaunted. He vaulted up the stairs, flames snatching at his trousers.

Scarcely aware of her actions, Narcissa elbowed Mattie aside, slipped past Drover's grasping hand, and lifted her nightgown. Flame seared her bare legs, but she ran faster up the stairs, choking in the thick smoke. Her eyes watered. Hot sand seemed to be pelting them. She felt rather than saw David darting from room to room, searching desperately for his bride. Narcissa took the other side of the hall, pushing as far as she dared into the rooms already aflame.

Then she remembered the stairs to the attic and was heading there when she saw Drover coming up from the first floor, his feet breaking through two of the burning steps. She ran to him and with an outstretched hand helped pull him loose.

"Get the bloody hell away from here," he said. "Leave this to David and me!"

Narcissa went her own way, onward to the attic stairs. She went up two steps at a time. On the top floor, the air was not yet completely fouled with smoke.

And there was another lamp.

Annie held it at her waist. She was almost naked and cowering in a corner, head bent as she retreated in the slanting room.

"Annie," Narcissa cried, "let's go."

But the girl cringed farther into the corner, an animal retreating the last few feet left to it.

"Don't let him see me," Annie muttered.

"What?" In the roaring from below Narcissa was not sure what she had heard. She had not realized fire would be so noisy.

"Don't let David see me."

Velvet Ass Annie was no longer pretty. Her velvety skin was bruised and cut with lash marks that would leave permanent scars. Her face was pocked with burns, as if she had been seared by a branding iron. Only a stubble that the scissors had missed remained on her sheared head.

A few rags hung on her body. The rest had been torn away.

Why? Narcissa asked herself.

Why had Mattie gone so insane? She had permanently disfigured the most valuable girl in her house. Not merely beaten her, but cut and burned her into ugliness. She had not just kept Annie from running away. She had made the girl useless as a whore.

Why?

To frighten the other girls so they would never dare break away? Possibly.

But this mutilation was born of baser emotions.

Mattie must have destroyed the living symbol of the life she could never have. A man. A lover. A family. She must have seen Annie about to escape with all that she herself had sacrificed for gold.

"Narcissa, is she up here?" David shouted.

"Don't!" It was Annie's agonized bellow. "Don't let him see me like this!"

"Annie, it's not that bad." Narcissa tried to close the distance between them. Time was running out. Smoke was rolling into the attic. The floor was hot. Only the thickness of the planking had kept the room from bursting into flames.

"Not that bad?" Annie laughed wildly.

A glass broke on the floor between them.

A mirror.

Annie had tossed it there, its wedge-shaped pieces telling all. She had seen herself, peered past the immediate burns, viewed the future. She saw the ugly, scarred face that people would look aside to avoid. Saw the face that she would have to show her David for the rest of their lives.

"Annie."

David bounded through the attic door.

The lamp rose, stopped in front of the tortured girl's face. "Don't come near me."

"Annie, it's David."

"Go away."

"Come with me. My God, what ails you? It's David!"

"No. No. No." A great canyon echoed and re-echoed her words. "I know it's David. I don't want him. I hate him!" The last was aimed at Narcissa.

David plunged forward. Narcissa's hand stopped him.

"David, she doesn't want to see you. Leave her and me alone. I'll bring her down."

"What's wrong with her?"

"For the Lord's sake, don't argue!"

"I'm not going with anyone," Annie replied. "Leave me alone!"

Drover had reached the attic door. He was coughing into a handkerchief held over his mouth. "You find her? Good on you, girl. Now let's get the bloody hell out of here while we still got a fair go of making it."

"She won't come," David said.

"Leave me with her," Narcissa pleaded.

"No time for earbashing," Drover called. "The stairs are falling like tenpins."

"Annie." David took a step toward her.

"Don't," Narcissa begged.

But it was too late. Annie had raised the lamp higher. He saw her face.

"Oh, good God!" he moaned.

"Burn. Let me burn!" His wife flung the lamp to the floor between them. The glass shattered and the flames gushed in all directions, a beautiful spectrum of yellows, reds, and whites, a design no artist could equal. Then it was just a wall of fire, separating Annie from the others in the room, forcing her farther into the slant-roofed corner. She held out her hands to block off the heat. The flames curled around her out-stretched fingers.

David dived through to her. When she fought him, they fell to the floor together.

Narcissa went next, halfway through the circle of dancing light before Drover pulled her back. Her night clothes had caught fire and he pushed her to the floor, rolling her over and covering her with his own body until the flames died.

"Got to get them out. Got . . ."

"Got to get you out," he replied.

She fought him all the way to the door until he slapped her hard across the face, powerfully enough to stun her. She lost her hold on the door frame, and he pulled her to the head of the stairs. The flight from the second floor to the attic was burning, so were the walls.

From the noise below they could tell the men were fighting the fire, but their buckets could reach only the first floor.

"Please. I've got to go back for them," she argued. As an answer, Drover dragged her to the little balcony at the top of the next flight of stairs.

"David will get her out of the dormer," he shouted over the sizzling, cracking flames.

"No!" She didn't believe him.

"Catch her," he yelled to the men below. He lifted her over the railing and bent down as far as he could.

Then Narcissa was screaming and dropping, fingers grasping for anything, finding nothing. But she fell into a cradle of the men's and the whores' upraised arms. She was hardly jarred.

They hustled her away from the building, to clearer air. They held her struggling body while man after man after man gave up and stumbled from the smoke-filled inferno. Mattie Lafayette was among the last to leave, then Drover, staggering and gagging, stumbling onto the porch, where he collapsed.

The firefighters tried to lift him. Unconscious, he was too heavy, and they had to drag him down the last steps, his boots bouncing off them one by one. When they had him braced against a tree, a miner splashed him with a pail of icy creek water. His smoldering clothing steamed in the night air.

Narcissa knelt beside him.

Her heart was pounding with terror. She could not see him breathing. She felt for a pulse and found none.

"Drover! Drover!" She was screaming the way she did sometimes at the end of an ugly nightmare. Only, from this there was no awakening.

"Not you," she wailed into the night. "Not you too!" She lifted her head and moaned to the sky. "No, God. Not him too. Please! Not him too."

Still he did not move.

A cry went up from the crowd as they pulled back from the doomed house of ill repute.

"Look up there!"

Narcissa raised her eyes slowly to the dormer that protruded from the ceiling over the attic. She knew what she would see. At first the figures were not clear. Then the fire silhouetted them more distinctly.

Annie and David.

They were standing arm in arm.

"Jump," the men cried.

"Break the window and jump."

The figures seemed rooted in place.

They're not real, Narcissa told herself. It was not the two newlyweds standing there waiting to be consumed in flames. It was some grotesque joke. Paper cutouts like the ones her schoolmarm taught her to make. Paper silhouettes.

"Why don't they jump?"

From somewhere a ladder appeared and was braced against the porch roof. If they could reach the roof, they could lift the ladder to the dormer.

It would not reach, that was obvious, but they felt compelled to try.

Narcissa sat helpless, cradling Drover's inert body in her arms.

Why don't they jump, she whispered the question others were shouting around her.

White Squaw answered the question for the tragic lovers. "They don't *want* to," she said.

The men stopped climbing the ladder. The buckets were set aside. No one spoke.

Narcissa watched. Did she only imagine it, or did David give his wife a reassuring hug just before the flames turned the window glass into an opaque spiderweb of cracks? ✒

"... and if I had known you were coming, I would have slowed and ..." He was leaning forward, willing to

15

THE rain, with no breath of wind to alter its course, dropped straight down, running off the two mounds of reddish soil and streaming in little rivulets into the shallow graves. The twin pine coffins being lowered into the flooding pits were soiled with mud. Three men stood on either side of each of the boxes. When the containers touched the bottom, the commandeered pallbearers on one side released their end of the ropes and those on the opposite side tugged them out from beneath the coffins.

One rope was so mired that no amount of pulling would dislodge it.

"Leave it be," Narcissa ordered.

The rope around David Ledbetter's casket seemed his last link to the living.

The coffin bearers tossed in the end of twisted hemp, picked up their shovels, and began pushing the gravelly mud into the hole while each scanned the stones for the glitter of gold.

Around the grave, beneath umbrellas and oiled tarps, the inmates of the whorehouse had watched the brief ceremony Narcissa conducted. None had cried. Only Cottontail betrayed a trace of emotion—there was a suggestion of satisfaction about the set of her mouth. She was now the prettiest girl in the house.

Madam Lafayette stood at the foot of the grave, MacIntosh and MacDermitt with her, one holding an umbrella over her head. The heavy woman's feet were sinking slowly into the mud. At the head of the gaping wound in the weeping earth were Narcissa, the judge, Drover and Walter King. That was all. Even the men who had performed the nauseating job of sifting through the burned rubble of the house had not come.

In the background, the only sound to interrupt the tympany of rain was that of the carpenters expanding the saloon. Mattie's girls had moved in there as permanent occupants. What had been the whorehouse was now a pile of sodden ash.

Before Narcissa could turn away, Mattie spoke to her across the coffins.

"Now you see what your preaching brought to Hangtown, bitch. Two dead. God don't live in no church. He's between a woman's legs."

"That's blasphemy," Narcissa retorted.

"Blasphemy be damned."

"Mattie!" the judge admonished sharply. The presence of death had pricked him with piety. "Not here."

The madam called to her girls. Together with her two armed guards, they marched off to the saloon.

"Are you going to let Mattie get away with this?" Drover asked the judge. "Little doubt she killed the pair of them."

"Suicide," Russell ruled, his brief and uncomfortable brush with religion forgotten in the return to business. "Double suicide. If you want to press charges against Mattie and her boys for beating you, that's another matter. Of course, they might charge Miss White with breaking and entering."

"Bloody bastard." He spat the words from his mouth like rotten food.

"And that's contempt of court." The judge took his hat from his head and brushed off the water with his sleeve. "I could have you fined."

"And I'll wear my bail on my hip from now on."

Walter King frowned. "We don't need any more men carrying guns in this town, Drover."

"Just those two bloody bastards that work for you and Mattie, right?"

"They don't work for me."

"Rubbish!"

"Drover, not here," Narcissa objected. "I just want to go home."

"I'll walk you to the church," he said.

"Mr. King will see me home."

"That ratbag won't take you anywhere. Come along."

Narcissa's gaze sought Walter's. With a nod he told her to go along. Now was not the time to be quarreling with the Australian, he seemed to be saying.

Drover took her arm when she slid in the unreliable footing of mud. She shrugged free and stayed a step ahead of him.

"What are you crooked on me for?" he asked.

"Speak English," she snapped, her head held high so that the rain could mix with her tears for the couple she had married.

"I am speaking English. I asked why you're so bloody down on me. You haven't said a decent word to me since those two died."

"You must have told someone they were staying at your house," she said coldly.

Still limping, he managed to get in front of her.

"So that's the burr under your saddle. Well, listen here, girl. I didn't tell anybody. Had no call to give them away after I offered them a place to hide. Those big jackeroos were waiting when the lovebirds rode off. Far as I can see, besides me, only you and King knew where they were staying."

"Who are you accusing?"

"King, damnit. I'm going to punch up that no-hoper if I have to kill his hired gunnies to get at him."

"You'll do no such thing. Walter had no reason to tell where Annie and David were hiding. He's supported me and the church from the beginning. He gave me the building, put up the cross, and printed posters. He paid to have them tacked up."

"How many of them stayed up?"

"What do you mean?"

"Must have been twenty of them float past my stake the day you had them printed."

"I don't believe you."

"Well, it's the good guts, I'm telling you. Those posters didn't stay up. And nobody much came to your shivoo on Sunday, did they now?"

"Shivoo? Now what's that supposed to mean?"

"Party. Your party Sunday. Don't you Yanks know English at all?"

"Well, we certainly don't say 'shivoo,' and that was no party. That was a religious service. It's not Walter's fault there are so many heathens in the camp. It's my job to convert them now that he's provided me with a place to do it."

"Well, there's a furphy going the rounds of the claims and town that church is no place for a bloke who wants to live to his natural age."

"A furphy? That's a rumor, I suppose."

"You pick up the language fast, girl."

She ignored his irritating praise. "Who'd say such a thing?"

"King."

"No. Mattie perhaps, but not Walter. He'll help me squelch that rumor."

"Sure he will."

At the church they found their way to the door blocked by the large wooden cross. It had been pulled from its place at the peak of the building. A lasso was still tied around it.

"Oh, no!" Narcissa cried. She dropped to her knees in the mud and wrapped her arms around the fallen symbol. "Who would tear down a cross? Why?"

Drover knelt beside her and untied the rope. "Well, whoever did it meant you to know it wasn't knocked down by the wind. They want to chase you off just as they did the Clappes."

"Is there no God here at all?" Narcissa covered her face in dry-eyed anguish.

"If there is, maybe you weren't supposed to reveal him just yet." He lifted the cross and leaned it against the church. "You want me to put it back where it belongs?"

"I don't know. I just don't know."

The door opened and the children peeked out.

"You all right, Cissie?" Adrian asked.

"Yes, dear one. I'm all right."

"Then why is your dress all wet and muddy? Were you bad?" Sarah asked.

"I must have been," her aunt smiled wryly.

She and Drover went into the church, the children beside them. Thunder and lightning had joined the morbid rain, and Narcissa's two young charges were afraid, reminded of days on the trail when they had huddled with their mother against the merciless elements.

"Did you put Annie and David in the ground?" Adrian asked, trying to keep his mind off the storm.

Sarah's eyes widened. "Did you put dirt on their faces? In their mouths and noses?"

"No, dear. They were in lovely caskets. Boxes made especially for them," Narcissa answered as she thought of the bed of rags that lined the bottoms of the coffins. She felt sick that she could do no better for their remains than she had for their living bodies.

She walked to the kitchen and poured coffee for herself and Drover. It was hot and bitter from sitting over the coals.

"Did you bury the boxes then?" Adrian wanted to know.

"Yes, we did. But enough talk about that."

"How can they get to heaven if you put them in boxes and cover them with dirt?" Sarah asked as she climbed into a chair and sat on her knees so that she could rest her elbows on the table top. The surface tilted as the child's weight pressed down on the shortest of the four legs.

"It's souls that go to heaven not . . . Oh, I can't explain now."

"Can we go to the cemetery and watch their souls climb up?"

Narcissa was grateful when Adrian changed the subject. He had news to tell. "Two men pulled the cross from the top of the church."

"You saw them?" Drover asked quickly.

"Yes."

"Who was it? Did you recognize them."

"Drover, the children wouldn't know," Narcissa said. And anyway, she didn't want them involved.

"It was the store man and the barber," Adrian reported. "They tossed a rope over the cross and tied it to the harness of a horse. It came down easy."

"Storekeeper and barber, eh." Drover pushed his cup of coffee away.

"You're not going after them?"

He grinned. "I got a hunch those two dills would like to do a little praying this afternoon."

"Drover, no . . ."

But he was already at the door, and she stayed behind when he went out into the rain. Although the thunder and lightning had abated, the rain came down in sheets, blurring the world beyond the toppled cross. She could only wait.

Twenty minutes later, like ghosts emerging from a grave, three figures appeared from the wall of water. The two on either side of the tallest figure were slipping and stumbling.

"They're not wearing any clothes!" the observant Sarah said in amazement. "Ooh, they must be cold."

Narcissa squinted, annoyed with the flush she felt rising in her cheeks when she realized what Sarah said was true. Only Drover was dressed, and he carried a ladder, but despite their nakedness, Narcissa stared at the embarrassed businessmen. They looked so strange. A close-cropped two-inch bare strip parted the barber's hair down the center from front to back and what looked like garbage was still draining off the storekeeper's head and body. He was covered in a paste of flour, jelly, molasses and salt that was melting away, leaving an unsightly residue in patches like dirty snow in the spring.

Both men were walking awkwardly, their hands below their waists, doing their best to cover their genitals. One of the barber's fists was wrapped around a hammer and nails. From nearby tents and shacks miners jeered the two opportunists whose exorbitant prices had long made them unpopular.

"Inside," Narcissa ordered Adrian and Sarah, but she had to pry them out of the doorway before she could shut out the rain. Against a background of men cursing and the ladder scraping against the church, she brought forth the lessons she had been preparing for her niece and nephew. Unfortunately, when the hammering started, there was no keeping their attention.

Eventually Drover stuck his head inside.

"Got a request from two gentlemen to do a mite of praying," he said, "now that they have done the Lord's work."

"Drover, you can't force men to pray," she objected.

"Oh, no, ma'am, I'm not forcing them. Am I, boys?"

Two bitter voices responded, "No."

"All right," she conceded. "The children and I will go into the kitchen."

"Just the kids, ma'am," Drover requested. "These gentlemen wouldn't put any stock in prayin' without a preacher's help."

"But they haven't . . ."

"If you're trying to say they didn't wear their Sunday-go-to-meeting clothes, you're right, Miss White. But then they didn't want to get their things wet, afraid they might not dry before they came to church next Sunday. Right, boys?"

"But Drover . . ."

"Come on in, lads. Heads low now. Mind your manners."

"Drover!"

She tried to shove the laggard children into the kitchen, but they were not to be denied the arresting panoply before them.

"Is that the way Adam looked in the Garden of Eden, Aunt Cissie?" Sarah asked, stifling a giggle with her pudgy hand.

"I suppose," Narcissa said agitatedly. "Now get outside. Go play in the rain."

The unexpected privilege was enough. They were never allowed to play in the rain. They yipped with pleasure and were gone.

Narcissa put her hand over her eyes but she still caught a glimpse of the two men, purple with cold, with their hands splayed over their privates.

"Preach, Miss White. Don't want the boys to catch their death."

Wishing she could suppress the hot flush in her cheeks, Narcissa thumbed through the bible open on the pulpit. She read passages that first caught her eye. " 'How amiable are thy tabernacles, O Lord of hosts! Blessed are they that dwell in thy house. I had rather be a doorkeeper in the house of my God, than to dwell in the tent of wickedness.' "

With the last "Amen," the men disappeared, and Drover approached her in triumph, proud of himself. He saw nothing wrong in forcing the vandals to replace the cross and to humiliate themselves in the process. If she knew Hangtown, the two would be goaded for weeks about their naked visit to the church.

"Oh, Drover, what am I to do with you?" she said. "You miss the entire point of Christian forgiveness."

"Well, I'm too old to stand in the corner," he said, "and too young to bury. So why don't you give me a kiss and say, 'Well done, there, Aussie. Well done.' "

"You humiliated those men. That won't help them to find God . . ."

He pulled her into his arms and kissed her soundly. Her heartbeat dipped and throbbed, and she felt the great rain-soaked warmth of him through his sodden clothing.

She wanted to stay in his arms, to lift her lips to his, but she could not. That she had made love with Walter so recently and out of wedlock, was bad enough. Letting Drover kiss her added promiscuity to her other sins.

"Drover, I can't . . ."

"Because of King?" How could he read her mind? "He's no good for you Narcissa. Why don't you marry me? Should be one married couple in town."

"Marry you?" He couldn't be serious. "You've hardly even . . ."

"Kissed you? We can correct that fast enough. Keep the kids playing in the rain and we'll give this kissing business a real go."

"You're moving too fast for me, Drover."

"Everything's fast in the gold fields, girl. A man finds a single rock, a twenty-five pound nugget over in Sonora, I hear, and he's rich over night. Gets in a card game with a fast dealer who white ants him in an hour, and it's hooroo to his swag. Edge over with your digging onto another man's stake, and it's farewell to the here and now. Sex is the same. Fast and loose, back to your claim to get out the gold before the heavy rain washes away your dust."

"I'm not like that," she said.

"You're no wowser either, Narcissa."

She shook her head, a wry hopeless smile tugging at her lips. "Now what on earth is a wowser?"

"A bluestocking. You know, straightlaced. Somebody that doesn't smoke, swear, drink, or whatever."

"Maybe I am a wowser," she said.

He shook his head firmly. "Whether you want to admit it or not, you'd like to be my Sheila. There's nobody else in town."

"There's Walter."

"How many times do I have to tell you he's not worth a bumper?"

"He's educated and refined."

"And I'm not. Well, let me tell you, Miss Prissy Priss. I come from a better family than that bloody bastard. My family goes back to royalty in England. If it weren't for one of my ancestors that got himself shipped off to Australia for doing the crown out of some taxes, I'd be living in a manor house with servants to tend me hand and foot."

"That's not what I mean. He's gentle and kind."

"You mean I don't come at you with enough patience."

"That's part of it."

"Well, give me another go at the kissing then."

He enveloped her in his arms again, more gently this time, and in spite of the odor emanating from his wet clothing, she began to lose herself in the dreamy state that came when she closed her eyes and a man's body was gently touching hers.

The sensations erupted freely, wantonly, uninhibitedly.

She did not want the feelings. He had insulted her so often, irritated her. She wanted to slap him as if he were a little boy who had pulled her hair or thrown mud on her Sunday dress. Still, although he was different from Walter King, he was surprisingly gentle in a strong, determined way.

Drover was trying to say something with his body.

What?

Was he taking her by force as the ignorant trapper had done?

Or was he coaxing her to the point that he knew she wouldn't be able to stop? Yes, that was it.

Then he would use her.

He kissed her into the bedroom. "Don't," she said when he began undressing her. "I don't want you."

"Yes, you do. You're just angry because I'm a man."

He tried to stifle her protests with his mouth against hers. She bit his lip.

"What's that supposed to mean? You know you love me. It's been there between us from the beginning. Even though I seem to raise your hackles at times."

"No." She fought his hands. He wasn't simply rolling up her dress the way Walter had. This man wanted her completely undressed.

"You do, and that bothers you because I'd marry you."

He was stripping off his own clothes, and she twisted free. He tossed her back onto the bed.

"That doesn't make sense."

"Yes, it does." They were both naked, struggling on top of the covers. "You're afraid I'd want a wife, not just a bible-quoting female trying to wear pants and pretending there's no difference between a man and a woman."

"I'll wash no man's shirts," she said. The inference might be stronger than her true feelings, but she had to refute him.

"Won't you?"

He rolled onto her and lay still.

"Tell me to go and I will," he said. "Outback to never never."

"Go," she said.

He had her wrists pinned to the bed, and she felt his hold loosening.

No, she didn't want him to go.

Yes, she hated him.

She opened her eyes.

"Go," she said again. "You said you would if I asked."

He studied her carefully, the hard manhood lying against her lower belly, waiting.

"You're a stupid, insulting foreigner that couldn't stop if I held a gun to your head," she hissed.

"Tell me one more time to go." He grinned.

She opened her mouth. His lips, gentle and seeking, kept her from speaking.

He was beginning to go soft.

"Oh, Drover, what am I going to do with you?"

"Lots of things."

Then he was no longer soft, and he was moving between her legs, and she kept her eyes open, wanting to know it was Drover.

"Oh, Drover . . . oh yes," she sighed.

"You'll marry me," he said. "You'll see."

They were in a whirlpool, spinning and swirling and floating. He was gentle and at once forceful. She wanted to be on top and he let her for a time, but as the pace of their lovemaking peaked he took the commanding position again.

When they were finally spent, he did not leave.

He lay staring at the windows, where the rain was giving way to sunshine. She rolled over and kissed him.

Neither heard the door or the small footsteps coming

through the house. She was putting her hand to the back
of his head, wanting to bring him closer, when she heard
Sarah's ingenuous voice.

"You kissing him, too?" the child asked.

Drover pushed Narcissa aside. He grabbed for his
trousers, his face saddened.

"Him too?" he said, shaking his head.

"Drover, listen."

He pulled on his shirt and boots, ruffled the child's wet
hair with his fingers, and stalked to the door.

"So King beat me to the gate. Should have known."

"Drover!"

"Aw, hell," he sighed.

When he was gone, Sarah observed, "I'd rather kiss him
than Mr. King."

Narcissa began to cry, burying her face in the pillow.

16

NARCISSA closed the bible on the pulpit and put her hands to her face.

"I cannot go on. This is a farce."

Only two worshipers sat in the pews, Walter King and four-year-old Sarah. Even Adrian had escaped unnoticed into the thin layer of snow that shrouded Hangtown. In the silence of the chapel she was taunted by the wild noises emanating from the saloon.

The laughter carried in the cold air, and the music from the tinny piano was crisp as a bell. The party had started late on Saturday and had continued through the night. There was no indication that it would end before Monday morning. In the cold weather the miners were more willing to admit that the dreams of easy riches were a reality of misery and disappointment.

Since Thanksgiving, weeks ago, a few had sneaked in to pray when their luck showed signs of needing transfusions of heavenly grace. But most had slipped into the habit of frequenting the saloon during work days. Only a few of the heartiest or the poorest were willing to brave the cold that froze the gravel and stagnant pools along the streams. Newcomers, and they arrived almost daily, also gravitated to the saloon, seeking reinforcement of their dreams before they plunged into the drudgery of extracting wealth from the soil. For the most part the old timers, those who had survived the summer without turning homeward or settling for odd jobs in town, fed the amateurs what they wanted to hear.

So it was that winners, losers, and beginners alike filled the saloon, spending what gold they had left or going into debt with the bartender, who accepted credit from any man young enough or strong enough to work or from whoever had a claim that showed promise.

Since most of the claims were valuable, the drinkers and carousers could spend their weather-induced vacations buying and selling titles from each other or putting them up as wagers for poker or three-card monte. It was not unusual for a man to trade his way to a small fortune, only to swap it away for a less valuable claim the next day. Periodically, according to Walter, the buying and selling metamorphosed the saloon into a miniature stock exchange. Although Narcissa knew little about the stock market, it must be an exciting place, judging from the gamut of sounds that erupted from the Hang Dog.

Enforced idleness brought with it the boredom and irritability which festered into fights. No grievance, real or imagined, was too trivial to warrant a battering.

In the past week alone Narcissa had bandaged two knife wounds, treated a bullet hole in the sheepish Placer Pan Sawyer's buttocks, and conducted a funeral for a man she did not know, the loser of a duel over a piece of pyrite he had sold to a quick-tempered novice.

She was making more money as a nurse and an undertaker than she was as a preacher.

Another trouble nagging Hangtown was the fear that Mother Nature would grow infertile, that her surface and streams were being stripped clean of her golden produce. More claims had petered out during the previous month than had been abandoned in all of the previous year.

It was due to the paralyzing cold, the men assured each other, but there was increasing talk of giving up the pan and going to placer mining when they started work again after the weather broke for the better.

More treasure waited below the surface for those who could afford the new equipment. They would need to wash away hillsides and funnel water down the intricate wooden sluices that would trap the gold. While they should not be squandering the stakes they would need in the spring, boredom was winning over good sense.

Those who did not save, the down-and-outers, might have to give up their dreams and work for daily wages rather than try to subsist from one day to the next on what they could find.

"We got a year of panning left," Narcissa had heard confident miners predict.

"No, six months."

"We'll be panning when I retire," one optimistic boy insisted.

"Pray," Narcissa had more than once suggested.

The boy seemed receptive. "I went to church faithfully at home," he said.

"Then why not attend here?"

"Yeah. Good idea, Reverend. Next Sunday I'll be there."

She had not believed him, and today proved that her skepticism was justified. Practically every miner she talked to agreed he would start coming to services, but the empty seats told the story.

"Sounds like the girls are still dancing," King remarked when Narcissa had ceased praying.

"Not even Drover came to services," she mused.

Walter led her from the pulpit with a reassuring arm around her waist.

"What I don't understand," Narcissa continued, "is why the town is still growing. New men arrive each day."

"Many of them will go broke," he said sighing. "I suppose I'll have to make work for them. Hard rock mining like we do at the King shaft will be making money for years to come. And I can't let the men go hungry. I'll just have to hire them."

"I wish I could pay men to come to church," she said

wistfully. When he cocked his head as if he might do just
that, she quickly demurred. "No, I'm not paying anyone
to come to God. I just wish the church held more appeal
to them."

He was sweet, though. Her only friend, really. Her
feeling for him had changed since that one afternoon with
Drover. She had sidestepped Walter's overtures since
then, and she knew his patience would not last forever.
Nagged with shame and guilt, she had done a lot of
thinking and had come to a decision that she knew she
must discuss with Walter. Too late though it might be,
she had vowed to become celibate, to save what she could
of her treacherous, sinning body for whomever she married, if indeed she ever did.

"We'll print some more posters," he said.

She said nothing. The posters would be torn down like
all the rest, by whom she never knew. But for weeks now
the pews had never been more than a quarter full. The
men who did come to her services were usually newcomers. They attended once, found it was not the accepted thing to do, and never came again.

Little or nothing reached the collection plate. She and
the children existed primarily on King's weekly donation
and her work as an unofficial nurse. With prices rising
daily in the town's thriving store, Narcissa served less food
each week, reducing her diet to the point that her slender
body was almost bony.

There was, of course, one reasonable solution to her
burgeoning problems.

Marry Walter.

Drover would never ask her again. With Walter there
had never been a formal proposal, only hints that he
would like to move out of the saloon now that it served its
dual role. Moving in with her was implied but she had no
idea whether marriage went with the arrangement or not.

"You could get out among the men more, too," King
suggested.

Shaking her head, Narcissa settled into a front pew. She
had done precisely that for weeks—walking among the
men at work, inviting them to church.

Uncomfortable in her presence, the majority had been quick to promise they would attend on Sunday. She understood. "It's a poor man who won't promise a dog a bone," her father used to say. Lately, however, even that courtesy came less frequently. Now some kept working, not so much as acknowledging her greeting.

And the pews stood empty.

"I'll have to take in washing," she said, "to get enough money together to move on."

"The Chinamen will merely undercut your prices," King pointed out. "Admit it, Narcissa, it's time we moved in together."

She lifted her eyes from her hands. "Here?" she asked.

"Or my place at the saloon. Until I can build a proper house."

The suggestion appalled her.

"It's noisy on Saturday nights," he admitted, "but I have more comfortable quarters there than you have here."

"You're asking me to marry you?" She put the challenge to him bluntly.

With his usual verbal skill he said, "Who is there to marry us?"

"I could."

"Think about it. The children could stay here. I know an Indian squaw who would make an excellent nanny."

"I could not leave the children alone."

"A saloon's no place for them. Perhaps I'll have a fine house built for all of us with a special wing for Sarah and Adrian. Think about it. I'll be back later to discuss it."

"No!" The vehemence in her response surprised her more than him.

No, she was not moving into a saloon. No, she was not going to live with a man outside of wedlock. And most emphatically she was not shunting the children off to live with an Indian squaw.

There was no denying Adrian and Sarah had been a millstone around her neck since the death of their parents, but again, no. They had been golden nuggets weighing her down, more precious than anything the most fortunate miner might discover.

"Think about it," King said again from the door.

"I have."

When he was gone, she sat staring at the wall. Although he had remained as pleasant as ever, there was something of an ultimatum in his gentlemanly tone. If she persisted in refusing Walter, if she lost him, how could she survive without his weekly donation? Even the church was his.

"Aunt Cissie." Sarah touched her arm. "Kin I go play with Adrian? He's building a snow man." The little girl had donned her warm, outdoor clothing herself. In the weeks here in Hangtown, she had become surprisingly self-sufficient. The frontier did that to people, even children.

When the door opened, the saloon's raucous merriment poured in. What a contrary place this world is, she thought. Sunday, the Lord's day, and the church is empty but the saloon's full. Borne on the crisp air were frequent references to the Lord—obscenities.

"By God, I'll . . ."

"Jesus Christ, Billy . . ."

On impulse she grabbed up her bible and started for the saloon. If they could use His name, even in vain, they could listen to His word. And if that turned out to be in vain too, so be it.

She entered unnoticed and went halfway up the stairs. The place was filled with men and women obviously enjoying themselves.

"Friends," she said from the doorway. No one heard her. "Children of God."

Placer Pan Sawyer stopped fondling the girl on his lap. He had shown a kind of grudging respect to Narcissa since the night he had seen her run into the burning pleasure palace in search of the girl she had befriended.

"Hold it, men," he shouted. "The little lady has something to say."

The din quieted slowly.

"Who's he talking about?"

"The preacher."

"What's she doing in here?"

"Goddamned if I know."

"Hey, lady, this ain't no church!"

"Quiet, let her have her say."

The piano stopped.

When she finally had their attention, she cleared her throat and started. "Thank you, gentlemen, ladies, I . . ." Her throat choked up and the words would not come.

Jake was impatient. "Speak up, lady."

"Yeah, let's hear it."

"I come here in the name of the Lord," Narcissa said.

"The Lord? Ain't seen Him around lately."

She waited for the laughter to die again. "Ladies . . ." More laughter. "And gentlemen. I come here to ask you to change your ways."

"What the hell for?"

"Because you're squandering your lives." She paused for the interruption that did not come. "You are working your hands to the bone, gathering a little gold, then wasting it on liquor, gambling, and sex."

"That's wasting it?"

"Yeah, what's gold for?"

More laughter.

"You should be saving, building a decent home, starting a farm, finding a wife, raising children."

No response. Had she hit a nerve?

She continued. "Find your relief from your labors in God's house, not here."

"She's saying we're demons," Cottontail giggled.

"Damn purty ones anyway," a gallant miner inserted.

"No," Narcissa said, "I judge no one. But you have a better place in the future through God than you do here, infecting your body with disease and destroying your mind and soul with liquor and sin."

"All right," Mattie Lafayette's coarse voice rang down from the balcony, "you had your say."

"Yeah. We heard it." MacIntosh said standing at her side.

"Let us pray." Narcissa bowed her head. "God, grant us

grace to rest from all sinful deeds and thoughts, to surrender our souls wholly unto thee, that we might do thy work. Keep our souls still . . ."

"That's enough."

"Piano player, let's hear it!"

"Max, give me another shot."

"Come again when you got women, pastor," Sawyer said.

Sadly, Narcissa let the words echo in the caverns of her mind.

Come again when you got women.

There was a fundamental truth in the words. It was too much to expect the men to remain celibate in this lonely place. She had failed, herself.

The men needed, craved, hungered for female companionship. And why not? Hangtown was as desolate as a desert in respect to women.

God had failed or denied the men that which they needed most.

She had failed too.

She had lost all sense of time and no longer could recollect when she had sent Old Gray off to San Francisco in search of the prized commodity—women and the love they would bring with them.

With each day, Narcissa lost another strand in the thin string that tied her to hope. She was almost certain now that Gray and his cargo had gone on to Sacramento.

Please, God, she said to herself from the perch of the steps. Please send women.

"If I could bring women to Hangtown . . ." she said aloud.

Men jeered. "Sure, turn the deserts green and the ocean water fresh. Then we'll know God gives a damn about us."

"It's true, Miss White," Placer Pan said loud enough to command silence in the teeming room. "We aren't scum just because we came searching for a better life. And we ain't completely selfish like you seem to think. We're opening up new lands. California alone could support more people than most nations. That's space which means there's more people who can live. It takes land for any kind of life to increase."

"More people to serve God," Narcissa said.

"If you want to put it that way, yes. So we ain't all bad. We opened the land. It ain't our fault there ain't more women."

"What's wrong with my girls?" Mattie Lafayette challenged him in her coarse deep voice.

"There's nothing wrong with them," Narcissa said. "Only there's too few of them. So they end up . . ."

". . . selling themselves," Walter King said from the balcony. "Plain economics, Miss White."

It did come down to that, Narcissa conceded. Plain economics.

"So produce the ladies, preacher," a voice said sarcastically, "and leave us alone until you or your God does."

The noise level rose.

She had lost her audience.

"Don't take it to hard, Miss White," Sawyer said. "Nothing much you can do about it."

"But God could," Narcissa said. God could answer her prayers and bring women to Hangtown, bring the ingredient that was essential for a normal life. She felt defeated. "Please, God. I can't do it myself. Don't punish Hangtown for my transgressions."

She wanted to cry out but she walked out with her head high. Outside, she breathed deeply of the clear, fresh air. Light snow was still falling, a coat of white paint that masked Hangtown's ruts and weeds and shabbiness. Even the unpainted shacks looked better re-roofed in white. The snow was an artist that beautified with a far-ranging brush—everything except human nature, she thought resignedly.

The snowman was almost finished, and its new parents came running proudly to her. "Oh, Cissie, isn't he beautiful?" Sarah asked. "Aren't you glad we did him? Can he come to supper?"

"Oh, yes, darling, he's beautiful," she said, scooping the tiny blond girl into her arms, "but not half so beautiful as you!"

Sarah wrapped her short arms around her aunt's neck. "I love you, Aunt Cissie," she said.

"And I love you, little Sarah." She kissed the round cheek and knelt to include Adrian in her embrace. "And you too, big fellow."

For a long moment she held them, gathering strength from their love and their confidence in her. We'll make it, she thought. Whatever lay ahead, this little boy and girl deserved something better than the women and men in the saloon. The three of them had survived much worse than this together. In fact, she had survived because of the children. Without them as motivation she would never have found the strength or the will to escape the trapper or . . .

"It's a pretty picture, isn't it, Cissie?" Adrian was saying over her shoulder.

He was looking at the house in the snow, and she turned to survey it with him.

"Yes, nature paints pretty pictures," she agreed, "and the most beautiful are children. Did you know that?"

Adrian, embarrassed and a little confused, ran off, shouting, "Come on, help us finish the snowman."

They had decided to build two children snowmen when the sound of wagon wheels stopped their labors.

"Haw! Haw!" She recognized Old Gray's voice, and a feeling of happiness swept over her. She had not realized how much she would miss the old man who had picked them out of the snow and brought them to Hangtown.

Taking the children's hands, she ran through the gray afternoon sunlight toward the wagons, realizing that the street was filling with men.

"Women coming! Women coming!"

The lead wagon was Gray's. It had the same six horses, and the old man was sitting in front. The two other drivers were strangers. Evidently the two who had left with Gray on the trip to San Francisco had given up the gold fields. Perhaps these newcomers were here to stay, full of hopes and dreams.

Piercing the gray gauze of snow were flecks of color, bits of ribbon and cloth that enlivened the plank sides and rounded tops of the wagons. The decorations and the excitement gave the scene a festive air, like the Fourth of July in Iowa or in the East where she had lived earlier.

Then she could see the girls with their beautiful faces, not the pathetic, painted masks of those whom fate had made prostitutes, but the clean beauty of fresh, courageous young women.

The carnival atmosphere escalated the mood of the Hangtown miners.

"Women in the pan!" Jake heralded the momentous arrival with a twist of another call that would set a man's pulse racing. And to the men of Hangtown, today's find was even more rare and valuable than the treasure that founded the camp.

Men clambered over each other leaving the saloon. They were waving their hats, the heavier drinkers staggering under the influence of their sixteen-hour binge. The more hesitant men, the shy ones who had tried to escape their inhibitions by coming west, found now that their insecurities had come with them, and they approached the wagons cautiously.

Even the bartender and the judge emerged from the saloon. The piano player was next and then the two gunmen, MacIntosh and MacDermitt. Mattie Lafayette and her girls were the last. In their short skirts, with their shoulders bare, they clutched themselves for warmth. They comprised an unsmiling contingent that did not leave the front of the saloon.

Narcissa was awed.

She felt as though the gray skies had opened up and allowed a beam of sunlight to spear directly toward her.

Her prayer had been answered, and so quickly, although she knew the arrival of women was not necessarily divinely timed. Old Gray had been gone longer than normal for a trip to San Francisco. If he were going to return at all, he would have arrived soon regardless of any heavenly intervention.

But she, the girl who had doubted, the girl who had doubted God, accepted Him now.

The arrival was timed by a force greater than she could ever have mustered.

"How'd you know they was coming today?" Placer Pan Sawyer asked as he passed her.

"You knew all along," Jake accused her good naturedly.

"Pretty clever timing," another remarked.

"You just converted me, preacher. Anybody who can produce decent women in Hangtown can have my soul anytime she wants."

"Be seeing you in church, Reverend White."

She could only stand and stare.

She felt enormous strength and enormous humility.

Could God have actually answered her prayer, urged her to make her speech in the saloon just now?

Was it pre-ordained?

She would never know.

Drover arrived from the opposite direction. At the rear of the second wagon he helped down a stunning blonde with slippers too beautiful to touch the wet layer of snow covering the frozen mud. He carried her to the plank sidewalk in front of the barber shop, where he backed her against the window and stood leaning forward with one hand bracing himself and the other helping to pull the girl's beaver skin coat up around her neck. Whatever he was saying—perhaps that ridiculous Australian English—made the girl smile, and Narcissa experienced a pang of resentment that could only be jealousy. It hurt to see him speaking to another woman. She had lost him, and only because of her own sinful ways.

In search of comfort for her battered ego, she looked for Walter. She need not have worried. He was there, standing some distance from the wagon. Unsmiling, hands on his hips, jacket pulled back to reveal the pistol strapped to his hip, he appeared to be anything but pleased with the arrival of the women.

Why, Narcissa wondered fleetingly as she ran forward to greet the wagon master.

"Mr. Gray," she said, reaching up to take his outstretched hand. "Welcome back! I'm so glad to see you."

"Hello. Mighty glad to see you too. Come here, now, and meet the ladies."

A motherly woman, well into her thirties, stepped forward first. She wore a long coat with a hood that covered her hair and made her sparkling eyes more noticeable. She was not pretty. Close up Narcissa saw the wrinkles around the eyes, hollowed cheeks, and skin dried by years of exposure to the weather. With one hand she held a boy Adrian's age and with the other, a girl perhaps a year younger than Sarah.

Seeing the little girl, Sarah ducked behind her aunt's skirt. The child had forgotten that other children existed. She did not know how to act.

Adrian hauled up short a foot from the newcomer.

"What's your name?"

"Alexander."

"That's a sissy name," Adrian declared.

"What's yours?" the new boy asked, in a tone that gave no quarter.

"Adrian."

"Ha!"

The two little stags might have locked horns then and there had not Narcissa dug her nails into her nephew's collarbone at the same time the woman spoke sharply to her son.

"Ouch, Cissie. That hurts!"

"Aunt Cissie," Narcissa corrected.

"Aunt? That's girl talk."

"Aunt," she corrected him. "It's time you learned some manners." And it was, too. She had been remiss. She dug her fingers in deeper.

"All right," he capitulated. "Aunt."

"Aunt Cissie."

"Aunt Cissie," he muttered at his shoe.

While the two boys took great pains to ignore each other, the little girls continued to peer from behind the women's skirts, studying what they saw as if they were peering into a looking glass for the first time.

"I'm Narcissa White, and this is Adrian. You can see he needs companionship. This is Sarah."

"Alex and Mary Frances," the woman smiled. "And I'm Mrs. Gunter. Nena Gunter. I suppose I ought to drop the Mrs. now."

"A widow?" Narcissa asked.

"Yes. Does it show? I know it does on my hands." She pulled off her glove and exhibited a callused palm. "We, my husband and I, had a ranch in Kansas. When he died, I had to take over. Herded cattle clear to Abilene on my own."

All of the women had left the wagons, and Nena Gunter surveyed them as if she had not seen them before. With men around they looked and acted differently, Narcissa guessed. She herself felt strange. Some of the newcomers were prettier than she and seemed quite sure of themselves.

There were introductions, names to be repeated and learned later when the excitement ebbed.

There was Prudence (tall and willowy), a Chastity (chubby and jovial), a Donna Mae (a natural blonde with a musical voice), and more than a dozen others.

"I hope I haven't made this trip for nothing," Nena said. "I could easily lose my confidence."

"Oh, no, I'm sure you haven't," Narcissa reassured her, smiling. "There are more than enough men to go around."

Standing on the wagon seat, Old Gray was calling for silence.

"Ladies and gentlemen, I know you're anxious to meet each other," he began. "But before you all start sparking . . ." He paused for an embarrassed ripple of laughter from his audience. "I want you to meet the little lady that arranged to bring you together. The angel of Hangtown, Narcissa White."

He made a theatrical gesture with his hand, and Narcissa blushed with everyone staring at her and applauding.

"Now," Gray continued, "we can't stand here in the cold, so I suggest we move this shivroo, as our Australian friend would call it, into the saloon."

He realized immediately that he had shocked the ladies.

"Hold your horses, ladies. No offense intended. But the

saloon's the only place in town with near 'nough room to hold us all, specially when the word spreads to the outlying claims and more of the boys hear what I brung to town. So grab your partners and let's get this social rollin'."

"Yahoo!" a cry went up.

"Women comin'! Decent women comin'!"

Inside herself Narcissa cringed. Decent women. It was an expression she had used herself too often. Not until now had she perceived its cutting edge. Didn't anyone think about Mattie's girls? How many of them wished they were one of the newcomers with hope for a fresh start in life?

The new ladies, each with a man or two holding her arm or escorting her, turned to face the saloon entrance. Only Narcissa and Nena Gunter were alone.

Then the new group reached the prostitutes standing near the door. Most of the whores were stony faced, arms crossed, eyes glazed. Only six feet separated them from their competition.

"Just where the hell do you think you're goin'?" Madam Lafayette confronted the first girl off the wagon, the young beauty escorted by Drover.

The parade came to a halt.

MacIntosh and MacDermitt flanked the madam. They had new guns in their holsters and their right hands rested arrogantly on the pistol butts.

Judge Russell ambled in closer from the position he had taken in the center of the street when Old Gray's wagon train first arrived. Walter King was off by himself, and he seemed to be glaring at Narcissa.

Why?

She could not comprehend his reaction. She had taken a few steps in his direction, intending to call, "Surprise!" the way people did at a birthday party. She had thought he would be pleased with her unexpected gift. Women, marriageable women who would help him build his town, the new Hangtown with a more inviting name, she hoped, that he had spoken about when they first met.

Why was he looking at her that way?

The confrontation at the door continued, the participants frozen in position.

Someone had to speak first.

"Miss, ah . . . Miss . . ." Drover was struggling with the name of the young blonde whose hand he held.

"Roth. Angela Roth." Obviously she had told him once already.

"Miss Roth, may I introduce you to Madam Mattie Lafayette, and Miss Cottontail, Miss Featherlegs, Miss White Squaw."

The girl held up under the shock of being introduced to prostitutes until she confronted White Squaw. The tattooed face was too much, and Angela whirled, ready to retreat to the wagons.

Narcissa sensed disaster. She rushed into the breech, clutched Angela's elbow, and turned her around again.

"This way, ladies," she said. "It's quite all right. Just follow me. Everybody inside." She held the heavy winter doors open and pushed the young blonde through while making sure that her eyes did not meet Drover's.

"Hey!" Mattie challenged in her coarse voice. "You lettin' these uppity bitches in the saloon?" She directed her question toward the judge, who seemed to be searching elsewhere for an answer.

His indecision gave Narcissa a chance to get the ladies inside. Bewildered by the unexpected, a few of the whores were objecting loudly.

"Hey, you bible belter," Cottontail complained, "we were here first. Way ahead of them hoity-toity scrubwomen with their noses in the air."

"You weren't here before me," Narcissa smiled. "Besides I'm sure there's more than enough men to go around."

"Never more than enough men," Featherlegs said.

The prostitutes were pushing their way inside too, and Narcissa could see the bartender gaping at the flood of women flowing into his establishment. Even the children went in.

"Sassafras," Narcissa called to him. "Get all the sassafras you can."

"Yes, Miss," he said, "if the judge says . . ."

"Get the sassafras," Drover ordered firmly.

"Coffee and tea too," Narcissa added.

"Ain't got but a quarter pound of coffee and no tea," Max countered. "Ain't much call for nothin' 'cept rotgut."

"There will be from now on," Narcissa said.

"I'll get some coffee," the storekeeper volunteered. He jumped up from the table where he sat with a plain woman ten years his junior. "Now, don't go 'way, Cecelia." He ran halfway to the exit and then returned. "And don't be talking to anybody else."

The woman looked at him with worshiping eyes. "No, I promise. No one else."

"Good. You make her keep her promise, Miss White, else I won't go."

"It'll be all right," Narcissa told him.

Seconds later, a miner with big rough hands and a stubble of beard settled into the empty seat. "Did I hear him say your name was Cecelia?"

"Yes, and you're . . ."

Narcissa looked on in mild dismay. Cecelia was as intrigued with the miner as she had been with the store man. Cecelia, whatever her last name was, was a kid turned loose in a candy store.

"You knew about this?" Walter spoke at Narcissa's side.

She looked up, pleased with herself. Old Gray had outdone her wildest expectations. The women, while certainly not all raving beauties, were generally attractive enough, and all except Nena Gunter were childless.

From the conversation around her, it was obvious that this was an extraordinary group of women. They were adventurous—they had to be if they were willing to travel into the wilderness. One openly admitted she was an actress. Another was a nurse who had served with President Taylor during the war with Mexico. Two sisters talked of running the family store in Pennsylvania until they tired of the gossiping neighbors who looked askance at career women. There was a milliner, and one especially knowledgeable woman who said she would like to open a bank. A trained lawyer. A newspaperwoman. Another was a daguerrotypist who planned to start selling likenesses as soon as she could get a camera and the other equipment she needed.

Their common bond was a desire to escape the restrictions placed on their sex in the more civilized cities and towns from which they had fled.

That and men. The unspoken attraction. Men as adventuresome as themselves.

"I said, you knew about this?" Walter repeated.

"Yes, I talked Mr. Sutter into letting the women come to Hangtown if they wanted."

"Without asking me?"

Narcissa was puzzled. She had thought he would be pleasantly surprised, and it had never occurred to her to ask anyone's permission to bring in some women. Not the judge's or Mattie Lafayette's. Not Walter King's.

"It was meant to be a surprise," she said. "I knew you'd be pleased . . ."

"Get them out of here," he said.

She tipped her head to one side quizzically. "Out of the saloon. . . ?"

"Out of Hangtown. Now."

"But why?"

"It isn't safe."

"For whom?"

"It isn't safe for you or them. Get them out of here, I tell you."

He strode purposefully toward the stairs that led to the second floor. Narcissa did not move until he had gone into the office and closed the door.

She shook her head, still puzzled, and then turned back to the increasingly noisy assembly. The oil lamps cast a warm glow over the place, softening the signs of wear and tear on furnishings and faces alike.

Joy had come to Hangtown.

17

THE mood of the welcoming party changed like a runaway fire. The saloon might have been a forest glade that echoed with the revelry of happy picnickers laughing on a warm autumn afternoon. Everybody, almost everybody, was having a good time sipping sassafras or warm coffee to keep back the chill.

On the outside of the circle, beyond the blanket of acceptance, were the outcasts, the school kids who did not quite fit. The prostitutes of Hangtown felt unwanted and out of place and the picnic was being held in their territory, on their property.

They hovered on and around the staircase. They watched men who had come to love them, men they thought they knew, men who they had thought meant nothing in their lives except the glitter of gold dust they left on the night stand by the bed as tips.

None of them was prepared to take a back seat. They had been the queen bees in Hangtown. And, although they had not realized they had created even shallow relationships with their clientele, what they experienced now was the age-old malady—jealousy.

The men ignored them. Not all the men. More than one

called to the whores to join the party. A few took the girls by the hand and tried to lead them into the group.

"Come on, Cottontail. Let me introduce you to Doreen. You can tell her about life here in the west."

The new arrivals looked up cautiously, like persons fascinated yet repelled by the sores on the face of a smallpox patient.

The whores scowled and returned to their place at the stairs.

Narcissa tried to meld the oil and water.

"Featherlegs, the rest of you," she pleaded, "join in. We're all going to be neighbors."

Cottontail made a damp, loud sniffing sound that was deliberately crass.

"You brung 'em here," Madam Lafayette accused. "We saved you and your brats from starvin' on the trail, and you brung them into our midst."

"Mattie, you'll like them. They're nice women."

Cottontail's laugh was sour and derisive. "That's the trouble, Miss Prissy Ass Preacher. They're nice women."

"And what does that make us?" asked the redhead who stood three steps up.

"It changes nothing," Narcissa replied. "In the eyes of God, you're . . ."

"In the eyes of God we're gonna burn our pussies in hell for eternity."

"I could have been one of *them*," White Squaw said, her fingers tracing the tattoo marks on her face.

"They think they're better than we are," said Cottontail. "The men think so too. Look at that fucking Spooner. Tipped me ten dollars dust last night. Now he won't speak to me."

"Cottontail, listen . . ."

The belligerent girl stalked across the room, elbowing her way through the men who surrounded the new women. She put her hand on the shoulder of a young miner by the name of Spooner and twisted him around in his seat.

". . . and if I had known you were coming, I would have shaved and . . ." He was leaning forward talking to a rather pretty girl his own age. She was shy and the boy was doing all the talking. He was emaciated, his cheeks sunken from too much back breaking work, too much drinking, and too much of Cottontail. He had already made a half dozen good finds and sold a claim for a tidy profit, but he had thrown it all away in Hangtown's looting monopolies. He had come to church several times, but not lately.

When Cottontail swung him around, there was a fresh excitement in his eyes. He had forgotten what it was like to be with a girl and just talk. He had forgotten you could spend more than a few minutes with a girl and not have her urging you to button your pants and leave as soon as you were limp because another man was waiting.

When he saw Cottontail standing above him, he blinked as if he did not recognize her at all. She was from another life, the life of another boy named Spooner who had vanished less than an hour ago.

"How about it, Spooner luv?" Cottontail said, her gaze fixed on the new girl. "Want to try again?"

"Try again?" He seemed honestly surprised at her suggestion. "Oh, hello there, Cottontail. Having fun? Great party, isn't it?"

He faced the girl across the table and laid his hand over hers. The broken, blackened nails on the upper hand and the ring finger that ended at the last joint were mute testimony of the youth's occupation. Shy and proper, the girl withdrew from the premature intimacy. Narcissa could tell she was having second thoughts. Weren't they all? Didn't everyone in California?"

"Come on, Spooner," Cottontail coaxed. "This one's on me."

"What?"

"Free, stupid," Cottontail said sharply. "That's the only difference between me and the fluff you're talkin' to, ain't it? I usually charge and she gives it away free."

"Cottontail, stop it!" Narcissa pushed forward.

The girl across from Spooner stood up, knocking over her chair in her rush to escape from the whore's vile tongue.

"I said, I'm giving it away. That makes me as good as her." Cottontail turned from Spooner and bellowed. "Anybody want to take Spooner's place? I'm giving it away to the first man that says I'm as good as any woman in the room."

"Hell, yes, Cottontail, I'll say it," a mousy little man said, turning from the bar. Still weak from his weekend binge, he stumbled over another miner's foot and splatted face down on the floor.

The lively voices of men and women discovering each other ceased as if a lid had snapped shut on a music box. The piano player left his stool and took an uneasy stance behind the instrument.

"Anybody else want a free trip around the world?" Cottontail asked.

"They're all free," Madam Lafayette announced from the stairs. She climbed a few steps higher. "You heard me, boys. The girls are free for the night."

"Yahoo!" cheered a pubescent miner whose sparse, downy beard betrayed his youth.

"Form a line, men. Girls, get to your rooms."

Narcissa blanched. She could feel the blood draining from her face, and she could sense the same reaction among the shocked, dismayed women rising from their chairs around the tables. They were ready to flee. The men nearest them offered reassurance.

"Wait."

Some added a second word. "Please." It was little used in Hangtown.

"I ain't goin' with them ladies of the night," more than one said.

Other pleas were broader, if unsubstantiated. "I ain't never been with any of them tarts, ma'am. Never. I swear."

"The shit you ain't," Featherlegs said to one. "We fucked last night. I cleaned your balls good. She ain't gonna get nothin' from your pooped pecker for 'least a week."

"Jesus Christ, Featherlegs!" The man was on his feet trying to silence the tirade. The woman he had been talking to intimately moments before was heading for the door.

Fearing a mass exodus, Narcissa positioned herself to block the exit.

"Listen, ladies . . . all of you." She addressed herself to whore and newcomer alike. "Listen. You have to learn to live with each other."

"The hell we do," Mattie snorted. "Up the stairs, boys. A cock in the bush is better'n a hand in your pants."

"Mattie, stop it!" Narcissa was furious.

Men, the shy ones mostly, were starting toward the stairs. A man Narcissa knew only as Dawes reached up from the table and grabbed the hand of his look-alike brother.

"Don't go with those bitches," Dawes counseled. "There's decent women here now."

"That's easy enough for you to say," the younger brother countered. "You got a girl. I haven't."

"No one *has* me. I'll be owned by no one," Prudence Patterson retorted.

Dawes said, "He didn't mean it that way, ma'am."

"Come along, boys," Mattie called over the agitated voices. "Don't let little Miss White order you around."

The newcomer with Dawes changed her attitude. "Your brother's right. Don't go. Join us."

Dawes toughened his hold on his brother's arm.

Featherlegs stepped into the brief stalemate. "Come boy. Around the world for free."

"Leave him alone," Prudence cried.

"Ladies. Ladies!" Narcissa tried to be heard above the tumult.

The picnic atmosphere had vanished. The forest glade had become a bed of dry leaves for the sparks of animosity flying between the two factions. The Dawes brothers and the two women were the first to ignite. Within seconds the picnic turned into a conflagration no bucket brigade could control.

"Tight-ass bitch," Featherlegs sneered at the girl.

"Two-bit whore," the girl hissed back.

"I ain't no two-bit whore. I charge plenty."

Featherlegs' fingers flicked out like talons and left four reg grooves in the girl's cheek.

What had appeared to be a helpless female moments before snatched the prostitute's hair and yanked.

Featherlegs shrieked, flailing against the painful onslaught.

Dawes, the older one, grabbed Featherlegs and pulled. Cottontail came to her friend's aid.

The other whores charged.

"Get those bitches," Mattie told her troops.

"Leave the ladies alone," Dawes yelled. He tried to pull Cottontail off, but the drunk who had slumped to the floor rose and took a swing at the man he thought was trying to get his free ride from the bawd. He missed and collapsed on a table.

At first the decent ladies cowered. Then some of the grit that had brought them beyond the fringes of civilization surfaced in a mighty crusade. Initially, Drover's lovely Angela went to the defense of the bleeding Prudence. Then in twos and threes, or one by one, they all waded into battle.

The fight originated with women against women. The newcomers started by trying to push their opposition aside, but it quickly deteriorated into scratching and hair pulling.

"Damn you, let go!"

"Oo-o-o-h-h-h-!"

"Throw the whore out."

"Go for the eyes."

"Kill the goddamn tight asses!"

"Stop! Ladies, stop!" Narcissa forced her way into the melee and tried to free a new girl who was pinned under a stack of three attacking whores. She pried one tart loose but before she could peel off the next, fingers snarled in her hair and snapped her head back toward her collarbone.

Incensed, lips pulled tight against clenched teeth, she stomped on the foot of her assailant. The girl yipped and released Narcissa's hair.

The whores went for the ladies' dresses.

"Strip 'em," General Mattie ordered from the steps. "Show the boys what little them snotty shills got to offer."

"Mattie, call off the girls," Narcissa yelled. She started up the stairs, but Madam Lafayette stuck out a foot and kicked her in the breast.

Narcissa tumbled down the stairs and the next thing she knew Drover was leaning over her.

"You all right?"

"Yes, but do something. Stop the fighting."

"Now?" he exclaimed. "The barney is just getting to be a ripper."

While he lifted her to her feet, Mattie charged past to do battle.

The fight had taken on form, the arena cleared. Tables and chairs had been given refuge in corners. Only the roulette table remained in place. The men had learned from experience that breaking saloon furniture was counterproductive. They would want the gambling tables and chairs as soon as the donnybrook was over.

The gallery of spectators was two rows deep, the shorter men jumping and squirming to see above around, or through the bigger ones in front. The women were in the center of the circle, half of them on their feet exchanging slaps or pulling each other's hair. Half were on the floor, grunting and thrashing and shrieking.

"Look at that!" MacIntosh intoned, pointing to a lady with her skirt hoisted to her waist—above bloomers and dark stockings.

Max the bartender had come around the counter, a belaying pin in his hand. He held it shoulder height and from time to time made feints at using it, but he always lost his nerve.

Sometimes a lull in the din would allow the sounds of ripping cloth.

"Well, I'll be a hawg-tied dude," Old Gray marveled. "I thought I'd saw everything."

He lifted his mug of beer in salute to a refined lady whose bodice had just burst like a tin of unbaked sourdough. One large, red-tipped breast spilled into the open, its premiere appearance hailed with cheers and applause.

The woman tried to cover herself while evading the prostitutes intent on plucking her bare.

The strategy of battle had changed. No longer did the opponents scratch and kick and tear at hair. They went for the clothing, to the delight of the cheering section. Within seconds a half dozen pairs of bosoms and legs were laid bare.

"That's it, girls," the men encouraged the belligerents.

Narcissa's attempts to stop the foolish struggle not only failed but also threatened to embroil her in the conflict. Unable to reach Drover—he had drifted over to the bar and was standing on it while he swigged beer and shouted advice to the fighters—she located Walter King observing from a commanding position four or five steps up the stairs.

Waving, she caught his attention.

"Walter, stop them. You can do it."

"I told you it was too early to bring decent women into this town," he said sullenly.

"All right, but stop the fighting."

He looked past her once more and walked to the balcony, where he leaned his forearms on the railing and continued to watch.

"Walter, please."

The young woman named Cecelia was knocked out of the fight and stumbled against Narcissa. She was sobbing hysterically and holding the front of her shredded dress in her hands, but when Narcissa tried to withhold her from the conflict, she twisted loose and stormed back into the thick of it.

"Judge!" The older man was close to the piano studying his crushed hat. It was covered with sawdust and sorely wounded. "You're the law. Stop them."

His expression questioned her sanity. "It ain't my clothes they're tearing." He went back to straightening his hat.

Nor did she succeed in coaxing the piano player back to his instrument. Failing that, she tried herself to play a hymn, the one type of song she knew, only to have Nena Gunter flounder backward onto the keyboard. Over the resounding chord, she looked at Narcissa and said, "I hope my children aren't seeing this."

"Mine, too," Narcissa agreed, scanning the place with quick eyes. At least the chidren were not in sight, and she returned to the immediate problem. "Nena, don't go back," she pleaded.

"No whore's going to chase me out of town," Nena pledged. Then she re-entered the fight.

The mother of two caught Cottontail by the wrist, sat on the floor, and pulled the prostitute down across her lap. Two enthusiastic males volunteered as seconds, one pinning Cottontail's legs, the other her arms and obligingly shoving up what was left of the skirt. She wore nothing above her stockings, and to her assistants' dismay, Nena pulled a thin layer of cloth over the milk-white buttocks before she began spanking the writhing, yelping younger woman. Nena was in no rush to finish.

Having exhausted all sources of help, Narcissa pushed through the men to the center of the ring.

The situation had worsened. Scraps of clothing littered the floor. Most of the contenders were stripped to their underwear or clutching to their bodies what clothing they had left. Hair was in disarray, scratches and bruises abundant. Shoes had been removed for use as weapons.

The men continued to cheer, quick to alert others to each new inch of exposed flesh or unmentionable.

All of the women were covered with sawdust. Two of them were fighting atop the roulette table.

Then Drover seemed to tire of the show. From his position on the bar, he swung his mug in a half-circle over the fight. The beer sprayed out and doused Featherlegs.

Surprised by the sudden drenching, she let down her guard and immediately fell victim to a female fist.

Other men liked the idea and began throwing whatever kind of drink they had in their hands: cold coffee, tea, sassafras, beer, even rotgut. When they needed more they charged the bar and returned with mugs, glasses, bottles, and pails of beer and booze.

They drenched the women, roaring approval as the sticky liquids flattened the remaining attire and revealed the curves and indentations underneath. Sawdust added mortar to the mix.

"You bastards!" Mattie shouted at them.

Her girls recognized the new enemy and flung themselves at the closest men. The decent ladies paused, realized they had been putting on a show for the voyeurs, and joined the prostitutes in a common assault. Furious and vengeful, they leaped on the men, who warded off the kicks and gouging nails as best they could without resorting to the brutal blows they would have used on their own sex.

Narcissa, too stunned to participate, fell back against a wall. From there she saw Adrian and the new boy fighting each other. The two little girls were standing in a corner holding hands.

Two gun shots roared, and splinter-lined holes penetrated the heavy front door.

The fighting stopped.

Everyone looked to the balcony.

Walter King towered above everybody else.

"Enough," he said.

The battlers looked at each other.

"Narcissa," King said, "get your women out of here. Mattie, I want your girls upstairs."

"But it wasn't my girls who started it," she protested.

"Do as I say. Get moving, Narcissa. You too, Mattie."

MacIntosh and MacDermitt pulled their new guns from their holsters. They did not point them at anyone in particular, instead using them as batons to direct the prostitutes toward the stairs. They went, limping, shoulders slumped. They mouthed obscenities at no one in particular.

"This way, ladies, the fight's over." Narcissa crossed to the door and held it open for the new arrivals. Cold air streamed in. The women clutched their tattered clothing and began flowing toward Narcissa.

The men they had been talking to before the fracas tried to accompany them, but King ordered them to stay where they were.

"It's not always like this in Hangtown," Spooner told his girl. "Believe me."

She walked away from him, her face averted.

As they passed Narcissa, each of the visitors had a comment.

"Never seen anything like this in my life."

"Whores, fighting. What kind of town is this?"

"Ladies, Spooner is right," Narcissa said. "Hangtown is not usually like this."

"Doesn't matter. We're leaving."

"This is no place for a decent woman."

"Where's that Mr. Gray who brought us here?"

Without exception the women walked back to the cold wagons and climbed aboard. Many were crying and groping for warm clothing.

Minutes later MacIntosh and MacDermitt appeared, stationing themselves between the wagons and the saloon. When the men came out, the two drew their guns and motioned the men to keep moving.

"The ladies is leaving," MacIntosh said.

"Who says?" a man challenged. Others chimed in.

"The judge says it. The ladies say it and so does this." He brandished his gun with a convincing wave of the barrel.

The miners grumbled. They moved on, however, a few of them trying to wave or talk to the women they had met earlier.

"Don't go," most of them urged.

The last was Drover. He paused briefly, and sighed. He did not so much as look at Narcissa.

The hurt brought tears to her eyes.

Everything was going wrong. The women wouldn't talk to her, not even Nena Gunter. "Find that Gray and let us get away before dark," the Gunter woman said.

"Please," Narcissa said. "Give the town a chance."

"No!" The response was unanimous.

And when Old Gray came away from the saloon, the women called to him, demanding he take them away immediately. They were leaning from the front and back of the wagon or peering from beneath the canvas.

Narcissa conceded. "I guess you'd better do as they ask, Mr. Gray. I'm really sorry."

Gray kicked at the frozen earth.

"Nope," he said.

Narcissa was not sure she had heard correctly.

Several women said, "What?"

And Gray said, "Ain't takin' you good women nowheres. Mattie's girls are good people in a lot of ways. Always the first women in a camp. They do their job."

"We want to be taken to Sacramento," Nena Gunter said. "We understand there's a fort and a growing city."

"They got whores there too," Gray added. "Excuse the language, but you come to the frontier, you're gonna find snakes, bears, Indians, outlaws, storms, and whores. Bet there's some among you that's worked in the reclining position once or twice in your lives too."

"But at Sutter's . . ."

"At Sutter's there's more women than need be for awhile. Hangtown's where the men are."

It was a sobering thought. The women pondered it.

"But there's no church here, no school," Nena Gunter said.

Narcissa stepped forward. "There's a church." She pointed proudly toward her home with the cross on top. "And a school. We have three McGuffey readers. We can get two more." She was determined. She was not going to give up now.

"Where's the preacher?" a girl asked. "Why didn't he come to meet us?"

"You're looking at him," Narcissa said with a glow of satisfaction.

"Old Gray's a preacher?"

"No, I am."

"A woman?"

"Yes, a woman. That's why you came west, isn't it? To get away from all the rules that say a woman can't do this and can't do that." She felt as if she had become a rock of determination.

"Yes, but a minister . . ."

"Look at yourselves," Gray said. "You been running

businesses, herding cattle, doing men's work that you dassn't of done when you were home. So why not a female minister? Got female evangelists traipsing around back east now, too."

"What about the men? They're a grubby looking lot," one of the younger girls remarked.

"You ain't so purty yourself right now, miss."

The women laughed. The girl's clothes hung in tatters. Her hair and face were covered with sticky soda pop and beer, her arms crusted with sawdust.

"The men will clean themselves up when they're courting," Narcissa promised.

Courting. It was the right word, the magic word.

"All right," Nena said. "The kids and me are staying."

"Staying where?" a timid voice asked from the middle of the wagon. "We can't very well stay in the hotel, that saloon with those women."

"In the church," Narcissa said, excitement stirring inside her. "You'll all bed down in the church until you get married."

"All them women?" It was Adrian who had appeared less than a foot away. "No, sir. Not in my house. You ain't neither, Alexander."

He pushed the Gunter boy, and his aunt wrenched his shoulder, spinning him around and swatting him hard across the bottom.

"All *them* women? *Ain't neither?* Where are you getting that kind of language?"

"Ain't nobody talks different," he challenged his aunt.

Narcissa swatted him again. "Well, you *will* speak better grammar. And you *will* be gracious to our guests."

"Who says?"

"I say. And tomorrow you start school in earnest."

"School!"

"You, Alex, Sarah. Mary Frances too, if her mother approves."

"She does," Nena answered.

Then the women were descending from the wagons, arms loaded with boxes and cheap suitcases as they followed Narcissa through the violet twilight snow to the church. Old Gray climbed to his seat and began turning the wagons, following the women along the short walk.

"We'll spend the week getting settled," Narcissa was saying. "We'll primp and sew. There'll be a party Saturday night. In the church, not in the saloon. The men will be standing in line along Suds Row getting ready for the big event."

Narcissa's mind flooded with ideas.

"On Sunday after church we'll have a picnic down by the stream. It's cold, but we'll pretend it's summer."

"And a potluck," Cecelia said.

"Bake sales and sewing bees and the Hangtown Ladies Club, a library committee, and . . ."

Narcissa looked down the street as they reached the church. The men were keeping their distance, but they could not take their eyes off the newcomers.

The only ones she did not see were Walter and Drover.

18

"I now pronounce you man and wife," Narcissa said with a satisfied smile, "or I should have said 'men and wives.'"

The four couples before her embraced and the church resounded with applause. Old Gray played "Here Comes the Bride" on his harmonica. People moved in to kiss the cheeks of the newlywed women and to pump the hands of the grooms.

"Look Aunt Cissie," Sarah said, nudging her aunt and holding the offering plate for approval. Then Adrian slid through the crowd, down the center aisle, and held up the second plate.

"I got more," he boasted. "I always collect more than Sarah."

"You do not."

"Yes, I do."

"You don't."

"That's enough!" Narcissa warned, but she was too happy to look angry.

The offering plates were liberally sprinkled with tiny bits of gold and even some silver dollars. And there would be more in special contributions from the grooms whom she had wed following the regular Sunday service.

It wasn't the money itself that mattered, it was what it would buy: slates and books for the four children. As soon as Mr. Gray could make a trip to Sutter's, they would have a real school.

Nena would teach it for a salary. That was the amazing part. In the weeks since the women had come to town, the church income had increased sufficiently to support Nena as well as Narcissa herself.

With today's wedding, only three other women remained unmarried. Two of them were engaged, the third waiting for a shy but pleasant country boy to finish his house before he set the date.

It was all legal. Narcissa had written to Governor Burnett, carefully listing the names of the couples she had married. The first official acknowledgement had arrived, giving her services semi-legal status.

She was a minister. Not ordained in any special church, although she still considered herself a Presbyterian. But she was a minister in the eyes of the law.

"Miss White," a voice from the crowd addressed her.

Silence fell over the room like a blanket.

In the flush of excitement that followed every wedding she performed, she had not been aware of MacIntosh and MacDermitt pushing their way to the front of the chapel.

Both wore guns.

She started to chastize them. Since the fight at the saloon more of the miners had taken to wearing guns. The camp had divided itself into factions—those who sided with Narcissa versus those who liked the rough wickedness of the saloon and the prostitutes who had recently lowered their prices. There had been a shooting or two, no one seriously hurt, but with winter making the men's work harder and jealousy growing among those who had not won a wife in the age-old mating game, tempers were honed to a razor-sharp edge.

That was why Narcissa had become more insistent on her rule—no guns in church.

No longer were the men allowed to wear them to the

house and hang them on the coat pegs at the back of the hall. Leave them home, she told offenders. Guns had no place in a church.

"Miss White," MacDermitt repeated.

She scowled at the guns. "You know better than to bring guns into this church."

"Ain't no proper church," MacDermitt answered.

"Ain't no church at all," MacIntosh added. "It's Mr. King's house and he's taken a mind to move in here. That's what we come to tell you."

Narcissa stiffened. Since the women had arrived, she had seen Walter King only at a distance. He avoided her, refused to see her. There was other trouble too. Men who attended services had been harassed afterwards by the two gunmen. The house of the first couple to marry had been burned.

The congregation had pitched in to rebuild the couple's home, yet the element of fear discouraged the timid from coming to the place of worship. There was talk of other trouble brewing.

Aroused by the judge, Narcissa figured.

That's why she had wanted to see Walter. If she could get him back into the church, she was sure some of the problems could be resolved.

But now this . . . Walter asking for his house. That she did not understand.

"Walter didn't say that," she insisted. "The judge did."

"Makes no never mind," MacDermitt said. "You're leaving before nightfall."

"This trash giving you trouble, Miss White?" one of the four grooms asked.

Others pressed in closer until the gunmen touched the butts of their pistols. The motions instilled caution in the challengers.

They had more to lose now. Even those who were not married or engaged were looking forward to the next shipment of women Old Gray would be bringing in.

"For a man who ain't totin', you do talk right smart," MacDermitt said.

"Right!" MacIntosh backed him up, drawing his gun and pointing it at the ceiling.

He fired once and the noise was stunning. It echoed off the walls and set the younger children crying. Men, the brave and not-so-brave alike, stepped back. The two troublemakers now had a vacant space around themselves, and MacDermitt had drawn his weapon too. He made a slow rotation, leveling the barrel at belly height. Wherever the gun pointed, the targets withdrew another few inches.

"Everybody out," MacDermitt ordered.

"No," one man protested.

Two guns turned on him and he went white, then stepped back to shield his wife of a week.

"Like I said, everybody out. Now!"

The chastened wedding guests started toward the door, their eyes still on the guns.

"No," Narcissa called. "Don't give in so easily." She had come through so much. Starved, baked in desert heat, frozen in the blizzard, suffered unforgettable abuse, lived and worked with prostitutes. It would take more than a gun to destroy her church.

Her supporters were still easing toward the door.

"Please," Narcissa begged.

Nena Gunter gathered her two children to her and spoke for the rest. "A building isn't worth dying for, Narcissa," she said.

Narcissa stepped forward until the muzzle of MacDermitt's gun pressed against her, just below her breasts. The tough Scotsman backed off. She moved right with him.

"Don't think I won't shoot," he warned.

"Go ahead," MacIntosh prompted. "Shoot the holy roller."

Narcissa again closed the distance between them. MacDermitt's free hand lashed out, struck one side of her head and sent her sprawling to the floor.

The congregation gasped. Several men and Nena Gunter stepped forward, wanting to put themselves between the guns and Narcissa, but the muzzles were too frightening.

Sarah and Adrian ran to their aunt.

"You bastards," Adrian hissed at MacDermitt.

"Adrian . . ." She was too stunned to finish the reprimand, and anyway he was probably right.

"Everybody out," MacDermitt repeated. He seemed embarrassed by what he had done.

His captives started to obey, then stopped. The door to the church had opened.

Drover stood there.

He held a double-barreled shotgun, its big twelve-gauge muzzles like the open mouths of diamond back rattlers ready to spew deadly venom. His aim concentrated on the two intruders, although the scattergun would probably take in some of the others.

"Put the guns on the floor slowly, very slowly," the Australian directed.

MacDermitt protested. "You ain't got no rights to draw down on us, you Aussie duck."

"And I suppose you have the right to go into a church and scare the bloody shit out of innocent folks?"

"Ain't no church, and yeah, we do have a right. A court order demanding Mr. King's property be returned to him forthwith." With his gun still in position, he cautiously fished in a shirt pocket and produced a piece of paper.

"Too bad I can't read from here," Drover said.

"I'll bring it closer."

"Won't do any good. Can't read that legal lingo in Australian, let alone in the words your Yank judge would write. So put down the guns."

"No," MacIntosh responded. "You ain't gonna shoot that scattergun in here."

Drover sighed. "Well, now, it looks to me like we can stand here all day until I think I see one of you boys twitch a muscle to point one of them six-shooters at me. Then I won't have much choice except to fill the air so full of shot that a ghost couldn't squeeze through." He thrust the gun slightly forward. "Whoa, there, MacIntosh. I think I saw you move."

"I didn't budge."

"Anybody else see him move?"

"Yeah."

"Yes."

"Drew down on you, Strine," a voice confirmed.

"Wait," a nervous MacDermitt said in a high, pale voice. "I'm putting the gun down. Look, I'm pointing it at the floor. MacIntosh, do what he says."

"Aw, shit," MacIntosh stooped carefully. "This is getting expensive."

They placed their guns on the floor and straightened.

They moved slowly up the aisle.

Having passed Drover, the two faced the congregation.

MacIntosh spoke for both of them. "Your Aussie friend here bought you folks as much time as it takes us to go to the saloon, pick up two more guns and come back here. Anybody still in the place is going to get shot for trespassing."

They ducked through the door, and the crowd began to buzz again. Others started for the exit, eager to be gone.

But Drover still stood there, the shotgun sweeping slowly back and forth.

With the exception of the gun, all movement ceased.

"Miss White, you care to lead these folks in a few more hymns? They decided to stay."

"Drover, you can't keep people in church with a gun," she said angrily. "It's not right."

"If the scattergun goes off, Miss, it's the devil's doing. And right now I feel him pulling on the trigger."

"Drover." She shook her head. "This *is* Mr. King's house."

"Where I come from, owning land doesn't stop another man from shooting pesky kangaroos wherever he sees the varmints."

"Have you been drinking?"

"Could be. 'Cause I think I see some roos right here in church."

"We'll stay," the biggest, burliest groom said as he took a revolver from the floor. He tucked it in his belt. Another man picked up the second gun, and the crowd began to settle into the pews.

"Drover, you're putting all of these people in danger," Narcissa argued.

"Pray then," he said. "Pray those dingoes don't have any more guns."

"You're impossible."

She stormed up the aisle, calling to the Gunter woman while she hurried toward the door. "Lead the folks in prayer, Nena. I'll be right back."

"Where are you going?" Nena asked.

"To see Mr. King and get this straightened out."

"Narcissa, don't . . ."

"I'll go with you," Drover volunteered.

"No you won't. You've caused enough trouble already."

She shoved past him, took a deep breath of the fresh, cold air, and strode along the deserted boardwalks.

Christmas was in the air, she mused as she walked. They would have a church by Christmas, her brother had promised himself. He had failed, but there was a church, and the cold that had settled into the lower altitudes was a reminder that she too had fulfilled a vow. She had promised to bring this town the church it desperately needed.

She would not give up now.

She did not hesitate at the door of the saloon. She opened it and entered purposefully.

Max was behind the bar. He was always there, deadpan, taciturn, sliding schooners of beer down the counter with a certain pride and pouring hard liquor with a deftness that let the dark-colored liquid rise a sip above the rim of a shot glass without spilling over.

He was still the same shapeless, featureless Max, but today there was a glint of guilt in his eyes.

"We missed you in church this morning, Max," Narcissa said softly.

He picked up a glass and set to drying it.

"You miss me, too, Tight Ass?" a female voice said from a corner table.

Cottontail sat there, a warm shawl pulled around her bare shoulders.

Narcissa studied the scornful girl, and for the first time she felt guilt.

"Yes," she replied, then admitted her lie. "No, I'm ashamed to say I never thought of you in connection with the church."

Cottontail sniffed and pulled a bottle of whiskey closer to the shot glass on the table before her. She poured a drink.

"Would you attend this evening?" Narcissa asked. "We're having potluck. It would be a good time to get to know the ladies of the town."

Cottontail laughed. "They'd like that, wouldn't they?"

"No." Narcissa shook her head. "They wouldn't. But perhaps it wouldn't take them as long to show Christian charity as it has me. I do wish you'd come. Any of the other girls, too."

Cottontail laughed again. "Me, Featherlegs, White Squaw, the others, in church? What's the gospel say about whores praying with the wives of men they've fucked?"

"Mary Magdalene was welcome."

"Who's she?"

"A follower of Jesus."

"She still around?"

"No, that was over eighteen hundred years ago. Jesus cast seven demons out of Mary, and she followed him the rest of her life. She stood at the cross when He was crucified. She was the first to see Him after He arose from the tomb."

"I probably got more than seven demons in me. Syph, crabs, who knows? And I don't want to see some trick risin' from a tomb. It'd scare the begeezus out of me. You promise me no corpse is going to come popping up at this church of yours, and I might just come around to take a look-see."

"The church is God's house, not mine."

"It isn't a church and it isn't God's," Walter King said from the balcony outside the door of his office. "It's mine."

MacIntosh and MacDermitt flanked him, their holsters noticeably filled again.

"I issued an eviction notice," the judge said from behind Narcissa.

She turned.

The judge was sitting at another table with a plate of food and a cup of steaming coffee in front of him. A napkin had been poked in his collar and hung like a white horse's tail down his shirt. His cigar smoldered in an ashtray. He bobbed as he ate, scooping the black beans and pieces of steak into his mouth with a minimum of spillage.

"Walter," Narcissa started reasonably, "it is your house. Certainly you didn't approve of our eviction."

"I want them out of town," he responded.

"Who?"

"The women."

Narcissa ran part way up the stairs. "But you said you wanted Hangtown to be more than a miner's camp. You wanted it to be a city."

"It's too soon."

Cottontail spoke. "Good women are bad for business. A married man don't pay for screwin'. He don't gamble as much or drink as much."

Narcissa was only two steps from the balcony. "But you don't own the saloon, Walter. The judge owns . . ."

"Give me a year," he said. "By then they'll have out all the gold they can get by panning or scratching the surface."

"You mean you'll have all the easy gold." Drover had said that all along. The saloon, the whorehouse, the stores. They all must belong to King. The judge was a front who enabled King to retain his good name. "You own everything."

King changed his attitude. It was no longer belligerent. "I wanted you, Narcissa. If you want to marry people, marry us, and when the mining has run its course, we'll let in all the women you want. Married men make better employees."

She tipped her head. "Wait. I'm not sure I have it straight. You don't want the men working for you yet."

"They're stupid dreamers, Narcissa. They're not like us."

"Who? The men standing in the icy streams six days a week from dawn to dark?"

"Yes. It's the same in every gold strike town everywhere in the world," he said. "The fools work themselves to death hunting for the big nugget. And when they find it, they spend it at the whorehouse, the saloon, the gambling casino."

"But married men would work harder."

"Believe me, Tight Ass," Cottontail interrupted, "it's harder getting a dollar out of a man when he's got a wife watching his bank roll. Add kids to be fed and he needs food for the table, not fallen angels and poker chips."

Walter had walked into his office. Narcissa followed, and he closed the door after her.

"You could sell them food and necessities," Narcissa said.

"The profits aren't big enough. Give me a year, Narcissa," King appealed. "I'll own the good mines. I'll give the men the steady jobs a family man needs. This is the way it is done everywhere. The smart men, and their wives and their associates, don't dig in the dirt or wallow in the mud. They run the stores, the . . ."

"But you don't just run the stores."

"Not in the beginning, no. There are better ways to get the money from the laborers in the beginning. Later they'll work for us in our mines and shop at our stores. You have to understand gold."

"Is that all you understand?"

His eyes were glassy, his fingers working at his palms.

"The earths moves, Narcissa. Slowly liquids and gases from deep underground rose, millions of years ago, bringing up minerals—gold locked in pockets of quartz . . ."

"Why are you telling me this?"

"Because it explains why we can't have married men here—not now. You see, they're picking up the dust and a few nuggets. Nobody gets rich that way."

"Except you."

"This." He took in everything with a wave of his hand.

"This is nothing. When the stuff on the surface is gone . . ."

"You'll have the men's money."

"Yes. Enough to hire Welsh mining experts and buy all the land in town from men like Sutter. Then we're going to dig down, Narcissa, down to the Mother Lode, one gigantic mass of gold. It can be mine, and yours, Narcissa, if we're smart and get the capital so we can hire the men who give up panning and settle for a salary. That's what men like George Hearst will do—go for the Mother Lode. Generations from now my sons, our sons, will still be presiding over my empire. So wait. Another year. Until I can get the capital I need. That's when we'll want married men with children to feed. I know how it's done, Narcissa. My family built a dynasty back east with just such tactics. Let the lone men in first. Let them clear the land. Buy their crops cheap, get the money back with booze and loose women at first, or any other way that works. When you've got all you can out of the single men, let in the wives."

Watching him, Narcissa remembered a comment she had heard the day she arrived in the mining camp.

"You're the promoter!" she said, finally comprehending. "You deliberately lure people to Hangtown."

"Yes, I'm the promoter, although not in the sense of men like Sutter who started out with massive land grants from the Spaniards and only had to sell off some of their holdings to get money for attracting more people. I started with almost nothing. Panned gold myself for a while. Then started a store and the newspaper."

"And you bring in people to make Hangtown grow, even when there aren't enough claims to go around."

"Yes."

"But, Walter . . ."

"My family cheated me out of my inheritance. Shipped me off because they wanted to forget how they built their empire. I was like my grandfather. I was a mark on their gentility, a reminder of their past. Well, I'm going to have it here. My mines, my stores, my town. Share it with me and we'll build a temple, if that's what you want. We'll have our own pew, the one with the padded seats down front, and no one else will ever dare sit in them. Nothing will be said, but the pew will be ours."

"Walter, if you think that's what I want a church for . . ."

"I'll build us a mansion, Narcissa. But you must let me run Hangtown my way."

"Without marriageable women."

"Yes, and you can't make me out to be one of your religious demons. I've been tough . . ."

"Burned houses, caused Annie's death. David's too."

"You can't blame that on me. It's a rough, wild town. Catch a lion and it takes a strong trainer like me to tame it. I'm going to make it a real town, a permanent town. I'm not ashamed of that. I'm a builder, and I say your women have to go. We're not ready for them yet, so send them away."

"Walter, I can't do that. Even Mattie's girls . . ."

"Some of them are already thinking of getting married. That's what precipitated my decision about the church."

"Walter, I won't help you chase off the good people."

"Then you'll leave with the other women and the menfolk you have already married. You're all leaving."

"You don't own us, Walter."

"I own your church. I start there. I want you gone by nightfall."

"No." She was pleased with the response and a little surprised.

"No?"

"I'll close the church when we have another built. That won't take long. Until then we will pay you any reasonable rent."

"I don't want rent."

"What are you going to do, Walter? Have your men shoot me?" she scoffed. "You'd never get your gentility that way, would you?"

He nodded and walked to the door leading into his private apartment.

"There are other ways of evicting you," he said.

He opened the door and Narcissa looked in.

She capped her mouth with her hand, trying to smother the cry before it escaped her throat.

19

She would have said the trapper lunged at her, his ugly face distorted, his cavernous mouth opened over broken fangs. She screamed and shrank back from him.

In fact he hardly moved.

She would have escaped through the door, but Walter King was there, pushing her forward, closer to the rapist. Still wrapped in his bear skin coat, to Narcissa he was a vicious animal brought up short by the heavy rope attached to his legs. With his hands tied behind his back he could not balance himself, and he fell at her feet, ugly mouth slobbering.

She screamed again, fighting the pressure of King's hands that was forcing her close to this living nightmare.

"Walter! In God's name, why are you doing this?"

Her reaction angered the trapper. He groped forward, trying to reach her.

The heavy mahogany desk moved a half foot, propelled by the hairy beast attached to it. With only one free leg and his hands restrained, he crept and squirmed against the oriental rug, a mammoth man-eating snail covered in bearskin. The smell of him was sickening.

241

"I'm turning him loose," King said. "Maybe you can invite him to your church."

There was a rifle leaning against the wall—the same one she had seen in the cabin. She snatched it to her shoulder and took aim at the trapper's head. Her finger touched the trigger.

The animal eyes were looking up at her, waiting for the killing shot. There was no rage in them, only patience and ... remorse?

"Go ahead, shoot," King taunted.

Her shoulders ached under the sudden heaviness of the gun in her hands. Its barrel drooped.

Defeated, she lowered the gun; she could not kill him, not while he lay trapped.

King took the weapon from her and leaned it against the wall.

"Help him up," Narcissa said.

"Not me. It took MacIntosh and MacDermitt plus three miners to subdue him."

"You went up into the mountains and brought him down?" Visions of the cabin flashed into her head. In what condition were the bodies of her brother and sister-in-law now? Was the snow covering them? She hoped so.

King said, "No, he came down looking for you. He was hiding, watching the church. What happened up there, *Reverend* White?" There was scorn in his voice. "You give him something he hadn't had before?"

She struck at him, and he caught her wrists, first one, then the other, bending her elbows and forcing her backwards until she felt herself falling.

"No. Damn you!" Her voice was coarse in her ears.

He dropped her to the floor, avoiding the knee she drove toward his groin.

Surprisingly, he rolled away from her, rising, drawing his pistol as he stepped back. It pointed at the bridge of her nose.

"Take off your clothes," he ordered.

"Never." The word was a dry, rasping croak.

Then he holstered the revolver and picked up the trapper's rifle.

"Strip," he said again. "Or you're dead and the trapper will hang for it."

She took a deep breath and looked up at him. "Walter, why this?"

"Nobody beats me. Nobody defies me. Not any more."

Was she dealing with a madman? Two madmen? "All right," she conceded. "I'll close the church, send away the married couples today."

He laughed.

"Afterwards. Now strip."

She continued to argue, but she moved slowly, fumbling fingers to her dress. She needed time; surely someone from the church would come looking for her soon.

"Faster. You're stalling."

Goosebumps covered her body. Her hands shook. Tears rolled silently down her cheeks.

The piano was playing downstairs; if she screamed, would she be heard? Would anyone come? "Drover, help me," she whimpered. But he wouldn't come. Nobody would. She stood, the dress loosened and ready to drop. She looked down at it. Wouldn't it be easier not to comply? Wouldn't death be preferable to this? But . . .

"Get on with it!" There was venom in King's voice.

"Walter, I beg of you, not this. Not this!" she beseeched. Her body quaked. Or was she crying without sound?

Each time she pleaded, he added to the threat. "What do you think will happen to those kids of yours if you're dead?" He reached out and yanked off the dress.

"But, Walter, why rape? You could have had me . . . you did have me . . . without this."

"I could have had you as a wife."

"Yes."

"This is better. Now finish."

"Not here," she begged. "Not in front of him," she begged as she glanced at the trapper.

"Especially in front of him." King took off his holster and worked on the belt and buttons to his trousers, with his rifle still in his hands. Not until he was naked, did he lay it on a table.

Then he approached Narcissa, cricling her appraisingly, savoring his power.

Hands flailing and clawing, she hurled herself at him. The trapper strained against his bindings, perhaps trying to help, but King grabbed her throat with his left hand while he tore away the last of her clothing with his right. She couldn't breathe. She clawed at his hands and kicked and squirmed as he forced her to the floor and fell on top of her, spreading her legs with his knees.

He had not released her throat. "You wanna die, keep fighting," he rasped. "We can hang the trapper for strangling or shooting you. Take your choice."

She forced her body to go limp. She had to breathe.

The room dipped and swirled. She could see parts of it as she rolled her head from side to side. The ceiling, the walls, King's leering face, and the trapper pulling the heavy desk forward an inch at a time.

With the dizziness came nausea. There was the smell of liquor on King's breath and the scent of a man perspiring with lust and exertion. There was also the odor of the trapper's coat.

King was mumbling, taunting her, putting off the inevitable, tormenting her with threats. She could hear the piano downstairs, the grunts of the trapper and her own whimpering.

"Look at him," King said, indicating the trapper with his eyes.

The beast was tearing at his restraints, trying to get closer, to watch, to take King's place. She could see the huge bulge on his front, and in his frenzy of voyeurism, he was rubbing his shackled hands frantically over his genitals. He was laughing, grunting, groaning, closer to climax than King.

"Watch him. Look at him!" King ordered. "You're servicing two of us at once. How do you like that? An audience. Like it, girl? Do you like it?" Then he turned his head toward the door and called to the people downstairs. "Mattie, Max, judge . . . all of you come here and watch."

"No, no, no. Don't. Please don't!"

She bit down hard on her lip and tasted blood. No one came, although King did not seem to notice. She felt his hand at her throat, the other cruelly pawing her breasts, and finally the pain as he forced himself inside her.

Then she was still, letting him have his way. He stopped choking her, cupping both his hands under her buttocks and forcing her to rise to meet each penetrating thrust.

It went on and on. Seconds and minutes lost in pain and helplessness. He kept at her, determined to make her like it.

He knew her better than she thought. She held out as long as she could. She would not give him that one last bit of satisfaction, but the man was a master of control. In the end she grasped him and urged him to increase his tempo.

There was no disguising the moment when she climaxed. Her entire body erupted in violent demand. In the frenzy she rolled him over, mounted him and drove herself onto him with piston-like motions, her hands on the floor for balance.

She continued long after they had both satiated themselves.

When he was limp and pushing her away, she persisted. There was perverse triumph in feeling the shriveled thing inside her. Only when she had him completely beaten did she rise and begin dressing.

She saw the trapper make a final effort to reach King and give up. She looked at the guns, then left them in place.

She paused at the door. There was only one revenge possible, only one way to redeem herself.

"I'll never leave Hangtown," she said. "There will always be a church."

Then she went down the stairs into the saloon. Max watched her with the same detached expression that he gave everything that transpired beyond the domain of his gleaming bar.

The piano player stopped playing.

The two gunmen—MacIntosh and MacDermitt—grinned knowingly at her disheveled appearance.

Cottontail looked up from her drink and said, "A woman's never free. You understand that now, Tight Ass. A woman never wins."

"I will," Narcissa said as she crossed to the door.

The judge said nothing. Did Walter King's front man see his own rape in her eyes? He would always be subject to King's demands.

Madame Mattie leaned over the balcony railing to ask without malice, "You ready to join our little ladies club now, girlie?"

She lifted her chin. "No, but the ladies club at the church would be pleased to have all of you as members."

She closed the door behind her and took a deep breath. She had just come back from hell.

20

NEARING the church, she could hear the voices singing a hymn. Despite their indecision about the words and the tune, the voices should have encouraged the young woman who approached from the street. Instead, her pace slowed.

Was this church worth the pain and danger?

What price must she pay to bring God and His ways to a ramshackle mining camp that might revert to nature when the easy gold pickings gave out? What price could she ask of others? The decent women and children she had brought here. The men who had married and thereby placed themselves in the path of Walter King's ambitions?

Did she have the right to ask them to risk their lives for her brother's obsession, the one she had made her own?

Drover must have heard her approaching. He opened the door and assessed her appearance. "You all right?" he asked, touching her shoulder.

She tried to straighten her clothing, but her dress was soiled and her hair was a mess. There were undoubtedly bruises on her neck.

"It was that bloody King, wasn't it?" Drover guessed. "I'll kill the bastard."

He moved as if to step around her, but she blocked his way.

As he always did, he misread her intent.

"Or maybe you let him mess you up," he said.

She was too exhausted to object. Let him think what he wanted.

She spoke to the congregation in a dry, throaty voice. "Walter King insists we vacate the church immediately."

Nena Gunter moved closer, her children on either side of her. "Where are we to go? Those of us who haven't married?"

"We'll put you up," one of the newlyweds volunteered. The bride glanced at the groom for approval and received a nod of assent.

"We'll make room for all of you," another voice promised.

Drover said nothing. He was glaring at Narcissa.

Why did he always interpret for the worse everything she did?

Jealousy? Disgust?

She deserved the latter. She was not lily white. She had given in to the lusts of the flesh. Breached her own religious beliefs. She was a hypocrite.

She was human.

But why did she care what Drover thought of her? Why did he have such capacity to hurt her?

More important, why hadn't she recognized her feeling for the Australian sooner?

She loved him.

He antagonized her like a little boy who pulled pretty girls' pigtails. That antagonism did not matter, however. She loved him.

"What did King do to you?" Nena asked. "How did he make you change your mind about the church?"

Narcissa pondered the question for a long silent time. The people around her quit talking among themselves. Every ear was turned toward her.

She recalled what she had told Walter King. She would not surrender. Oh, he could use her body, abuse her, threaten her, even humiliate her by rousing a primitive pleasure inside her at the very moment she hated him most.

He could kill her.

Worst of all, he could threaten the children.

But she would keep her promise to him. Her promise to God.

"I'm not leaving," she said.

The congregation was puzzled.

"What?"

"But you just said . . ."

"I intend to remain here and keep the church open alone."

"By yourself," Drover said laughing.

"I have a gun. I'll use it if I must."

"You won't," Nena insisted.

"Oh, but I will. I have already turned the other cheek."

"But what about Adrian and Sarah?" Placer Pan Sawyer asked. "They wouldn't be safe here."

"They can stay with me," Nena mused, "temporarily. What's two more. That is if someone would take us all in." Several couples volunteered quickly. "But this isn't right, leaving Narcissa to face King alone. We should stick together."

Spooner agreed. "Give King his damned building. We can build a new church down the street sooner or later."

"It goes farther than that," Narcissa told him. "King wants all the married couples to leave Hangtown before sundown today."

"Leave?"

"Move out?"

"Who the hell does he think he is?"

Narcissa heard the string of irate voices. It was like a snarled skein of yarn . . . unintelligible.

"I think you'd better obey his wishes," she said. "He is capable of anything."

And he was. He was unbalanced by an obsession to prove himself to the family that had disowned him. And perhaps, most of all, to disprove his own self-doubts.

He had to triumph in his own eyes. The lengths he would go to build his city—one he owned and controlled—surpassed normalcy. Still he was probably right, from a practical standpoint. He could build a city out of Hangtown while miners scratched the surface in camp after camp, moving on, leaving buildings as gravestones, victims of the lack of capital which left the Mother Lode untouched.

He would get his way by force, if necessary. Although he would prefer to be subtle, anyone who disagreed with him or presented a threat would be chased away.

A married man lured into a brutal beating.

A claim jumped and validated by his shill the judge.

A couple's house burned.

A child . . .

What would he do with children if he could force them to his will? Adrian and Sarah. Nena's children.

King was clever. He wouldn't get caught. He would have the judge, MacIntosh and MacDermitt, and his other hirelings on his side. Practically all of the unmarried miners too. Those who worked for him already would have no choice except to go along with anything he wanted that would send the women and the married men packing. She doubted that any of his employees had put away enough money to reach the next camp, let alone to hold out until a new claim began paying. The same was probably true of the independent gold panners. With King's prices for food, tools, liquor, and women, few would be able to fight the determined King.

There was another factor, a significant one.

Ironically, Narcissa had, without meaning to, allied the vast majority of the men in the area to King.

She should have brought in a great many more marriageable women or none at all.

Except for those in the church now, all the men were, in a sense, rejects. They had not found a girl or wife among those Old Gray had brought from San Francisco. Either they had courted one of the women and lost, or they had been too unsure of themselves to court at all.

Then too there were the drunkards and gamblers who wouldn't want their camp changed in any case.

They knew decent women brought rapid change.

In all, an indomitable number stood with Walter King and against Narcissa. He had known that when he forced her to submit.

"Mr. Gray," she said to the old wagon master who still sat in one of the back pews.

He came to church regularly on the Sundays he was in town. Usually, though, he was on the road, bringing in supplies and new miners, taking out gold and those who admitted defeat and those who were moving on to new dreams.

"How soon can you be ready to take these people away from Hangtown?" she asked.

"Hey, wait," a man said.

"Two hours?" Narcissa suggested.

"Ain't taking nobody unless they want to go," Gray answered.

"And none of us do," Nena responded.

"That's right."

"We're not leaving."

"Us either."

"King can't force us to leave. This is our home."

Narcissa spoke above the determined voices.

"You don't understand. He can force you."

"How?"

"Lots of ways. There'll be fights, claims jumped, houses burned, prices raised and children harassed."

They listened in silence. The truth of what she said became more vivid with each moment.

Drover broke the quiet. "Got myself driven out of Gundaroo by a stage coach driver who stole his own cargo and needed a bushranger to blame it on. Got myself chased out of Sydney by a gambler who couldn't win if I got in his game and made him deal from the top. Took a dozen of his mates to put the hard word on me—leave or let them beat me to death. Even got myself ejected from San Francisco because some other ducks were setting fires and the Yanks were tying a noose for me because my accent was jackeroo. The way I see it, I can leave Hangtown and file a new claim, break my back and freeze my feet there until the claim starts to pay off and some other bloke puts on a crack hardy and drives me off again, or I can stay put and pull this boomer King down to size."

"In other words you're staying," Gray translated.

"You can wager a hundred bob on that, mate."

"That's easy for you to say," one man remarked. "You're not married."

"I'll be getting a cheese and kisses of my own soon," he said and shot a glance at Narcissa. "Maybe from the next crowd Old Gray carts in."

If he meant to hurt her, he succeeded.

"You'll change your mind," Placer Pan Sawyer said.

"No, I won't."

"Now, when it counts most, though, you're single. King will leave you alone."

"If King so much as sneers at one of my mates, I'll toss him head first into the saloon's own dunny, and you can believe me, that's one outhouse that is really full of shit. Excuse me, Preacher Lady."

Why did the Australian persist in joining her fight, Narcissa wondered. Was he as tormented as she, drawn to her and repelled at the same time?

"We're staying," Sawyer's wife said softly.

Her husband turned on her. "Who do you think wears the pants in this family?"

"I'm beginning to wonder. In any case I'm staying."

Women's voices rippled through the group. A consensus was arrived at quickly.

They were staying.

The men were quick to echo their wives' position. If they were not otherwise convinced, Narcissa suspected, they were afraid to appear weaker than their women.

"I can't let you do this," she said. "You don't seem to realize this is a battle we can't win. King has time on his side."

"Then we fight it right now," Drover said.

"How?"

He turned to Gray. "Get your wagons and get out of town. I want to see that wagon hop like a joey leaving its mother's pouch."

"Why?"

"Go for more girls. I'll shout for the bill."

"Cost double if I gotta go to Frisco with empty wagons."

"I'm good for it. You know me. Now get on with it."

Gray shrugged and stretched. "Don't know what I'll round up this time of year. But I'll give it a try."

"Bring back one wagonload of supplies. We may be hungry by then."

"I can still hunt good enough to keep us from starving," Sawyer volunteered.

"So can I," another male agreed.

"Have it your way then, Aussie," Gray said as he snugged his coat to his body and went out into the afternoon sun.

When he was gone, Drover confronted Narcissa.

"So now what, Preacher Lady?" he asked sarcastically.

"Sing," she said. "Loud. Loud enough for King to hear good and clear."

They sang with gusto, powerful, determined gusto. Walter King could not help but hear. He knew instantly the angel of Hangtown had not wilted under his threats.

ஜ

21

THE window exploded and showered the worshipers with shards of glass.

From the pulpit Narcissa saw it happen before she heard the sound of shattering glass. The concussion of gunshot came a fraction of a second later.

Then the screams—some were high pitched shrieks that began while the congregation was still singing. Those at the back were the first to feel the glass spears penetrate their shoulders and the backs of their necks. Those at the front twisted around to see the final splinters falling among the rear pews.

"Mama!" Sarah's pathetic cry carried above the rest.

"I'm hurt," a male voice said.

He was not alone. Others were staring in shock at blood, their own blood. One big man pulled a glass spike from his shoulder and studied the sticky red point.

"I'll be damned," he said. "Excuse me, Reverend."

"What was that?" somebody asked in the instant before the second window exploded and showered another group of parishioners. The wiser and less curious had sought shelter behind the protective pews before the second shot came.

"Somebody's shooting."

"Get down!"

The cries tumbled over each other like dry leaves fleeing in the wind. ". . . going to kill us all . . . do something . . . I'm bleeding . . . Drover . . . you and your damned church . . ."

"Don't throw a willy. Let me through!" It was Drover. He had been in the front pew, having moved around and even outside the church during the long afternoon and into the evening while the congregation defied Walter King's eviction order. He and the others, men and women alike, had checked often and reported the street to be quiet. In fact, no one stirred. It was as if Hangtown were deserted, except for Drover's irregular patrols.

He wore a pistol in the holster strapped to his waist. For once Narcissa did not object. Now he drew the gun and carefully pointed it at the ceiling while he worked his way along an aisle blocked with crouching men and women. Some were trying to tend the wounded.

A man cursed him when he nudged his bleeding wife. Another pulled at his coat.

"Don't go out there. There'd only be more shooting."

He hesitated; the decision was not his alone. Would he provide more protection here or in the street?

"Drover, do as they say," Narcissa said.

Before he could move, the wailing of Nena Gunter's little girl stopped him. All eyes turned to the sound. The child lifted her head; the entire side of her face was covered with blood.

"She's hurt!"

"My God! Look!" The last came from a man huddled on the floor near the child. He might have been pointing an accusing finger at the unseemly way Nena Gunter had let her dress ride up on her legs. Then everyone saw the wound. Most of her right breast had been blown away.

By some primeval communication, the crowd forgot minor hurts.

They sensed death.

Narcissa knew before she reached her friend that she was gone. Her fingers on the pulseless wrist told a story she already knew, and when she leaned over Nena's mouth to check for breath, it was a gesture that gave her something to do until she could regain control.

For a long moment she knelt there, feeling Nena's blood soaking into her bodice. Then she lifted the dead woman's little girl and passed her off to the man who had risen from the floor.

"Take her and the boy to the other room," she said.

A woman caught the boy before he saw the disfigured body of his mother.

Then slowly the people began to rise. It became a point of pride.

"Stand up for Jesus," someone said. "Stand up for the Lord."

"Rock of ages, cleft for me . . ." A hymn started with a man who held a hand over his bleeding eye.

A single timid voice failed to dampen the growing determination. "Maybe they were only trying to frighten us," a bony weasel of a man breathed.

"They?"

Whoever asked the question did not expect an answer. "They" meant everybody, everything beyond the door of the church.

"Whoever they are, they're going to get done like a burned dinner," Drover said and marched up the aisle.

"No, Drover," Narcissa said. "It's me he wants."

He waited for her.

"What do you mean?"

"Wait," she said.

Narcissa went into the kitchen and found the gun King had given her. Then, with Drover, she walked into the darkness of the unlit street.

Light flowed from the back rooms of stores and shops where the clerks lived, and already the street was filling with men and the girls from the saloon. The two shots had been heard beyond the rows of stores. Miners were running toward the town center, shouting, questioning each other.

"What happened?"

"Who got shot?"

"Where is the bastard?"

"Heading toward the mountain."

The gaggle finally had an answer, and the men became a mob, forming without leadership at first and then following two shadows that appeared to be MacIntosh and MacDermitt. Most of the miners carried rifles or picks and shovels as weapons.

"Get back inside," Drover told Narcissa. "I'm going after him."

"After who?" she challenged.

But he would not be diverted, and he disappeared into the massive posse whose path was marked by torches which dripped fire and cast shadowy shapes of the disappearing searchers.

The whores, the judge, some of the clerks, and even Max the bartender remained in the street.

Walter King was approaching from the direction the mob had taken, apparently having joined the chase only to return.

"That you, Narcissa?" he asked. He held a torch higher so that he could see her face.

By now the parishioners were spilling out of the church, their fear overcome by curiosity.

"It was the trapper," he said. She wondered if he were smiling to himself in the darkness.

"You let him loose with a gun?" she demanded.

He talked over her to the church members. "I told your preacher here to get you people out of town . . . that there was a madman loose with a grudge against her. She spent some time with him in his cabin."

"I don't believe it, not Narcissa."

"Ask her. Spent at least one night with him," Madam Lafayette confirmed from King's side. "Old Gray will tell you. She was coming from the trapper's place when we rescued her and the kids. Probably wouldn't give the ugly bastard any more honey so he tried to sting her like a bee. She's why your church got shot up."

"You didn't tell us that, Narcissa," Spooner said. "You didn't say nothing about a madman with a gun. She blamed you, Mr. King."

"Me?" His pretense of incredulity was transparent only to Narcissa. "Why did you tell them that?" he asked her.

"You know why."

Again he spoke directly to the parishioners. "In any case, you married men better get your womenfolk out of town. Now. That crazy trapper could easily escape the posse. He might double back. You'd better go, don't pack, just get on Old Gray's wagons and head for Sacramento or San Francisco."

"Gray is gone," a woman said. "We have injured people that couldn't ride a horse."

"If we had a horse."

"Gray's gone?" King turned on Narcissa. "You sent him away? Why?"

"For more women. We're staying."

"Not us," a miner replied. "We'll walk if we have to."

"Us too."

"And us."

"We're all going, Narcissa," a woman said. "You'd better go with us. You should have told us the truth."

"No," Narcissa cried. "Don't you see? This is what King wants."

"To save lives," King said. "Is that so bad? You escaped with a few cuts this time. If he comes back, he's liable to kill one of you."

"He already has." Several spoke at once. "Nena Gunter. The woman with the two kids."

Walter King was silent. Narcissa could sense the sudden tension in him. He was gouging the fingers of his free hand into his palm. He had not expected the trapper to kill any one. That put the entire incident into different perspective. A different jurisdiction. A shooting could go unnoticed outside a mining camp. Even a knife fight was too common to trouble the officials of the burgeoning state, but a wanton murder in a recognized church . . . that could attract attention.

He turned on Narcissa. "You, damn you!" he barked. "I told you to send the women away!" His voice cracked with emotion.

"You let him go," she lashed back. "You let trapper go, even gave him his gun back."

"I don't know what you're talking about." He was ready to deny any part in the crime.

"You liar." Narcissa stepped toward him, her mind still seething with the sight of Nena Gunter's body, the thought of her orphaned children. She wanted to scratch and kick him, but suddenly Sarah and Adrian were there, clutching at her. "Get back inside," she ordered.

"No, Aunt Cissie," Sarah whined. "Mrs. Gunter's all bloody."

"She's dead. I don't want to be with her," Adrian said. "And her kids, they're crying something awful."

She spat the words at King. "You see what you let happen. They ought to try you with the trapper."

"Look, the posse's coming back. Get a rope. I think they got him." One of the parishioners was the first to call for a lynching.

Narcissa's protests were lost in the general turmoil. The returning men were jubilant in mood, shouting and laughing, bunched together, each trying to get a hand on the powerful man they pushed in front of themselves.

It was the trapper. With his heavy fur coat, he was a monster from a fairytale, but even a mythical beast could not have escaped the numberless hands pushing and beating him. Men with burned out torches were using them to jab him in the ribs or smash him on the head. They had already beaten his arms so badly, he couldn't lift them to defend himself, and he barely shuffled along on his crippled legs. Had they been that way before the traps? Narcissa wondered.

Like an ugly tornado funnel, the mob grew in size as it swept along, sucking up fury in its path. The people from the church crossed the street cautiously and then unleashed their venom on the recluse when they realized he was unarmed and helpless.

Narcissa ran with them, elbowing and scrambling, pulled as if by a magnet until she stood before the atavistic fiend. He looked down at her and she struck him with all her strength. The ugly face was turned aside by the blow. "Killer!" she shrilled. "Murderer!"

Remember Christ, something spoke inside her. What would He have done? Been forgiving?

She could not forgive. But she could perform the role she had chosen for herself. The man had not been proven guilty. She could not judge.

She stepped back. "I am sorry," she said.

"Sorry!" She had angered the crowd and now she absorbed some of its anger.

"He's an animal."

"A killer."

"But we aren't," she said. "God made him what he is. He's one of God's children, too. We must show mercy."

"Nonsense."

His lips tried to form words. From his expression it was obvious that whatever he had to say carried no malice. Suddenly Narcissa felt pity.

"What?" she asked, sensing that the words were important. He tried again.

She thought she could discern two of the words he was mouthing. "Not my . . ."

"Not your what?" she asked.

"Forget it, Tight Ass," Cottontail said from a few steps away. "He can't talk."

"But maybe he can write. Somebody get a pencil and paper."

"No!" King said. "String him up."

"Yeah!"

"Build the gallows."

"No time for that."

The groups which had opposed each other had found a common cause, a vendetta to unite them. Her congregation joined the others in lust for retribution.

"Get a rope from the store." King began directing the crowd with the authority of a born leader. His men had the trapper by the arms. "Hang him from the balcony of the saloon."

The cheer sounded unanimous.

"He deserves a trial," Narcissa argued.

"Judge! Get over here," Walter King called while the crowd prodded their captive toward the saloon. Two men came running from the store with a rope, one of them forming a noose as he ran. "Give the man a trial fast, Judge. Say he's guilty."

"No," Narcissa shouted. "That's not a trial. There has to be a jury and lawyers and . . ."

"You men," the judge shouted, pointing to a group of the lynchers. "You're the jury. You, Cottontail, you're his defense lawyer."

The men were laughing as Cottontail spoke to the deaf mute. "You guilty, trapper?" The prisoner grunted. Cottontail interpreted for him. "Pleads not guilty, your honor."

"Not guilty?"

"Yep, says he done fired the gun all right, but it was the damn fool bullet that killed the woman."

"Gentlemen of the jury." They had reached the front of the saloon, and the two men with the rope had gone up to the balcony. Others ran in to help them. The noose dropped in front of the trapper's face. "How say ye? Guilty or not guilty?"

A hundred voices chorused, "Guilty!"

The trapper fell to the ground, with his crippled legs and battered arms fighting for his life. His captors crawled over him, one producing rope to tie his ankles and cinch his arms to his sides. He dodged and bobbed, trying to avoid the noose lowering over his head.

"Stop it!" Narcissa pleaded. "Please, in the name of God." Her people brushed aside the fervent request.

Even Adrian was with them. "Let them be, Cissie. He ought to hang. You should see what his gun did to that lady."

Gun? Where was it. "Just a minute," she called out. "You can't hang a man without evidence. Where's the gun?"

"The Australian stayed behind looking for it," a man said. "He'll be along in a minute."

"Then wait."

"Sure, lady, we'll wait."

"Drop the rope!"

"Well, it's gonna take us awhile. Having a helluva time getting the noose on him anyway."

The trapper's jerking legs and butting head sent a man staggering from the center of the mob, his hands cupping his genitals and vomit pouring from his mouth. Another flew out and landed on his back. He didn't get up.

"Leave the men alone, Tight Ass," Madam Lafayette called. "Let the boys get this over with. I'm losing money."

Narcissa broke away and ran across the street and between the buildings opposite the church. She was fifty yards down the path when she met Drover loping toward her.

"You've got it?" she asked.

He did not stop and she fell in behind him. He was breathless, and held up the rifle to tell her what she wanted to know.

"It's a single shot," she said as they ran.

"Right."

"And he couldn't have reloaded and fired twice, not so quickly."

"You guessed it, girl."

"Hoorah!" The cheer blasted from the direction of the saloon.

At the sound Narcissa went limp and staggered. Drover forged ahead while she recovered herself and followed at a distance.

The semi-circle of people around the saloon was packed tight, shorter men and women craning their necks to see past the inner ring of torches. The light illuminated a huge body being pulled upward by a gang of men working in unison.

"Heave. Heave. Heave," their self-appointed leader called in a set cadence.

With each "heave" the trapper was pulled higher. His body convulsed, bound legs kicking, shoulders tossing in a vain attempt to feed his tortured lungs.

"We're too late!" Narcissa cried. She lifted King's pistol, pointed at the sky, and fired.

The shot shocked the crowd.

She turned, backed away, but the men on the balcony merely stopped pulling.

"Drop him," Narcissa demanded. "Drop him."

The men did nothing. The trapper's body was in its last convulsive shudders.

Lowering the barrel, she fired at the peak of the saloon roof. Splinters sprinkled the men below. One ducked for cover. The others crouched, but they kept their grip on the rope. She fired again, this time holding the revolver with both hands, the way her father had taught her. Aiming an inch or two above the tallest executioner's head, she fired.

"Jesus Christ." The oath came from the balcony. All hands released the rope. The trapper fell to the ground.

Drover had already reached the mob and was plowing through. With the armed Narcissa behind him, nobody blocked their passage. They knelt beside the trapper, working quickly to loosen the noose. She tensed as the rope finally released its grip.

The giant chest did not move. There was no gasping intake of air.

The trapper lay still.

Drover eased her aside to check the pulse.

"He's dead," the Australian pronounced. A light moved closer, and others checked, then stepped aside in mute agreement.

Now Narcissa knew what the rapist, the cannibal, the recluse had been trying to say with his tongueless mouth.

"Not my fault. Not my fault."

She took the rifle from Drover's hand and held it up for the crowd to see.

"The trapper's gun," she said. "Drover found it."

"Just where we thought he dropped it?" MacIntosh asked.

Drover said, "Yes."

Narcissa passed the rifle to the nearest man. He sniffed at the barrel.

"Ain't been fired lately. Clean as a whistle. Still loaded."

"And how many shots were there?"

"Two." The crowd had become a class of school children, all eager to recite the right answer.

"Does everybody remember how close the shots were together?"

"Yeah."

"Damned close."

"Could the trapper have fired, reloaded, and fired again that fast?"

"No."

"With that old blunderbuss? Impossible."

"We hung the wrong man." The realization was mouthed by Max the bartender. As if he had been saving his voice for something important, the laconic barman stepped forward, took the gun, checked it, and repeated himself. "We hung the wrong man."

"Oh, God!" MacDermitt sounded sick.

"And I was his attorney," Cottontail said. She was serious, the weight of the man's life heavy on her conscience in spite of the recent mockery of justice.

"He weren't no good, anyways," MacIntosh said. "We all know what he done. He ate people."

"Dead people," the judge said softly. "Nobody ever knew him to kill, no matter how hungry he got up there in that cabin of his. He always had plenty of game and corpses left along the pass." Pondering briefly, he sucked once more on his cigar, then pitched it away, as if he never intended to smoke again. Solemnly he said, "I never hanged an innocent man before."

"But he was a cannibal," MacIntosh argued.

"He was a man," Narcissa said, suddenly forgetting the hate pent up inside her since the trapper had violated her body. She could almost forgive him, a lonely man taking the only kind of love available. Now that he was dead, she could forgive him. She knelt beside him, her eyes closed in silent prayer.

"Then who did do it?" MacDermitt asked. "There's a woman dead. Somebody's got to pay."

Eyes turned to MacIntosh, whose disparaging remarks had made him suspect.

"Hey, it wasn't me. You men, don't look at me like that."

"You figured he was just an animal."

The thought quickly festered in the crowd.

"Called him a cannibal."

" 'Weren't no good anyways.' That's what you said."

"You shoot into the church?" Drover asked.

"Me? Why the hell would I do that?"

"You said you'd be back. You work for the judge."

"The hell he does," the judge objected. "We all do what Mr. King orders. I just front for him. But hanging an innocent man . . ."

"Mr. King wanted us out of town," the youngest bride remarked. "Maybe MacIntosh was doing like he was told."

"Mr. King?" Drover and Narcissa looked for the saloon owner. When they failed to locate him, they returned to the crowd's reasoning.

"Give me your gun, MacIntosh," Drover demanded.

"Why?" The Scotsman faltered, then agreed. "Sure, sure. Look at it all you want." He would have extracted it from his holster, but without warning he was surrounded, arms pinned behind his back, the weapon removed for him.

The debate was quick.

"All six bullets."

"He could have replaced them."

Max sniffed at the barrel before passing the gun around. "Ain't been fired."

"And I didn't have time to clean it," MacIntosh pointed out anxiously. "You all got to admit that."

Now MacDermitt became the center of attention.

Without protest he handed across his weapon.

"Look, maybe MacIntosh and me have played rough sometimes," he said. "Mr. King demanded that. But neither him or me . . ." he pointed to his cohort, "would kill for him. He don't pay enough for beans and a good screw once a week, let alone for killing."

"This one's a Whitney-Walker .44 so he could have changed cylinders fast." The man sniffed at the barrel. "But it ain't been fired. Hell, it's rusty. You big bullshitter,

MacDermitt. You don't even keep your weapon clean. Some gunslinger you are."

"I still think he had a part in this," the man named Ben insisted.

MacDermitt admitted it. "Mr. King told us to turn the trapper loose. So we did. At the saloon door. He run like a wounded bear. But MacIntosh and me never came outside until the shots were fired. Fact is, I was with Cottontail, just getting ready for a good screw."

"And I was headed to the outhouse for a shit," MacIntosh said.

Suddenly Drover interrupted, calling out over the men's shoulders.

"Hold it there, King."

King had surfaced mid-stride toward the door to the empty saloon. The men holding his hirelings' guns swung them, taking aim at King's belly.

"Going somewhere, Walter?" Narcissa asked.

He laughed. "No." He cast a disdainful glance at the crowd. "You looking for another scapegoat to lynch?"

"You was the one wanted him hung," a guilty voice pointed out.

"You wanted us out of town, didn't ya?"

"Did I? How about it, Judge? Mattie?"

"Well . . ." Mattie tussled with her answer and never did get it aired.

The judge hesitated too, searching either his memory or his conscience. "No. Can't say as I ever did hear him say anything like that."

In turn, the girls from the whorehouse nodded, divorcing themselves from whatever King might have said.

Max remained silent. No one asked MacIntosh or MacDermitt. Any answer they gave would be suspect, regardless of what side they took.

"There!" King said with satisfaction, but his fingers were working in his palms again. "Nobody ever heard me say you good folks had to leave town except when we had to let the trapper go free."

"MacDermitt and MacIntosh told us. They work for you."

"Miss White put you up to that, right boys?"

Their response was not fast enough for him.

"Right, boys?"

The two nodded dutifully.

"Why would Reverend White do that?"

King smiled coldly. "Because Mattie made her a good offer." Mattie Lafayette's head jerked up but she said nothing. "Your pretty little preacher lady got tired living on the dust you folks have been giving her. And Mattie offered her the lead girl spot in the new parlor Mattie is going to build. And a bigger slice of the cake than any of the other girls get if she'd scare the marriageable women out of town. No offense, ladies." He smiled. "But you are bad for Mattie's business."

"I don't believe it. Reverend White is . . ." Spooner's voice trailed off.

"She's no more ordained than I am."

"She's what we got."

"And what you got is an ex-whore who thought she could make more money from a pulpit."

"You bloody, lying bastard." Drover started to lunge, but Narcissa placed a discouraging arm in front of him.

King smirked. "You think I'm lying? Give Mattie fifty bucks and take the little lady upstairs. If you still think she's a virgin, I'll refund your money."

"Being a virgin is no . . ."

King cut off Drover in mid-sentence. "An unwed preacher lady who isn't a virgin? Come on, duck. I'm a religious man myself. I financed the church, didn't I? Supported it for months until I heard what the little lady is really like."

Narcissa withered under the attention focused on her. No one spoke. Her parishioners were the worst. Not only did they scorn her with questioning eyes, but they moved away from her as if she had cholera.

She wondered how many of the women had reached Hangtown as virgins. Very few, she would guess. There had always been a question in her mind when she married off the newcomers; which of them were bawdy girls escaping whorehouses and seeking respectability in a town where they were not known?

The question was irrelevant.

But a preacher, a woman preacher in particular, had to be above reproach.

She wasn't.

By saying nothing, she had lied to all of them.

"Is what he says true, Miss White?" a man asked.

Decent of him, she thought ironically. He was giving her a chance to deny King's claims.

She was tempted to lie. For herself. But for the church too. And the chldren. She had four now to think about, unless someone else offered to take in Nena Gunter's boy and girl.

"It doesn't matter," she said finally.

"But it does," the man insisted.

"She's already told you," King replied. "She doesn't deny it. Question her. Maybe she knows who did fire into the church."

She responded fast enough to avoid further questions, turning attention back on King himself.

"First, we'll have a look at your gun, Mr. King," she said.

"Certainly." He pulled it from the holster at his side.

"No," the judge interrupted. "First we question you, Reverend White." His manner had reverted to the slithery, cynical veneer he had always worn before. A better side of him must have surfaced briefly inside him, fought, and lost the battle. Obviously he had decided to stick with King. "Bring her inside, boys, before she puts us all under her spell."

"The gun," Drover said. "That first."

"Fine," King agreed. "But I suggest you take the one out of her hand first. And you check the street, the trail. The trapper could easily have had a second gun."

Two miners moved in to disarm Narcissa, but they drew up short as reined-in horses when she swept the muzzle toward their bellies.

"No," she said.

"Need any more proof of the fact that she's involved . . . of what kind of woman she is?"

"Take his gun," she said. "I think you'll find two bullets spent. He didn't have time to clear or reload either."

"No, damnit. You first," MacIntosh argued.

Drover held out his hand. "Give me the gun, King."

"Stay out of this, you fool foreigner," Mattie said.

"Yeah, stay out of it, duck."

The crowd fumed with frustrated hostility.

"He's sweet on her anyway," a woman said. "He'd do anything for her. Even get us to hang another innocent man."

"Let's discuss this inside," King said.

"Where you can switch guns? No," Drover said.

He reached for the weapon, but King pivoted and started for the saloon. "Go to hell," he said. "I don't have to prove anything to a bushranger like you."

Drover grabbed for him.

The gun in King's hand rose by a few inches. It fired, and Drover's left shoulder jerked back, slamming him to the ground. The crowd flowed backwards.

"Maniac," King barked. "Somebody help the fool Aussie into the saloon. I've got some bandages upstairs in my office. Hurry, before the poor love-struck fool bleeds to death."

Narcissa had not moved. Although her instinct was to help Drover, she knew what King was conniving to accomplish. He was starting for the saloon. If he could get upstairs and exchange guns, he'd be clear of Nena's death.

Because Walter King was a power in town, the crowd welcomed the excuse for not pressing the issue. Many of the men worked for him. All were dependent upon him for supplies and for safe shipment of their ore to a refinery.

Let it be the trapper, after all. Search for a second gun.

It was a solution that would leave their tenuous lives intact. To destroy Walter King, even if he were guilty, was to destroy much of themselves.

"Stop," Narcissa said softly. She was wrestling with contradiction. Why was she so sure Walter had done the shooting? He had his twosome of Macs for such dirty work. Still, as MacDermitt had said, they may not have been paid enough to shoot into a church. Or her second idea might explain it, Walter King was not going to have anyone around who could hold a major crime against him. Shooting into a church. That he might prefer to do himself and avoid extortion. Especially when he was sure the crime would be blamed on the notorious trapper.

She pointed the gun directly at King's heart, her finger laid lightly on the trigger.

He halted, looking back over his shoulder. He laughed. "You're not going to shoot anybody, Miss White. Boys, take that gun away from her and get the Australian inside. I'll get the bandages."

Lowering the barrel, she blew a hole in the boards just three inches from King's foot. Slivers of wood settled over his boots. No one came closer.

In response King's voice was still sardonic, if somewhat quieter. "All right, if you want to see the Australian bleed to death, that's one more mark on your phony soul."

He started toward her, the gun in his right hand deliberately held low along his leg so that she would have no excuse to shoot him.

When he kept coming at her, she began to realize she must be wrong. He couldn't have shot through the church windows. The clyinder of his six-shooter must be full.

She moved the pistol in her hand so that it pointed slightly to one side. She feared her shaking hand might pull the trigger accidently.

He was innocent. She just wanted him to be guilty. She wanted to see him hanged for what he had done to her.

Repent, girl, she told herself. Cleanse yourself. Lust not for vengeance.

Dear God, lead me, tell me, show me what I must do.

The gun stayed pointed at Walter King.

Was it God staying her hand or her own craving for revenge? ◆§

22

"I *will* shoot you, Walter. One more step and I *will* shoot you."

She watched his expression change as he weighed her religious beliefs against her secular responsibilities. The smile that curled his lips died. His voice was dead serious.

"You'd do that. Some preacher." But she had made a believer of him.

At such close range it would be all too easy for her to wound him, just as he had deliberately avoided killing Drover.

The crowd would get its chance to check his gun.

"All right," he said. "If it's so important to you that you look at my gun first, so be it."

Then, like a cat, he leaped behind Adrian. The child, though startled, was quick. He jumped into the crowd, leaving his sister behind. King grabbed for the girl as Narcissa swung her gun with him, reluctant to shoot.

Her hesitation and Sarah's crippled leg was all he needed. Even MacIntosh and MacDermitt trained their pistols on him. Men in the street leveled their rifles at him, ready to shoot.

They were all too late. Sarah's right shoulder cringed

under his grasp, the barrel of his gun pressed against her head.

"Don't shoot, anybody!" Narcissa screamed.

It was an unnecessary warning. Every man in the street who carried a weapon could have put a slug into King's body. They were close, good shots most of them, and the target was exposed. But a hit, even in the head, might give King's brain that instant needed to pull the trigger on his own revolver. His finger might move by reflex action alone.

They dared not shoot for fear of losing Sarah.

"Put the guns down, boys," King said coolly.

They were reluctant to obey but they were sure—surer, at least—that they had their man. Obviously King couldn't chance having his gun examined. He must be guilty. He had murdered and made murderers out of them.

"I'm innocent," King was saying. He spoke slowly. If he could say it right, the men would capitulate, some with relief. "I just fired this gun. I can't defend myself like MacIntosh and MacDermitt."

"How many bullets left?" Spooner asked.

"Five."

"Let us count them."

"You'd just say I reloaded and tossed aside the other cylinder. You're a hot-headed mob with blood boiling for somebody to lynch so you can clear your own consciences. I don't intend to be the next innocent man you string up. When you've cooled, we'll clear this up. So put the guns down, boys. And you, MacIntosh, get my horse."

Their guns wavered.

"You can't believe him," Narcissa said. "If he were innocent he would show us his gun."

They didn't want to hear her argument. King's explanation had given them an out. They would not have to gamble a child's life.

"You take that child anywhere," Drover said through teeth clenched with pain, "and that's kidnapping. We'll hang you for that."

"Yeah."

"Right."

"Kidnapping's a hanging offense."

Again the mob's mood shifted, this time to side with Drover. Now they would not be cowards letting a possible killer go free—they would be saving a child. And King would not return to present them with a moral dilemma: was he a killer or not? Somebody, the judge probably, would take King's place. Their lives would go on. It was easier to lay down their weapons.

MacDermitt chose to make a stab at negotiating. "Our guns are down," he said. "Now let go of the girl and you can ride out of town with an hour's head start."

"Sure," King mocked. "I can trust you, MacDermitt. What kind of ass do you take me for? The girl goes with me."

"All right. As long a start as you want," MacDermitt said. "I'm rotten. But I don't want no little kid killed. Just leave her. Nobody's going to chase you."

"No," Drover said from the ground. He was pressing hard on the wound in his shoulder and trying to crawl toward the horse MacIntosh was leading.

King inched slowly toward the animal too. Sarah was crying, "Momma, momma."

Then Adrian came around to his aunt's side. "Kill him, Cissie. Don't let him take Sarah. Kill him."

Narcissa pushed him behind her.

"Put your gun down too, Preacher," King ordered.

He was beside the horse now and ready to lift the girl into the saddle just behind the horn.

"Don't let him go, Narcissa," Drover said in a low, weakening voice. He tried to move closer, to relieve her of the decision. "You know his kind. He'll keep the child with him until he has disappeared over the mountains or across the sea."

"I'll let her go," King promised.

"You'll kill her so there'll be no tracking you." Drover reached a hand toward Narcissa. "Give me the gun. Leave this to me."

She started to pass the gun to Drover. Let a man do it. He was probably a better shot. He probably knew what was best. Let a man do it.

Then she saw his head bow as a shudder of pain wracked his body.

She's your niece, Narcissa, she told herself. This is your problem, your decision.

Like so many of the women here, the whores and the others, she had come through hell without a man. Fighting, working, praying. Without a man.

She had both hands on the gun. It would be more accurate that way. Using one hand made a man look better, but she did not have to pretend or display bravado.

The gun was no longer aimed at King. In the moment of indecision when she considered turning her problem over to Drover, she had lost her aim.

It worked against her. It worked for her.

Noticing her hesitation, King used the moment to swing up into the saddle behind the girl. The movement required both hands, and for an instant the muzzle of his gun slipped from Sarah's head. Narcissa could now choose between Sarah and God as she had been taught to see him.

Thou shalt not kill.

She swung the pistol upward and saw King's startled expression begin to form on his face. The sights were on the target, the moving gun passing Sarah's small chest and bracketing her kidnapper's mouth.

Shoot.

Don't shoot.

He'll let her go.

He'll kill her.

Thou shalt not kill.

A hundred voices spoke at once, each one clear, each countering the other.

Then she pulled the trigger and Walter's handsome face exploded like a bursting bag of grain. He fell backwards off his horse, hitting the ground before Sarah tumbled forward into the arms of MacIntosh.

Narcissa looked down at the gun smoking in her hands and wondered if she should use it again.

This time on herself.

23

THE church was dark inside. Boards had replaced the broken glass. There was a lamp that had not been lit.

She sat in the front pew. Alone. The children were asleep at last. All four, Nena's and her own, were still so bewildered by what they had seen and experienced that they were quarrelsome and overwrought. They would bear the scars for a long time.

Someday, perhaps, Adrian and Sarah would really comprehend why their aunt had killed a man. And perhaps, with time, Sarah would forget the dead man on the ground beside her, his blood smearing her new dress. She rarely talked.

Nor did Narcissa.

The townspeople had been sympathetic. They boarded up the windows at the church and insisted that she officiate at the funerals for Nena, the trapper and Walter King. At Narcissa's insistence, they were buried close together in the tiny cemetery.

"They were all victims," she said over them. "Nena wanted a father for her children. The trapper, God forgive us, we don't even know his name, what did he want? A few minutes with another human being. And Walter."

The silence lengthened while she searched for words. "He probably meant not to kill but to frighten. He had his own battle to fight, the family outcast trying to prove his own worth." She took a long, shuddering breath. "And me," she finished, "God forgive me most of all."

They had trudged through the snow back to the church, filling it . . . miners, whores, families. They brought in food and ate together, speaking infrequently, a few trying to cheer the solemn mood by mentioning Christmas.

"It will be better after Christmas," a woman said. "I'll make mittens for the young ones."

Only Drover did not come. With fever threatening his life, he did not leave his house. Cottontail and the church women tended him. Narcissa stayed away.

"We'll all be at church on Sunday," people promised.

Narcissa nodded, but once inside, she locked the door. Knocks went unanswered. By Sunday a few tried to rouse her. They left after awhile and spread the word.

Hangtown no longer had a church. The cross was still there, but it was no longer a church.

In the weeks that followed, Narcissa peered through the cracks in the boards across the windows only when she thought she heard the rattle of heavy wheels in the frozen street. She was waiting for Old Gray to return. When he left again, she and the children would go with him.

To where?

Wherever he was going. She no longer cared.

Days later, or weeks, time had no meaning, the wagons finally rambled into the street.

The cry of "Women comin', women comin'" confirmed her expectations, and she went to the boarded window. From there she could see the covered wagons with the draw strings tugged tight to close off the front canvas.

Old Gray sat on his usual perch, tying the reins. He was bundled in a heavier coat than he had worn when he left, and he climbed down with arthritic stiffness. Men converged on the small convoy, not running, but moving at a brisk pace, hunched against the cold.

Narcissa stayed at the window until she saw the first

women climb from the wagons. They were a tired lot. But the brides from the last load were hurrying to greet them.

They'll all go to the saloon, she thought. There would be a party in Hangtown tonight, a party she would be glad to miss.

Walking to her bedroom, she took her heavy coat and wrapped it around her body. If she timed it right, she could talk to Mr. Gray alone and arrange for her passage. She would wait until the rest of the people had gone into the saloon—the saloon and town hall, they called it now.

Peering again through the boarded window, she watched the women disembarking and the men closing in. They were a shyer lot than the first. Only one walked directly up to the prettiest girl among the passengers.

It was Drover, walking a bit sideways because of his wounded shoulder. He was smiling, chatting animatedly, attracting the attention of several newcomers. Then, all of a sudden, he took the arm of a woman his own age. He was all smiles.

Narcissa turned away from the window, surprised at the pang of pain in her heart. Until now she had been too numb to feel. But it was too late now. Why hadn't she gone to see him while he lay sick? Why hadn't she told him she cared?

Why? Who knew why?

What Walter King said about her was true enough. She wasn't the virgin so many of the men who were handsome and appealing enough to hold out for the top prizes expected for a bride. Or at least they liked to think of their brides as virgins.

The way the church people expected their pastors, especially their female pastors, to be unsoiled.

The knock on the door was not unexpected.

Old Gray, she thought. Good, I won't have to go outside.

"Yes, who's there," she said, close enough to the door to be heard.

"It's me," Drover said from the other side.

"Go away, please. I don't want to go to the party."

There were others with him. She could hear the voices rising in a party mood.

"I'm not asking you to the party," Drover responded. "There's got to be a wedding."

"I'm no longer a preacher." She closed her eyes. Figuratively, she had always closed her eyes where Drover was concerned. She did it now to close out the fact that the last thin thread of hope that tied her to anyone was broken.

He was taking a wife.

Somebody he had met only minutes ago when the wagons arrived? Fool. Was he that uncaring about who shared his life?

No, he must have known the woman from before. She should have guessed he was waiting for someone to come, from Australia, perhaps.

"Go away," she said.

"Nope. I'm not sleeping alone tonight, and I'm not living in sin. So open the door or I'll break it down."

Wearily Narcissa unlatched the door and swung it open. The woman with Drover was a surprise. She was older than she had appeared at a distance, and she seemed quite uncomfortable with him.

"Narcissa, this is . . ." He stumbled over the woman's name.

"Evadene Lawrence," she said for him.

Narcissa shivered even though the warm coat was still warpped around her. Drover was so close.

She wished she could speak up, to warn him of marrying in such haste.

He was smiling broadly, a happy, jovial adventurer . . . but a blind one. Couldn't he see that she loved him? Shouldn't he sense it? She wanted to tell him, but that was impossible.

Mixed with the pain inside her was anger. She had done nothing that would hurt a marriage, nothing that would keep her from being a good and loving wife. Theirs would have been a good pairing, she knew. Even so, she could not, would not, say the words. Pride had built a solid wall. She did not need his forgiveness. If she had God's, that was all that was important.

But she did want him so.

"You going to keep us out here much longer?" Drover asked. "Can't you tell, I'm wild as a brumby to get married."

"Marriage isn't something to be rushed," Narcissa said seriously.

"It is when you got a Sheila that's as extra grouse as mine. So can we come in or not? You're kind of crueling my wedding."

She shook her head as if to clear it. What's the matter with you, she scolded. Stop stalling and get on with it. You're acting as much the fool as ever where Drover is concerned.

She stepped back and smiled at the new lady. "Do come in. I didn't mean to be inhospitable," she apologized.

The crowd was funneling toward the church. The entire town, plus the recent arrivals, seemed intent upon invading the sanctuary that she had declared off limits except for herself and the children.

"Miss Lawrence . . ."

"Mrs."

"Mrs. Lawrence, perhaps you'd like just your friends who came with you to attend the wedding. The chapel is rather small." She did not allow her eyes to meet Drover's.

The tall, statuesque woman spread her hands slightly. "Have whomever you like."

Drover seconded the idea.

"Have 'em all. Give everybody a bo-peep."

"Well, all right, but give me a moment. I must see Mr. Gray to be sure he has space for me and the children on his return trip."

"That can wait." He took Narcissa by the elbow and propelled her toward the pulpit.

Again she was angry. He did that to her. So peremptory. So intent on getting his own way. "I don't mean to delay you, Mr. Drover," she said stiffly, "but . . ."

"Broderick Jacob Outlander, that's my real moniker. Didn't you know?"

She did not succeed in keeping the irritation out of her voice. "How would I know that? I supposed it was a secret."

They had reached the front of the chapel. The Lawrence woman was scanning the room, apparently looking for something.

"Where's the bible?" she asked.

"Over there on the chair," Narcissa said, turning to Drover and forcing a smile. "Did you know each other in San Francisco?"

Drover said, "Nope. Never set eyes on the lady before tonight."

"Have you thought that perhaps you're being a bit hasty?" she asked carefully. She had to raise her voice. The church was filling with people. She could hear crying, and Adrian appeared, looking cross for being disturbed.

"Nope," Drover said. "I'm dead set on this."

"And you, Mrs. Lawrence?"

The woman had the bible and was thumbing through it. "It's all right with me," she said. She too sounded irritable.

"Miss White." It was Cottontail speaking from the aisle. She cupped her hands around her mouth and spoke in a stage whisper. "I'm getting married too. Tonight if you don't mind. I been putting this nice boy off, but with more women coming in, you know what I mean."

"All right, Miss White," Evadene Lawrence said rather officiously, "let's get this over with."

She was a pushy one all right.

Drover took Narcissa's arm and moved her toward the altar. "Start saying the words, Reverend Lawrence, before my Sheila drops her bundle."

"Drops her bundle?" Narcissa and others in the audience misunderstood. The tall, slender Mrs. Lawrence certainly did not look pregnant.

"Loses her nerve, as you silly Yanks would say."

"All right," Reverend Lawrence said, opening the bible.

"Do you have any preference concerning the services, Miss White? It's your wedding."

"My . . . Reverend Lawrence? Did you call her Reverend?" Narcissa snapped at Drover.

"I'm ordained," Mrs. Lawrence said. "I had a little church of my own down in San Francisco until I got burned twice and tired of preaching in a tent."

"But if you're an ordained minister and I'm not . . ."

"You have any religious preference?" the tall woman asked.

"Presbyterian."

"Close enough. Hold hands, you two. I do this my own way."

Narcissa felt Drover's strong hand engulf hers and she suddenly understood.

"You . . . me . . . oh, no!"

"Oh, yes," the Australian said with a grin.

She tried to pull loose.

"You aren't leaving this altar until we're hitched," he said, squeezing her hand more firmly and smiling down into her eyes. "And the four nippers are thrown in with the deal. I made up my mind days ago when I found there was a preacher lady coming to Hangtown."

"Made up your mind! And mine, too, I suppose. Well, Mr. Drover, Broderick whoever-you-are, when will you learn that . . ."

"Marry him before he changes his mind."

Narcissa turned to see the tattooed White Squaw at her elbow.

"You ain't gettin' away this time, Narcissa," Max the bartender said.

Even Madam Lafayette was there, smiling and crying at the same time. At least she dabbed at her cheek with the back of her hand as if to stop the tears before they showed.

"Drover, I don't come to you clean," Narcissa said. "Some of what Walter King said . . ."

"I don't want a wowser for a wife. No bluestocking, straightlaced bible belting prude could put up with me."

"But you didn't want a . . . , somebody who . . . , well . . ."

"And I'm not getting one." Then he took her in his arms and pulled her tight against his chest. His lips covered hers, warm and seeking, and she felt the strength of him, the power and the safety. When she leaned away to look at him, he drew her close and kissed her again before she could speak.

Happiness washed over her like warm rain, and she relaxed in his arms, giving herself to his kiss. Their appreciative audience was applauding.

When at last he released her, there was still something she had to confess. "Drover, no matter what, I have to tell you. You won't like it, but . . . Well, I know I won't change. I'll always be a bible belter. I've learned to be self-sufficient. I . . ."

"I'm not bailing you up, girl. I'm marrying you. Besides, I don't think we have much choice. You see, I love you. Nearly killed me every time I saw you with that piece of pyrite King. And if you aren't a bull artist, you'll fess up you love me too."

"Marry him," MacIntosh shouted.

"Go ahead, Aunt Cissie, marry him," Adrian said. He stood with the other three children. He must have awakened them so they wouldn't miss the party.

"See?" Drover said. "We try to back out now, we're going to get knuckle sandwiches from the ockers. So, will you marry me and quit bunging on the act?"

He kissed her again, hard and fast.

"Oh, yes, Drover . . . I mean, Broderick Jacob Outlander. Oh, yes, I love you and I'll marry you . . ." She stopped and smiled up at him. "But please. Promise you'll learn to speak English."

WOMEN WHO WON THE WEST

Dodge City Darling

by Lee Davis Willoughby

Bold and beautiful, a penniless Lucia Bone sells her body at a Dodge City bordello rather than give up the search for the mother she has never known. Dubbed "Dodge City Darling", Lucia softens the heart of the legendary gunslinger, Bat Masterson. A tough private detective named Brooker and a hardened Dodge City madam also succumb to Lucia's fatal charm. The stakes are high, the dangers great, but the determined young beauty stops at nothing in her relentless search for the truth. But a terrible secret may mark Lucia as the daughter of a murderess—and as the next victim of a ruthless killer....

From Dell/Bryans

WOMEN WHO WON THE WEST

Duchess of Denver

by Lee Davis Willoughby

She came from the river towns of the East and crossed the wide open plains to the rich land of California. Posing as the beardless "E.J.", Elsa Jane toils and sweats to lead a stubborn breed of sailors and pioneers. Her beauty and bravery makes the young widow the "Duchess of Denver" when she tames the wild heart of an English Duke. Despite the hazards of the land, Elsa struggles to survive. She must fight the jealous Daris Jamieson, who seeks to destroy the woman he cannot possess.

From Dell/Bryans